THE SECRET OF ROVER

THE SECRET OF ROVER

RACHEL WILDAVSKY

AMULET BOOKS

NEW YORK

Library of Congress Cataloging-in-Publication Data

Wildavsky, Rachel.
The secret of Rover / Rachel Wildavsky.
p. cm.
Summary: Twelve-year-old twins Katie and David Bowden evade foreign militants and make their way from Washington, D.C., to their uncle's Vermont home, hoping he can help rescue their parents, who were kidnapped because of their secret invention, Rover.
ISBN 978-0-8109-9710-3 (alk. paper)
[1. Kidnapping—Fiction. 2. Brothers and sisters—Fiction. 3. Twins—Fiction. 4. Uncles—Fiction. 5. Voyages and travels—Fiction. 6. Inventions—Fiction. 7. Washington (D.C.)—Fiction.] I. Title.
PZ7.W64578Sec 2011
[Fic]—dc22
2010023450

Book design by Maria T. Middleton

Printed and bound in U.S.A.
10 9 8 7 6 5 4 3 2 1

Amulet Books are available at special discounts when purchased in quantity for premiums and promotions as well as fundraising or educational use. Special editions can also be created to specification. For details, contact specialmarkets@abramsbooks.com or the address below.

THE ART OF BOOKS SINCE 1949
115 West 18th Street
New York, NY 10011
www.abramsbooks.com

This book is for my parents,
Arnold and Nancy Flick.

CONTENTS

PROLOGUE

The guns seemed out of place in a country as beautiful as Katkajan. There was the village nestled beneath the snowcapped mountains; there were the sweet and spicy blossoms and the towering pines. And then there was the small band of men and women with guns, passing by on the dirt road. They scanned the fields as if searching for something, or someone.

The villagers heard the people with the guns before they saw them. They heard the clanking of their ammunition belts. They heard the stomping of their boots and their loud, laughing voices. Not again, thought the villagers as they heard these sounds. Not again.

The villagers thought this, but they did not say it. The women looked up from their work in the fields. They saw the guns, and they looked away. The men stopped briefly to stare and to lay their hands protectively on their children's heads. Then they, too, turned away.

There is nothing you can say to a man or a woman with a gun.

Farther down the dirt road and outside the village was a cottage, separate from the rest. The young husband and wife who had built this cottage were happy together. They needed no one but each other—each other, and the baby who would soon be born to them.

But that morning, catastrophe had struck this couple.

Inside her small home, the young wife had felt the first of the labor pains that meant their child was on its way. Her husband, who was outside tending their crops, heard her calling. He ran to her across the field. In his haste he did not see the deadly snake that lay in his path. The snake struck. The man fell. Within minutes he was dead.

His wife never knew why her husband did not answer her call. She faced her own mortal struggle, alone. It was a difficult birth, and no doctor or midwife was near to help. A few short hours after her husband collapsed in the field, the young mother delivered her baby. As the little girl drew her first breath and let it out in a piercing newborn cry, the mother drew her last.

Inside the cottage the mother lay dead with her baby by her side. And now the small band of armed men and women came up the road. They saw the father's body, dead in the field. And they heard the wail of the orphaned child.

The strangers stopped and looked at one another. They shared a quick, low conversation, and then—in a slow-moving pack—they approached the house.

They crowded inside, and their voices rose in glee. They had been looking for a baby.

One of the women gave her gun to her companions. She wrapped the baby in the soft cloths that the mother had prepared for the child she was expecting, and slung the little girl next to her body.

The armed strangers continued down the path, moving faster than before. Now that they had the baby, they would have to hurry. They were headed to an orphanage in Taq, the capital city, and it was very far away. They carried the little girl carefully. It was a piece of luck that they had found her so easily. They had plans for this baby— important plans. Nothing must happen to her.

Lulled by the motion of the woman who carried her, the baby slept. She had no idea how much drama she had already experienced, at just one hour old. And she had no inkling of the vast global adventure that lay in store for her.

THEO

Baby Theo's luggage lay open in the hall outside her room. The plane was taking off at sunup the next day, but there were just a few last items that needed to be packed, and David and Katie could not seem to make them fit.

Their parents' luggage wasn't ready either. Each had an enormous blue duffel, not yet zipped but already stuffed. These lined the wall like bulging blue sausages, spilling rain gear and papers, pills and sweaters.

That was their problem. But David and Katie were packing for Theo. Her things were to go in a pair of trunks, each hard and square and the size of a coffee table. Nonetheless, it was not at all clear that the baby's many belongings would fit inside.

"How come the littlest person has the most stuff?"

Katie fretted while struggling to wedge a camera between the back wheel of Theo's new stroller and the edge of her collapsible cradle.

David did not look up from the other trunk, where he was trying to balance a small pink giraffe on top of a tottering stack of tiny pajamas. Concluding at last that it would not stay put, he toppled the tower, stuck the neck of the giraffe into a baby bottle, and slammed the trunk decisively shut. "Whatever," he announced cheerfully. "It works."

Katie glanced at David's trunk, annoyed. They were twins so he wasn't older or anything—they were both twelve—but David often finished things first. That was because she was careful and he was not, she reflected. She could be done too if she did it like *that*.

Their parents were in their room and Katie could hear them laughing. Peeking around the corner she could see them both: her mother's dark oval face with its high forehead and deep eyes, and her father's fair face, ruddy, round, and softened by a golden beard.

Both faces shone with pure happiness. Sandra and Alan Bowden had just adopted a baby from the far-away country of Katkajan, and the next day—Monday morning—they were flying off to get her. When they returned one week later, Theo would be with them.

Katie felt a pang of unease when she thought about the week to come. An ocean would lie between herself and two members of her small family—no, three, she corrected herself. She and David would be with a stranger, a new nanny who was coming to dinner that night.

But Theo was worth it. Life had been good lately—very, very good. But with Theo, life would be perfect.

Things hadn't always been good for the Bowdens. Before Katie and David's parents and their uncle Alex invented Rover, the present had always been bleak and the future had always been uncertain.

The family had been poor—just poor. There had never been enough of anything. Their house in Washington DC had been small. That was OK, but the rats that infested it had not been—not for anyone but the cat, Slank, who had roamed in and out through his private cat door, feasting. And because of neighborhood thieves there had been bars on their windows. They had needed the bars, but what had kept the thieves out had usually kept the family in, and alone.

The Bowden parents had been busy with Rover all the time, and their work was totally private—secret, even. Even the name of their invention, "Rover," was a code name. That was because Rover was for spying. When dangerous people started trouble far away, Rover was supposed to discover it and stop it.

Rover was important, and David and Katie were proud of it. But it was hard to know so little about it. Although they often asked exactly what Rover did, their parents never answered. Though they often asked how it got its strange name, they were never told.

Rover had meant other things for their family, as well. Though all four Bowdens liked people, there could be no guests, so there were few friends, sadly. Nor did the family ever go anywhere, not even to see their uncle Alex. Alex was their mom's brother, and he was a hermit who lived on a mountain far to the north in Vermont. Alex had taken to his mountain after a mysterious quarrel with a girlfriend long ago, and he had never left it. In the busy days when Rover was nearing completion it seemed as if one parent or the other was constantly heading off to meet with him.

David and Katie had heard about this long journey north so many times that they felt they knew the way by heart. But their uncle Alex was a riddle. Ever since that quarrel he had been shy—very shy; and private—very private. He was a scientist, but he lived a simple life. He invented machines, but he did not like to use them. Their parents said he cared about his family, but he did not come to visit. Katie and David had seen pictures of Alex as a boy. But though he was their only relative, they had no idea what he looked like now, and they had not been to his house.

Worst of all, in the old days there had always been just Katie and David—only two children in the Bowden family.

Both of them felt strongly that four people were simply too few for a family without even any cousins. They watched other families roll through parks and malls in noisy packs. They tried not to stare as older brothers and sisters manhandled tiny siblings with a practiced air. In their lonely house—huddled around their lonely table—Katie and David had pleaded. But they had pleaded to no avail.

"I know little kids are very cute," their mother had said unhappily.

"It's not that," replied David testily. "I mean, they are, but that's not really it." He looked around at the tiny room and his tiny family. "It's just that it's always only the four of us. Don't get me wrong," he added quickly. "I mean, I like you and everything."

"Thanks," said their father shortly.

"But with another kid or two this family could eventually move from man-to-man to zone."

It was never any use. Their parents could not buy shoes for one more pair of feet or sandwiches for one more mouth, and there were no babies.

One amazing day, though, Rover was finished. And then the government bought it.

Though Rover was still top-secret, its sale led to many excellent changes for their family. After it was sold they left the small house with the bars on the windows. As far as any of them knew, no one had been in it since. They

5

moved to the other side of town, to an enormous house full of light and space. In this house, windows swung open to a neighborhood they could roam at will. Katie and David each had their own room and bathroom and a special room besides, where books and projects could be strewn and abandoned where they lay. There were long slippery corridors where they slid in their socks, whooping.

The children had always wanted a cuckoo clock, and their parents bought one for the kitchen wall—a real one from an antique store, with a bird that popped from a door and chirped out the hour. They had always wanted piano lessons but had never had the money for either the teacher or the instrument. Now they had a piano and an instructor, Mrs. Ivanovna, who came once a week. And in a sunroom off the kitchen they had coaxed real orange trees to grow in earthen tubs. Each morning Katie and her mom selected the day's fruit, and Katie never tired of the ritual: the stroll amid the trees, the pleasure of plucking her breakfast from the branch.

They had moved in the spring, just a few weeks before summer. There had not been enough time to get to know anyone at their new school. There had been enough, though, to leave them hopeful about the fall. Now, in August, David and Katie stuck with each other, swimming in the glittering local pool, throwing their football on their own endless lawn, and eyeing the potential friends who wandered past their house and who sometimes glanced curiously their way. Not even rain could dampen David's and Katie's spirits. In bad weather they played indoors, sending long passes sailing across their new home's cavernous open spaces and kicking the ball to great heights without ever hitting their towering new ceilings.

Only the cat was dissatisfied with their new house. To his immense disappointment he ate canned food now, from a dish.

Best of all, though, was Theo.

Just two days before, Katie and David had wandered home from the pool to find their mom and dad awaiting them at the kitchen table, clutching a small photo and looking ready to burst. The photo was of a tiny baby with warm, coppery skin, dark black eyes, and a rosebud mouth. She had a slightly startled look, as if the light of the camera had surprised her. She was just three weeks old, and she was their sister.

Katie was round-faced and blond like their dad, and she had been named for his mother. David had their mom's oval face, with her dark eyes and hair, and he had been named for her father. But the baby's face was from far away, and she, their parents said, was Theodora: "Gift from God."

With the last few items safely stashed, Katie slammed Theo's trunk shut. As she did so she found herself wondering yet again about the person who was going to care for them while their parents were away. This woman was not only going to stay with her and David while their mom and dad were overseas; she was also going to stay on after Theo came home, to help.

They had not yet met this nanny. They couldn't. Everything had happened in such a rush. Their parents explained that that's how Katkajanian adoption works. You apply for a baby far in advance. Then when your baby is available, you're expected to go get it *fast*.

Fortunately, the orphanage where they'd adopted Theo had helped. It had strongly suggested that a nanny from Katkajan would ease the family's adjustment to its newest member. It had even recommended the agency where they'd found the woman who was coming that night.

Katie turned again to her parents' room. "When's she supposed to get here?" she called for perhaps the fifteenth time. "When did you say she was—"

Before she could finish the question, the doorbell boomed its deep notes throughout the house.

"Now!" her mother sang.

"Please get the door!" called their father. But David had already smacked his hands onto his sister's back and leapfrogged over her where she hunched by the trunk. Katie sprang after him, threw herself across the slick banister, and shot ahead.

"*Off* the banisters!" Hearing the familiar command behind her, Katie dropped to her feet on the landing, just as her brother serenely launched himself into a slide down the next flight.

"We each ride one or it's not fair," he said, shooting back into the lead.

"You can't do it after they've said no!" Katie cried. But he was already on the ground and was skidding toward the massive front door. He thudded into it as she collided into him. Still struggling for position, they seized the heavy knob and threw their bodies backward, tugging the door open. Breathless, they crowded into the doorway to peer at their guest.

She looks just like Theo, thought David, taking in the nanny's warm, coppery skin and thick, glossy hair. But— no. No, she's different.

Katie stood motionless. Her round face grew solemn beneath her disheveled blond hair as her eyes absorbed the woman in the doorway. It took less than an instant and the verdict was dismaying.

I don't like her, thought Katie.

TRIXIE

While the Bowden children stared at their new nanny, the woman herself stared back from beneath straight black brows. She was short and squat and everything on her crackled with newness. Her neat skirt and blouse, her sensible low-heeled shoes, and even the twin suitcases that she clutched in each fist seemed to have been slipped from their plastic packages and arrayed on her person just moments before she appeared at their door. Her eyes flickered over them and for an instant her straight brows drew together.

And then she smiled. It was a smile that seemed to glide out from the middle of her face on a slick coat of syrup. Wearing this slippery grin and gripping her suitcases, she leaned toward David. They were almost the same height.

"Hi, sweetie?" she said. "I'm your nanny?"

Her English was nearly perfect, with only a trace of an accent. But for some reason both comments came out as questions. Was David supposed to confirm these facts? "Right," he said.

The nanny laughed a tinkling laugh, as if he had said something adorable. Then she leaned toward Katie, her interest in David apparently exhausted. "And you?" she asked in the same sugary voice. "You're the sister?"

No, she's the brother, thought David as Katie took an involuntary step backward. Luckily their mother arrived at just this moment.

"How nice to see you—welcome!" Mrs. Bowden's warm voice sailed over their heads from behind as she joined them in the doorway.

Their visitor abandoned her pleasantries with the children and directed her gaze upward toward their mother, who was eagerly beckoning her in. As David and Katie scrambled out of the woman's way, she put one foot heavily across the threshold and reached back to close the door.

It was then that something went wrong. A black streak shot across the slick wooden floor and darted between the woman's feet, headed for the great outdoors. Both children gasped and threw themselves on the escaping cat, tumbling against the woman's legs as they did so. She stumbled and, piercingly, she shrieked. The sound ricocheted off the walls and ceilings of their enormous home.

"Slank—*no*! Did you get him?" Mrs. Bowden cried. The children hunched over the struggling animal. "Oh! I'm so sorry!" She turned her attention back to their guest. "Are you all right? He's *not* supposed to get out!"

The sugary expression was gone, wiped away like so much spilled syrup. A stony fury had replaced it.

"He wants to go back to our old house," offered David apologetically. The dark oval of his face gazed up, worried, from the floor. "Cats have a homing instinct. If we let him out, he'll run back to where we used to live and that's not—"

"He could be hit by a car!" pleaded Katie. "He's not safe outside!"

"Kids," said their mother, cutting in, "we'll tell our visitor about Slank later. Just put him away for now and we'll all get acquainted." She turned back to the still-glaring woman. "I'm Sandra. And please," she added, reaching for her guest's bags, "let me help you with your things."

At the sound of Mrs. Bowden's voice the woman seemed to remember herself. The angry lines relaxed. "No thanks?" she said. "I'd prefer to keep them?"

By now Mr. Bowden had arrived to join everyone, and his hearty voice boomed into their awkward circle. "Welcome!" he called. "I'm Alan Bowden. You must be . . . ?"

There was a short silence, then the smile slid back

into position as the nanny craned her neck upward. Mr. Bowden towered above her.

"I'm Trixie?" she answered. And then she laughed, revealing her sharp white teeth. "Nice to meet you!" she sang.

For days the Bowdens had talked endlessly of what they must tell Trixie. But now she was with them and Katie and David could remember none of it.

It was *her* fault, thought Katie as the five of them sat at the dinner table. Every time you tried to talk to her, you got that icky smile.

David didn't like the smile, but he could have lived with it. He just couldn't stand how everything had to be a question, as if they'd be mad if she just said stuff or something.

They tried to chat with her. While their dad slid the pizzas from the oven and their mom tossed the salad, Katie timidly displayed their orange trees and described their morning ritual. But Trixie's reply stopped her cold.

"And you're the little gardener?" she asked.

David found that although she asked a lot of questions, Trixie was strangely uninterested in their answers. She asked about their new school, but when he started to tell her about it, her eyes went skittering around the room. He stopped answering and she did not seem to notice.

Then as they took their seats for dinner the cuckoo

13

clock chimed. A woman who made a question of her own name would surely ask something about the small bird who popped from a door to warble six chirps. Not Trixie. She did not even seem to hear it.

But their parents were, if anything, even more puzzling than their guest. They did not seem to notice how weird Trixie was. They plowed straight ahead, eating their pizza, enthusing about their new daughter, and filling Trixie in on the nuts and bolts of the family's life.

Mr. Bowden reviewed their weekly routine. The garbage was picked up on Tuesdays, he said. The piano teacher came on Thursdays, and the children—here he turned to them and smiled jovially—were to practice for half an hour every day. While he talked, Mrs. Bowden ran her fingers through her dark bangs, trying to remember what else they must discuss.

"Yes—the children," said their mother. "Let's see. It's still summer, so there's no school, of course. But they can walk to the pool. And a little TV in the evenings is fine. Of course," she added, brightening, "when it's evening here, it will be almost morning in Katkajan." Her eyes lit up as they always did when she thought of Theo. "Two days from now we'll be with her!" she exclaimed.

David cut a sideways glance at Trixie, then turned to his father. "Just keep that phone *on*," he said.

"Always," answered Mr. Bowden. "You know our ring-tone!" he added.

Now that they had piano lessons, Katie had learned to play "You Are My Sunshine," and she and David had to sing it for their first recital. Their parents had loved it so much that they'd demanded a repeat performance later at home, which they had recorded and loaded into their phone. Now their children's supposedly adorable voices could be heard every time somebody called their number.

Both Katie and David found this excruciating and usually supplied a sarcastic retort when it was mentioned. Now, though, they exchanged a look that said neither of them cared to share this family joke with Trixie.

"Yes," said Mr. Bowden, perceiving it was best to move on. "Well. And you also know, of course, that if you can't get through on our cell you can try our hotel. The hotel's in Taq—that's the capital city."

"We know!"

"The number's—"

"The number's on the refrigerator. The number of the hotel in Taq, capital of Katkajan. We know." David sighed.

"Trixie." Mrs. Bowden spoke brightly. "Tell us about yourself. You speak such beautiful English! Were you born in Katkajan?"

Trixie's honeyed smile had not so much as faltered since the family sat down to dinner. Now, though, David thought he saw a flash of annoyance behind it. It only lasted an instant, but it had been there.

She doesn't like questions, he thought.

But Trixie's smile had already slid back into place. "Katkajanians?" she said. "We're very good at languages?"

No one knew quite what to say to that. There was a pause, and then Mrs. Bowden called out, "Kids! Dishes." Trixie began to lift her plate. "No, no!" said Mrs. Bowden, stopping her with a polite hand on her arm. "You'll be working hard, starting tomorrow. Tonight you're our guest." She began clearing the table, and David and Katie rose to help her. Trixie wandered into the adjacent rooms. Though she was short, she was solid, and they could hear her heavy, thudding walk as she paced.

Both kids drew a sigh of relief now that the family was left alone. And why, thought Katie, was that? Their guest had been perfectly nice. If anything, she had been too nice. There was no reason why tears should fill Katie's eyes as she scraped her uneaten pizza into the garbage.

The nightly news murmured on the TV that glowed in the kitchen wall. It was the new secretary of state, and she was talking about Katkajan. Mrs. Bowden paused from her cleaning to listen.

"What is it?" asked Katie dully.

"Katkajanian politics," said her mother briefly. "Some people there don't like their government. I like this new secretary of state, though," she added softly, sharing a rueful glance with her husband. "It's very sound, what she's saying."

Katie gathered up the trash and set off through the pantry to carry it outside. But as she rounded the corner, she collided with the sharp edge of an open drawer. It was a special drawer lined with felt and it contained the family's new silverware: fancy silver, expensive silver, for company. Staring into the drawer and poking amid the forks and spoons was Trixie.

They had bought this silver when they moved to the new house. They were going to use it this year at Thanksgiving. That drawer was always kept closed.

A thick, uneasy feeling was in Katie's throat. Trixie looked up and their eyes met. They were alone together and the pantry was very small.

"That's for our new dining room," said Katie awkwardly.

Trixie stared. The smile was completely gone now. For almost the first time that night, she said something that wasn't a question. "You have a lot of stuff," said Trixie.

Sunlight penetrated through Katie's closed eyes and she awoke. With the first drowsy blink she remembered.

They were gone. *She* was here.

This almost hadn't happened. After dinner, Katie had crept to her parents' room and asked them not to go. She did not like Trixie, she said. Maybe Theo could wait for just another couple of days. Maybe they could find another nanny, and go then.

Her mother and father were concerned. What had

bothered Katie about Trixie? The nanny was a little stiff, her father acknowledged. She had perhaps been over-eager to please.

"She was a little on the smiley side," Katie's mom admitted. "But that's not a bad thing, honey."

Katie did not want to tell them about the silver. It would be so hard to explain what that moment was like. "I don't like how she makes everything a question," she said instead.

But even to Katie this had sounded sulky and inadequate. And unfortunately, David had walked in while she was saying it. He dismissed her discomfort at once.

"Trixie's fine," he said to his mom and dad. "I don't figure we'll be best friends, but you'll be back in a week. Go."

Katie was annoyed. David had butted in, and he was bossy, too. But she did not want to be the only bad guy. So she had said good-bye to her parents and slunk away to bed.

Now she groaned and, punching her pillow, rolled away from the light that crept beneath the shade. It was so peaceful here in her room, and outside it was all weird. It would be an uncomfortable day, with their mom and dad gone and a stranger there instead. Maybe she could get up late—very late—and skip breakfast with Trixie.

But she heard David moving in his room across the hall. A moment later, her door swung open and he walked in.

"Get up," he said cheerfully and without ceremony. "Breakfast!"

Katie stared at the ceiling, not replying. Just what she wanted. Her brother had been replaced by an alien channeling a camp counselor.

And why was that? she wondered, feeling suddenly more awake. David did not usually stop to get her before going downstairs to breakfast. He had acted unconcerned last night, when they talked about Trixie after dinner. But he must feel strange too.

Well, they could not avoid the kitchen for a whole week. Sitting up, Katie swung her feet to the floor. It must be faced.

"Maybe she isn't in there," said Katie in a low voice. "I think I'd rather eat breakfast with just us."

Both kids were hovering outside the kitchen door, reluctant to go in.

"I figure she is there," replied David. "And the sooner we get used to her, the better." With that, he shouldered open the swinging door and both of them walked in boldly.

But no boldness could have prepared them for what they found in the kitchen. Trixie was there, and she had . . . changed.

Gone were the skirt and blouse. The sensible low-heeled shoes were nowhere to be seen. Trixie was dressed like—like—

"A soldier?" whispered Katie.

"Wow," said David. "She changed her clothes."

The neat matron of the previous night now sat before her breakfast with her chair tilted back and her feet on the table. And what feet! They were huge, as today they had been laced into real-life, waffle-stomping combat boots. The rest of Trixie was largely concealed by the newspaper that she held open before her short person, but the children could see enough to know that a pair of worn fatigues printed in a camouflage pattern went with the boots. On top of her head, just visible over the edge of the newspaper, was a squat military-style hat with a jutting brim.

Trixie must have heard them enter, because a corner of the newspaper flicked down, revealing her face. They waited for the syrupy smile and the sugary greetings that sounded like questions. But these did not come. Instead, the kitchen was silent, as the kids stared at Trixie and Trixie stared right back.

Then the newspaper snapped back up, and the new nanny returned to her reading without a word.

Were they supposed to talk first? "Good morning," said Katie stiffly. But Trixie said nothing.

David and Katie stared at each other. They were too astonished to speak and, frankly, they were too uncomfortable. But eventually David, shrugging, proceeded into the kitchen, opened the cabinet, and took out a bowl.

This was certainly weird, but it wasn't going to stop him from eating.

Katie followed and poured herself some cereal. Her back tingled with the certainty that peering eyes were upon it.

This would never do. Resolutely, she put down her spoon and addressed her brother in a normal voice.

"I forgot my orange," she announced. Then she headed to the sunporch where the trees basked greenly in their pots. Feeling awkward, but willing herself to act normally, she strolled amid them, searching for the brightest color that hung from their boughs.

Something soft slinked past Katie's ankles. She stooped to scoop up Slank and kiss the top of his sleek head. Setting him down again, she plucked an orange for herself and carefully picked one for Trixie as well.

Bearing a heavy, round fruit in each hand, Katie marched awkwardly toward the table and planted herself at Trixie's side. Reluctantly, the paper came down and the woman's eyes met hers. Katie smiled and held out her offering.

Surely no one could refuse a fresh-picked orange in the morning.

No one but Trixie. There was a brief silence.

"Does it look like I'm reading?" Trixie asked after this icy pause. "You're interrupting my paper?"

The rudeness! Katie felt as if she had been hit. Astonished, she let her arm fall to her side. From across the room David spoke. He had heard the whole thing.

"C'mon," he said with a faint, indignant tremor in his voice. "C'mon, Kat. Let's eat in the family room." With his bowl in one hand and the cereal box in the other, he turned his back on Trixie and walked away from the kitchen. "Get the milk," he said, departing.

With dragging feet, Katie followed. Well, she thought to herself, so much for breakfast. Only about twenty meals to go.

Breakfast turned out to be the worst part of that day. The remainder was OK—not fun, but fine. Trixie was awful, of course; there was no longer any doubt about that. That subject was closed. But they soon learned they could avoid her. This proved to be easy to do. In fact, it was shockingly easy, David pointed out, considering that she was there to look after them.

After their hasty breakfast the children retreated upstairs, and by the time they crept down again, late in the morning, their visitor had vanished into their parents' offices. These were a pair of rooms joined within by a connecting door.

"She shouldn't be in there!" said Katie indignantly, finding both outer doors shut tight. She could faintly hear

Katkajanian music playing inside. She recognized the soft, wailing sound of it.

"Probably not," agreed David, pulling her toward the living room so they wouldn't be overheard. "But let her. She's listening to music—I don't care. If she downloads something weird or messes up their computers, they'll fix it when they get home. Let's go to the pool."

And they did. They stayed at the pool all day and eventually felt almost normal. A few kids they recognized from their new school were there as well. Katie had already met one of them, but that girl was tightly clustered with others who were obviously her best friends. They were giggling and whispering and tearing around, and very definitely not noticing Katie. There was no way she would try to break into *that*.

Floating wistfully in the water, Katie found herself forgetting about Trixie and wondering whether next summer she'd be part of that group. It seemed impossible.

"Today's Monday," said David, drifting lazily on his back beside her. High above his furrowed brows the sunlight flickered through the leaves. "If Katkajan is . . ."

Oh. So he was thinking about their parents and Theo.

"If Katkajan is nine hours ahead of us, and the flight takes—"

Katie cut him off, anticipating where he was going. "They won't even get there till tomorrow," she said. She had worked all this out days ago. "We can call them when we wake up—it'll be Tuesday afternoon for them. But they'll be really tired. And they won't be getting Theo until Wednesday."

"At ten o'clock Wednesday morning," said David. Privately he was glad that Katie had figured this out. He didn't like to admit it, but he found time zones sort of confusing.

"Right," said Katie. "They'll get her on Wednesday, at ten their time. But that'll be the middle of the night again for us. We'll be asleep. If we get up at seven, though—"

"Eight," corrected David.

"I'm saying seven," continued Katie. "If we get up at seven on Wednesday we can call them again, and they won't even have eaten dinner yet. And they'll have the baby. David," she added.

"What?"

"When we call them tomorrow? When we wake up Tuesday morning and call them? I really want to tell them about Trixie. About how mean she was this morning, and the weird clothes and the offices and stuff."

"You know we shouldn't bug them with that."

"I know. I'm not going to *do* it."

"They're going to be really tired, Katie. They'll have been flying for, like, forty hours or something."

"Twenty-two!"

"Whatever. They'll be wiped out. So if they ask us how she is—and they will ask us—we're going to say she's fine."

This bossiness annoyed Katie. "Since when are you in charge?" she retorted. "I said I'm not going to do it! I just want to, that's all." She kicked irritably off the side of the pool toward which they had drifted.

"Anyway, I get to talk first," said David. "When we do call."

At this Katie seized his ankle and jerked it sharply downward. He went under, sputtering, and she shot off before he could get her back.

"Sweetie?" The voice crackled and sounded as far away as, in fact, it was. "Katie, it's Mom—is that you?"

"Mommy! Just a minute." Katie had slept with the phone by her bed so she could call her parents first thing in the morning. But she hadn't even needed to. Their parents had called them, and though they had woken Katie from a deep sleep, still she clutched the receiver tightly to her ear. She wanted to hear every word.

Slank was curled in front of her bedside clock so she could not see the time. With one elbow she shoved him aside. It was just seven a.m.

"How are you, darling?" came the voice. "We're here in Katkajan; we landed just a few hours ago. Is everything OK?"

Katie's door burst open and David, in pajamas, hurried in. He'd heard the phone too. He started to speak but Katie, intent on the receiver, shushed him with a wave of her hand.

"We're fine," she said. "It's normal here. Are you at your hotel?"

"Yes—oh, you sound good. I'm relieved. Here's your dad." Apparently satisfied, their mother handed the phone to their father, who began the whole conversation all over again.

"Honey? Everything OK?"

"We're great. What's it like?"

"Well, we're tired, of course. But the hotel's beautiful—very small. I think we may be the only guests."

The line crackled. "What?" said Katie.

"I said," repeated her father, loudly, "we may be the only guests! So the whole staff knows us. We're getting lots of attention and we're going to be very comfortable."

"Have you seen Theo's orphanage?" David leaned over Katie's shoulder to speak into the phone that she still clutched tightly to her ear. His breath stank and she pushed him away.

"Not yet," Mr. Bowden said. "We tried to drive past it but we couldn't. There were some army guys blocking off the street."

"Army guys?" David had pushed his way back.

"Yeah—you know, there's political trouble here." Their father spoke through rising static. "So there are soldiers everywhere, and a lot of places you can't go. They'll let us through tomorrow, though." They heard him chuckling over the sputtering line. "I don't think they're going to keep your mom away from our Theo."

"Do they have guns?"

"What's that? Katie, say it again; I can't hear you." Their father's voice was breaking up.

"I said," Katie raised her voice slightly, "I said do they—"

"*What?*"

The line had gone very crackly. This time David tried. "*Do they have—*" But the line went dead.

"Call him back!"

"Katie, it was a terrible connection!"

"Oh!" In frustration Katie threw herself backward onto her bed, sending Slank scampering. It was too hard, after waiting a full day to talk to their parents, to be able to say so little.

"We'll try again tomorrow," said David.

"Yeah, and talk for about another five seconds!"

"In which we'll hear about Theo, 'cause they'll have her by then. C'mon." David was already over it. He yanked on his sister's arm and once again assumed his annoying camp-counselor voice. "Upsy-daisy!" he cried. "It's time for"—he paused, as if for a drum roll—"*Breakfast with Trixie.*"

Katie moaned.

"Yesterday wasn't that bad," David offered. "We know the deal by now. She's a jerk, and she ignores us! So today'll be better."

■ ■ ■

But today was not better. Today was worse.

It started at breakfast. Trixie, again in camouflage, had fixed herself an enormous meal with eggs and bacon and some kind of mushy gunk they didn't recognize. After she ate she clomped in her booted feet to the family room where the children had retreated with their cereal. Standing in the doorway she ordered them to clean up the mess she had made.

"The kitchen? It's all icky? I want it clean?"

Then she disappeared once again into the offices.

Fearing to contradict her, Katie and David resentfully complied, tiptoeing about their task and murmuring their protests only to each other. Trixie had clogged the drain with whatever that weird stuff was, and it was revolting to put their hands through the stagnant water to clear it.

Katie fled upstairs as soon as they were finished, but David wandered to the living room to practice the piano. When their mom and dad were home, piano practice was something he generally tried to duck. But today—with them gone and Trixie around—he felt a surge of loyalty to the normal rules.

Besides, his father was right. Though David wouldn't admit it, some days he actually *did* enjoy the piano, and he could tell that today was going to be such a day. The instrument they'd bought for this new house had a velvety sound and the keys were cool and responsive beneath his fingers.

It was good to think about something that wasn't Trixie. David moved into his first piece and the familiar sound and feel began to soothe him.

But then the door to the office burst open. Trixie appeared before him. Her boots were thumping and the eyebrows that too often crawled up her forehead as she asked one of her sugary questions were plunged, low and menacing, over her nose. "No noise!" she barked.

For a moment David was startled into silence. Was this Trixie? Then he found his voice. "But I'm supposed—"

"I'm on the *phone* . . ." Trixie exaggerated the word, as if she were talking to someone very stupid. "On the *phone*, see? And I. Can't. Hear."

"But you can close the doo—"

"You can close your mouth."

David's jaw dropped. Silence rang in the wake of Trixie's words. Katie, who had run to the banister at the first sound of commotion—clapped her hands over her ears.

"You can't—you shouldn't—" David had risen to his feet, but he found himself at a loss for words.

Now Trixie raised her hand and pointed one fat finger threateningly at David. She leaned in toward him and shook that finger right in his face.

"You need to go to your room," she commanded. Her

brows drew down even lower than before and she hissed, "*Skedaddle!*"

Skedaddle?

But apparently that was that. Trixie turned on her heel and marched her short, squat self back toward the office. With her hand on the doorknob she delivered her parting shot.

"Later, when that pool opens?" she said, without even turning to look. "You're going. Till then, don't be in my face. I've got work."

Work? Now David found his voice.

"What work?" he demanded.

Katie had found hers, too. She leaned far over the railing and her indignant words sailed down at them from above. "We'll go if we want to!" she cried. "And we're your work! You're supposed to take care of us!"

At this Trixie let go of the doorknob, put her hands on her hips, and pivoted to confront them. Her face was twisted in anger. She glared up at Katie, drew a deep breath, and opened her mouth. They braced themselves. Katie had surely pushed it too far.

But the shout they anticipated did not come. Instead, Trixie stopped. As if she had suddenly remembered something, she composed her angry features. While they watched, fascinated, the oily smile again stretched itself across her face.

"I am taking care of you?" she said. "You're just fine!"

She forced out her tinkling little laugh. "But we have a relationship? So you have to do your part."

"What part?" demanded David. His breathing was barely under control.

"The part where you be really, really good," said Trixie. And with that she was gone. She stepped inside the office and closed the door. In the silence that rang in the hallway, both kids heard the lock snap shut.

They retreated to David's room to confer.

The pool did not open until ten. They would be there when it did; they needed no further urging to swim today. In fact, they did not plan to return from the pool until the gates were shut for the night. But for now, they concentrated on what had just happened, struggling to figure it out.

Katie sat on the floor, leaning against the bed. In a way, she explained, this fight was an improvement. At least the truth was out there now. "If someone's going to hate my guts," she said, "I'd rather just have them hate me, you know? I mean, it was bad when Trixie told us to shut up."

"'Close your mouth,'" David corrected. He was also on the floor, but with his back to the wall and Slank draped around his neck like a stole. With one hand he idly rubbed behind the cat's ears.

"Right; it was bad," said Katie. "But that smirky stuff, and those questions that are all, like, sickly sweet?"

"That's worse. I know," said David.

Katie shuddered, remembering. "But we're wasting time, David," she said, moving to a new topic. "We're worrying about the wrong stuff."

"What are you talking about? And as for time, by the way, we have plenty. We're grounded till ten, remember?"

"We should be worrying about this 'work' thing, is what I mean," continued Katie.

"What are you talking about?"

"Trixie's work. In the *offices*. In Dad and Mom's offices." Really, David was sometimes slow to catch on. "What's she working *on*?" pursued Katie. "What's that about?"

"She's in charm school," said David. "She's studying for a test. She's not ready for it either—it's the least of our problems, Kat."

Reaching over, Katie lifted the limp cat from David's shoulders and settled him in her own lap. He began to purr.

"You're wrong," she replied, stroking Slank's silky back. "It's a very big problem. What's she doing in there?"

"She's getting away from us, is all. She goes there 'cause it's private. She listens to her music and she doesn't have to look at us. She doesn't want to be with us any more than we want to be with her. We just have to keep our heads down for six more days. We can do this, Kat."

"Well, I'm not going to tell Mom and Dad or anything."

"You got that right!"

"I *said* I'm not. But I'm telling you it's more than that. I'm just betting, that's all."

And when they tiptoed past the office door half an hour later—with towels over their shoulders and backpacks loaded for the day—they did indeed hear sounds from within. They were faint, rapid, clicking sounds, barely audible beneath the drone of the music. They were the sounds of someone typing on their mother's computer.

That night Katie and David set their alarm clocks, and by six forty-five the next morning, they were in Katie's room awaiting their call from their parents. Neither of them wanted to miss a word. By now their parents would have Theo.

They were not disappointed. The phone rang just a few minutes before seven. Both children snatched at it and together they huddled over the receiver. On the other end of the line—on the other side of the world—was a voice they knew as well as their own: their mother's. And behind her elated hello—snuffling and murmuring and sounding very near—was a voice they had never heard before but loved right away. It was the voice of Theo.

"She's there! Mom, that's her—I can hear her!"

"Mom, put the phone closer!"

Mrs. Bowden laughed for pure joy. "More Theo! Just put on the baby! Never mind *me*."

"Mom, is she cute?"

"Can't you hear?" their mother replied. "She's adorable! She's as cute as she sounds and more. It's all so worth it! This whole horrible trip and all the trouble—"

Mrs. Bowden broke off as, in the background, an unknown man with a foreign accent made an inquiry they could not hear.

"Not for another three days," she said, her voice muffled, half away from the phone. "There's still paperwork. We'll be here till Saturday." Another murmur came from the unknown man and there was rustling and shuffling as their mom moved off, handing the phone to their dad.

Katie looked at David. "That was short," she said.

David shushed her. "Dad's coming on," he said.

Mr. Bowden's voice sounded muffled too, as—like their mother—he was speaking to the polite voice in the background and not to them. "Right," their father was saying. "Saturday." Then much more brightly he added, "Oh thanks. Yes, thanks; she's beautiful."

At last their father raised the phone to his face and spoke to them. "Hello? Hello, kids? You have a sister! She's a sweetheart!"

David leaned in. "Does she look like her picture?"

"Dad." Katie clutched at the phone so tightly that her knuckles were white. "Did it go OK? Did you have any trouble?"

"No trouble is too great," sang Mr. Bowden happily. "We would have fished her out of a volcano! We would have snatched her from a tiger's jaws! She's—"

But now a warble chirped across his words, briefly drowning them out.

"What?" said David. "We couldn't—" A second warble interrupted David.

"What's that sound?" asked Katie. "Is a phone ringing?"

"It sounds just like our cuckoo clock, from our kitchen," said David, again over the chirping noise. "Do they have a clock like ours, Dad? At your hotel?"

"Clock? I don't know. Never mind; I can hear you. You won't believe this baby!" But though their father could hear, Katie and David missed much of the description that followed, thanks to the series of warbles that continued to interrupt them. Frustrated and perplexed, they gazed helplessly at each other as their father spoke.

"And the most adorable little sneeze!" he was saying. The chirping had stopped now; at last they could follow his words. "I think she must be allergic to my sweater— aren't you, honey?" Mr. Bowden asked in a voice that suddenly went itsy-bitsy.

David rolled his eyes.

Now their mother returned to the phone. "Are you two OK?" she asked anxiously. "How's everything going with Trixie?"

"Fine," said Katie shortly, wanting to say more but seeing David's face.

"Oh, I'm glad!" their mother said through the static. "Well, I hope we won't be long. Theo is a love and they're very nice at this hotel—the whole staff's talking about the Bowden baby! They can't do enough to help us. But I must say that outside our hotel it's awful here. There are men with guns everywhere and I don't like the looks of it.

"We'll tell you the whole story when we see you—it's just too hard on this lousy international line. We miss you so much. Daddy and I can't wait to get home."

"Me too," said Katie, her eyes filling.

"We'll call again tomorrow, but you know you can also call us," her mother continued. "We'll hear our special song and we'll know it *is* our sunshine. We'll know it's you."

Now Katie's eyes spilled over.

"We'll call you really soon, Mom," she said.

"Bye," said Mrs. Bowden softly, and with an even softer click, she was gone.

Katie sighed and reached over to hang up. But just as she did so, the receiver clicked again.

"Mom?" asked Katie, putting the instrument back to her ear. "Mom, are you still there?" But no one replied. Instead she now heard the flat tone that indicated the line was dead.

David was looking at her. "What?" he said.

"Somebody just hung up," Katie replied sharply. "Somebody else hung up after Mom. Who was that, David? Who else was on the line?"

"Are you sure?"

"David, that was the most frustrating call! We barely heard a thing! And somebody else was listening! I heard them hang up!"

David had grown slightly pale. "It was her," he said slowly. "It was Trixie. She must have been listening on the phone in the kitchen."

"That explains the clock!" said Katie. "That wasn't a clock in Katkajan; it was *our* clock, striking seven."

"And she's a nosy little snoop," said David, heating up. He could feel his anger rising just thinking of that woman, eavesdropping on their call.

"David, you don't get it!" Katie was practically shouting. "Of course she's a snoop—the question is why?"

"She's a snoop because she's a creep," said David. "Next?"

"What's the matter with you?" cried Katie. "She's *up* to something, David!"

"Like what?" he said. "You read too many books! She's mean, Kat; she's not an alien."

"I didn't say that!"

"What did you say?"

"I don't *know*. Get out of my room."

"Fine. You can eat with Trixie. I'll eat by myself."

But when Katie crept downstairs a few minutes later, Trixie was not in the kitchen. She had already vanished into her regular haunt, the office. The door was once again shut and the usual music trickled out from beneath it. David, though, was in the kitchen, and he didn't look well. His face was ashen and he was staring into the garbage can.

"What?" Cold fear clutched at Katie.

"She threw them away," he replied, bewilderment in each word.

"She threw *what*?"

He tipped the can so she could see inside it. Wadded up amid the usual eggshells and plastic bags were the skirt and blouse Trixie had worn the night she arrived at their home. Poking up from beneath the discarded clothes Katie saw the sole—barely worn at all—of a sensible low-heeled shoe.

Katie stared at her brother. "But they were new," she said softly.

"It's like they weren't even really hers," he said. "It's like she bought them just for one night."

"She doesn't need them anymore," said Katie. "She's done." She understood it all; it came to her quite suddenly and she took his arm and shook it urgently.

"They were a costume, David. Like for a play. Like for pretend."

"And now . . . ?"

"And now the pretending's over."

YOU ARE MY SUNSHINE

David and Katie did stay all day at the pool. But the pool was not open all night. And when evening fell and the final whistle blew, they felt something they had never felt before, and had never in their lives expected to feel. They felt afraid to go home.

It was nearly dark by the time they cautiously entered the house. Inside, the familiar rooms and corridors were cloaked in shadow. No light shone from beneath the office door, no music trailed its wailing notes, and Trixie was nowhere to be found.

"We have to put away our stuff," whispered David. "Our water bottles and junk."

"Why are you whispering?" asked Katie at normal volume. Her voice sounded frighteningly loud and it trembled a bit, but she refused to lower it. Take charge, she thought. Take charge; you live here.

Katie marched smartly across the towering foyer and flicked on the light. Hesitating only briefly in the sudden brightness, she willed herself to march straight back to the kitchen without even looking to see if David would follow.

It was lucky that he did, for yet another shock awaited them.

The kitchen was a mess. Four empty pizza boxes were piled in the center of the table and greasy plates were strewn everywhere—eight plates, she counted quickly; no, nine. Chairs had been pushed roughly back from the table and left scattered about the floor. Boxes of crackers, empty bags of chips, and half-eaten tubs of dip overflowed the counters. Over by the refrigerator, a sticky, dark drink had been spilled on the floor and a puddle of it oozed, unwiped, toward the center of the room.

"She had a *party*?" David was sputtering with amazement and rage. "How many people were here?"

But Katie's mind had moved in a different direction. "I think," she said thoughtfully, "I think it's time to tell Mom and Dad."

"They just got the baby today!"

"OK, so not this minute. We don't have to call them tonight. But tomorrow I think we should. Enough already! They need to know this stuff, David."

"OK," he said. "OK." It was a relief, after all, to give in.

Tossing her backpack onto the counter, Katie marched to the refrigerator, removed the slip of paper with the number of her parents' hotel, and pushing past her brother in the doorway, headed for the stairs.

"I'm going to bed," she said over her shoulder. "I'll make the call myself, first thing in the morning. You don't even have to wake up."

But he did wake up. He awoke from a strange dream.

David was on a truck, rumbling down the highway. He was on the roof of the truck, then he was inside the back, and then he was outside of it, clinging to the door with the wind whipping through his hair. From somewhere he heard a radio playing. Bits and pieces of music and voices came to him through the roaring wind.

The radio was bothering him. Where was it coming from?

The driver of the truck must turn that music off, thought the dream David. From his perch on the truck door he pounded on the window, but he could not catch the driver's attention or even see who the driver was.

Bam! Bam! The wind whisked away the sounds of his fists on the thick glass. "Open up!" he cried. *Bam!* "Open the door!" *Bam-bam-bam!*

David's eyes flew open. He was in his room, and someone was pounding on his door.

"David—*open up*!"

It was Katie. Uncharacteristically, he had locked his door the night before and now she urgently wanted to come in. And there *was* a radio, and it was tuned to an unfamiliar station. He heard it in real life now, from very nearby.

"I'm coming!" David rolled out of bed and cracked open the door. Katie slid in and slammed it behind her, refastening the lock.

The music had been loud in the hallway in that instant when the door was opened. Where was it coming from?

"David." Katie's face was anguished. "She's *in their room*."

"What?" David rubbed his eyes. He had just woken up and none of this made sense.

"She's in their room! Trixie is. She's in Mom and Dad's room—*she slept there*!"

Now David was awake. "How do you know?"

"I saw her! I woke up and heard that music. Don't you hear it?" David nodded. "So I walked in to turn it off. I was mad 'cause I figured she'd been snooping there last night and turned it on. I didn't want it bothering me when I try to talk to Mom and Dad. So I just walked right in and she was still there! She's in their bed!"

"Did she see you?"

"She's awake! She looked right at me!"

"What did she say?"

"Nothing. She just kind of . . ." Katie searched for the

right word. "She kind of smirked at me. Then she rolled over and shut her eyes. And I was so surprised, I just closed the door. Then I came here.

"But she's awake now. Don't you hear her moving around? She's getting up, and soon she'll be out. We have to call them right away—before she tries to stop us!"

"The phone's in your room," said David, reaching for the door and pulling it wide open.

But they were too late. Standing in the doorway—filling it; blocking their exit—was Trixie.

She was wearing their mother's bathrobe. And she was wearing the smile.

"Morning time!" Trixie sang.

Even granted that Trixie had said very little to them in the three days that they had spent together, they could not help but notice the change in her voice. Always before she had been either syrupy or furious. Today she was ebullient. Today she was triumphant.

But Katie was beside herself. She had been outraged when she saw this woman in their parents' bed. But that was nothing compared to what she felt at seeing her in their mother's robe. She leaped to her feet and shouted, *"You take that off!"*

Trixie's eyebrows arched upward in mock surprise. "Oh?" she asked. "Are we cranky today? Did we get up on the wrong side of the bed?" And she laughed out loud.

"Please move," said David tightly. "I need to leave." They must get to the phone!

"Go ahead!" said Trixie, stepping ostentatiously out of his way and gesturing him out the door. "You go on and call them. You'll see!"

See what?

Phone, phone, to the phone. Both kids dashed beneath Trixie's outstretched arm and across the hall to Katie's room. As soon as they were in, they slammed the door behind them, but it would not shut. Trixie had stuck her foot in it. Now she elbowed it open and poked her grinning head into the room.

"'You Are My Sunshine!'" she called. "It's not quite so sunny anymore, I think!"

In a rage, Katie stomped on Trixie's foot. Trixie withdrew it, laughing, and the door slammed.

"It's getting a little cloudy!" she called through the door. "I'm thinking it looks like rain!"

Katie turned the lock and through the walls they heard Trixie's heavy, stomping feet and her snorts of laughter in the hallway.

David, frantic, was scrambling on the floor for the phone.

"David, how does she know that? How does she know their ringtone?"

"He told her. Dad told her at dinner, that first night."

"No, he didn't. He never named the song! I remember he didn't—I was relieved! But how does she—"

"Shhh! I'm trying to dial!"

David peered intently at the phone and punched in the familiar series of numbers. Then he clutched it to his ear with both hands.

Somewhere on the other side of the world, a piano plinked and two children sang a tender, sentimental song.

And sang, and sang. There was no answer.

"Let me try!" Katie snatched the phone from her brother and redialed with urgent fingers. Again the phone simply rang.

"They're napping or something, and they've turned it off," she said. "Where's the hotel number?"

She had stuck it on the wall by her bed, and now David read out the series of digits as she punched them into the phone.

"Anybody home?" Trixie called merrily from the hallway.

Katie's fingers shook at the sound of that voice and she messed up the long international number.

"Give it—I'll do it."

Katie thrust the phone at David, who began the number again.

"It's ringing!" he said to Katie, then returned to the phone.

"Hello? Hello. I'm calling from America." David spoke loudly, remembering the expanses of land and ocean that lay between himself and his listener. "I want to talk to Alan and Sandra Bowden."

There was a brief silence.

"Bowden, please. Sandra and Alan—they're staying there. They're guests."

Another silence. Now David was frowning.

"You do—they are. They have a baby. They're the ones who just adopted!"

"David, ask to speak to the manager." Hadn't their father said everybody there knew them?

"May I speak to the manager?" said David. "Hello . . . hello, I want to speak to someone in charge—is that you?"

For a moment David was silent, with the phone still clutched to his ear. Then the blood drained from his face, and slowly, without saying another word, he hung it up.

"They have never heard of Mr. and Mrs. Bowden," he said woodenly. "There are no such people at their hotel."

"Did you speak to the manager?" It simply could not be. "Give me that!" demanded Katie. "I'm trying their cell again!"

"Is it raining yet?" called Trixie from the hallway.

"Oh!" cried Katie, and her fingers once again stumbled.

"Thunder and lightning!" added Trixie.

Now the trembling in Katie's fingers was so wild that she almost could not dial at all. With an enormous effort she mastered herself and again she heard her parents' number ringing. And this time—on the third ring—someone picked up.

"They're there!" she cried. "Mom? Mom? Trixie, she's—"

But Katie broke off. As David watched her face, a pit seemed to open in his stomach.

"What?" she gasped. "Where? Where are—" Katie gave a short shriek and dropped the phone. David lunged for it, but he was too late—he could already hear the tone that said it had been hung up.

"They're gone," said Katie desperately.

"What are you talking about?"

"A man answered. A foreign man. He told me he and some other guys have them—the baby, too. He said to stop calling. He said to tell no one or we'll never see them again. He said they'd kill them if we do—oh, David! He just said that and then he hung up! He sounded awful—David, they're gone!"

"You mean like kidnapping?" said David. "They're kidnapped—Mom and Dad and Theo?"

At this, a triumphant voice floated through the door from the hallway. "How are Mom and Dad?" sang Trixie. "How're they doing?"

"Trixie," said David, as the terrible realization washed over him. "They're kidnapped, and she knew. She's probably in on the whole thing! That's probably why she's here! She's *not* a nanny! She's—she's a—"

"David, who cares about her now?"

"Because she's one of them, Kat! Mom and Dad are kidnapped, and one of the kidnappers is here and she's in charge! And—" The many pieces of this nightmare now

47

flooded into David's understanding; everything suddenly made sense. "And she's spent hours on their computer. She knows everything about them now. She knows all about Rover—Rover!"

David grabbed Katie's arm and his words tumbled out. "That's what this is about. It's a political thing in Katkajan; they're insurgents or something and they want Rover! They—"

"Rover? David, what if they kill our parents? What if Mom and Dad never come home?"

"They will come home. We'll get them home."

"How?" Now Katie, too, began to understand. "David, think! It's not just Trixie and the guys in Katkajan. It's got to be all those people who were here last night—they're all part of this!" Yet another dreadful truth occurred to Katie. "And they were celebrating! They all did this, and then they had a party! That's what that was!"

"And the agency's in on it too—the agency that sent Trixie. And the people at that hotel," said David. "They all knew. No wonder Mom and Dad were the only guests! We're going to fix this," he continued wildly. "We're going to save them. We're going to bring them home!"

"David, *how?*"

"We'll get help. We need to call the police."

"David, that man said they'd kill Mom and Dad! Mom and Dad and Theo, too! We can't tell anyone!"

"That's right!" called Trixie from the hallway. "You want your mom and dad to live? You don't—tell—*anyone*!"

"Oh!" cried Katie in fear and distress. "She's listening to every word!"

"True that! And now she's *opening the door*!" retorted Trixie. As she spoke they heard a pin twist in the keyhole and indeed, the door burst open.

Trixie's squat frame filled the doorway. The weird, slippery grin was stretched across her face, but now, for the first time, it betrayed a maniacal trace of actual pleasure. And while the phony Trixie had been awful, the happy Trixie was infinitely worse.

She put her fists on her hips and the grin faded as slowly, appraisingly, she looked around Katie's room. Her eyes came to rest on the phone, which lay on the floor where Katie had dropped it. She held out one hand.

"I'll take that," she announced. "Since you don't really need it anymore." Her grin returned as she expanded on this apparently comical idea. "You don't need that phone," she amplified, "'cause you're not calling anybody. Seeing as how there's no one *to* call. Since there's nobody *there*." And she laughed.

Her laugh sounded like splintering glass. So this is humor Trixie-style, thought David, appalled.

"Phone!" Trixie commanded, as they had not yet complied. Slowly, eyes down, Katie handed it over.

"Now, just you listen," said Trixie, pocketing the phone in Mrs. Bowden's robe. "You listen to my rules. You're all done with that pool. Today you're staying home. Tomorrow, too. It's time you did a little work around here. That way you won't be in my hair."

This was too much for David. "Like we've been bothering you!"

"We've barely seen you!" cried Katie.

The black brows rose. "Oh, are you talking back?" asked Trixie. "Let me see . . . where exactly are your mother and your father? Who has them, anyway?"

It worked. Katie shot an anguished gaze at her brother and both children fell silent.

Trixie observed their cooperation with satisfaction. "Now," she said, "you mosey on down and fix up that kitchen. It's just a mess!" And laughing her brittle laugh, she turned to waddle from the room.

But their mother's robe was too long for Trixie's short body and the fabric tangled about her legs as she did so. At the very moment when she reached down to jerk it into place, the familiar black shape slithered silently between her ankle and the doorframe and the soft fur brushed her hand.

Trixie shrieked in terror and withdrew her hand as if it had been burnt. Leaping aside, she drew back her leg and dealt Slank a swift and vicious kick.

He yelped and fled under Katie's bed.

"Oh!" Katie's hands balled into fists and, enraged, she turned on Trixie to deliver a piece of her mind. But she stopped short with her mouth open as she remembered Trixie's threat: Don't talk back. Remember who has your mother and your father.

Katie turned her burning gaze to the ground, breathing deeply.

It was not even possible to find and comfort Slank. Instead she and David slowly followed Trixie from the room and downstairs to the filthy kitchen.

They would not talk back—not yet. But they would get rid of her. They would send her packing, they would free their parents and their sister and they would get even.

They would find a way.

INVADED

That day people came.

The first to come was Katie and David's piano teacher, and with her went their first hope.

Not, of course, that this hope had been very specific. It had been more of a feeling that the teacher's presence in the house would be an opportunity for *something*. The feeling had begun to stir in them in the kitchen, as they had scooped the revolting mess from the previous night's pizzafest into the trash. That was when Katie had reminded David in low tones that today was Thursday and Mrs. Ivanovna would be ringing the doorbell at nine thirty.

Each of them would be alone with her at the piano

bench for forty-five minutes. Neither of them was sure what they would say or do in that time. After all, they knew that telling was forbidden and might mean danger for their parents. But Mrs. Ivanovna was an adult and she was not from Katkajan, and they awaited her arrival with desperate eagerness.

By nine fifteen they were back upstairs and were straining their ears for the sound of the bell. It rang at 9:31.

Trixie was in the hall and they heard her sharp response to the sound. "Who's that?" she called.

With studied casualness, both kids emerged from David's room and headed for the stairs. But they were not to reach them.

"Where do you think you're going?" demanded Trixie, clomping into view and cutting them off.

"It's just Mrs. Ivanovna, Trixie," Katie said. "It's our piano teacher. Today's our lesson."

"I don't think so?" said Trixie, and their hearts sank.

The bell rang again and Trixie thumped downstairs toward the door. Creeping to the landing, the children heard her open it and inform the startled woman outside that lessons had been permanently canceled. Hadn't Mr. and Mrs. Bowden told her? Katie and David no longer studied piano.

Their teacher's words did not carry upstairs, but the

consternation in her kind voice did. Tears smarted behind Katie's eyes at the sound of it. Good Mrs. Ivanovna! What would she think of them? And who would help them now?

Their teacher's voice was the last kind sound that David and Katie heard that day. The others—the Katkajanians—began to arrive at noon. The children, who watched these arrivals unnoticed from the top of the stairs, observed with surprise and alarm that they all brought luggage.

The first to come was a woman, as squat and square as Trixie herself. Trixie emerged from her usual haunt in the office and met this unknown person with a snort of recognition and a rapid slurry of foreign words. The stranger tossed a bulging and battered suitcase under the hall table and at once retreated with Trixie to the kitchen. The sounds of cupboards banging and chairs scraping immediately followed.

Soon afterward a man rang the bell. Just as if it were her own home, the new woman wandered out from the kitchen to admit him. She gestured to her suitcase and the man dropped his long, lumpish duffel beside it. Exchanging rapid chatter in Katkajanian, these two left the door slightly ajar before retreating again to the kitchen, where they were greeted with shrill ecstasy by Trixie.

"The door's standing open!" whispered David. But Katie, hearing wheels and brakes on the driveway, hastily shushed him. And indeed, moments later another man and another woman let themselves into the Bowdens' house.

"We're up to five," said David grimly.

"There were more than that last night," replied his sister. "How much do you want to bet they're all coming back?"

It was starting to sound like a party in the kitchen. They heard the TV snap on and the sound of someone reading the news begin to drone beneath the rising chatter of voices.

"David, did you see that last woman — the one who came with the guy?" Katie was sprawled on the hall carpet. She stared downstairs between two railings that she gripped with both hands.

"What about her?"

"She's not Katkajanian. She's American. Or at least," Katie added, recalling the woman's lank, colorless hair and gray face, "she looks like she is."

"So? So they have an American with them. Big deal."

"It's a very big deal," said Katie testily, "because maybe she won't speak Katkajanian."

"And this is important because . . . ?" David raised his brows and spoke with elaborate patience, as if dealing with someone very dense. Katie's anger flared.

"Because then they'll have to talk to her in English! Which we understand. So maybe we can hear it and figure something out, *duh*! Don't start on me, David! You aren't that smart."

"*You* aren't that smart. I already thought that about the English—it's obvious," said David, lying.

"Right."

"But it won't matter what language they're using, because we won't hear. They're not going to let us listen. You think we're going to get within earshot of the kitchen?"

"Aren't you forgetting something else?" said Katie acidly. "Like, um, the vents?"

"Oh!" This idea was too stunning in its excellence for David even to pretend he'd also thought of it. "That's great," he admitted, excited. "Let's go."

The kids had discovered soon after moving to their new house that the same vents that carried heat and air-conditioning from room to room also carried sound. You couldn't hear anything just by walking around, but if you lay on the floor and pressed your ear straight to them, sometimes you could.

Katie was still thinking. Each vent connected only to certain rooms. The vent in the kitchen connected to their parents' bedroom. "We'd have to be in Mom and Dad's room," she said. "And that's where all Trixie's stuff is. She really wouldn't want us in there."

"She wouldn't want us listening, period," reasoned David. "If she found us, she'd be too mad about that to care where we were doing it. We just can't get caught, that's all."

"Then let's go now, while everyone's still arriving," said Katie, as yet another car door slammed outside.

Stealthily they rose from the rug on which they'd been sprawled and crept down the hall to their parents' room. The door was unlocked and they slipped in. It was awful to see Trixie's things strewn about.

"How much camouflage does she own?" asked Katie. One of Trixie's suitcases lay open on the floor, and there seemed to be nothing but army clothes inside it.

"Look!" David was pointing at the other case, which was also open and half under the bed. It bristled with walkie-talkies, cell phones, and small flat computers.

"No wonder she didn't want help with her luggage," said Katie bitterly, remembering the night of Trixie's arrival. "It looks like she raided an electronics store."

"We'd better be quick. What if she comes for that stuff?" David dropped silently to the floor by the window seat and rested his ear on the vent.

This was her mother and father's room and Katie loved it. But it was creepy thinking Trixie might walk in at any moment. "Move," she said. At her command David wriggled over to make room and she laid her head beside his on the small vent.

The air-conditioning was on, and at first they heard just the whooshing of cool air through the big house's many ducts. But after a moment this shut off, and suddenly they heard a man's voice droning on the kitchen television, the opening and closing of drawers, and the sounds of unfamiliar voices.

Then a woman's voice could be heard on the television. A derisive hoot of laughter followed.

"Oooh, 'dere she goes!" sneered one woman, who spoke with a Katkajanian accent.

"David, they *are* speaking English!" hissed Katie.

"Shhh!"

"How she secretary of state? How dat girl get dat job?" pursued the voice, indignant.

"That's so disrespectful!" Katie was truly upset. "She's not a girl! She's a grown—"

"Shhh!" David silenced Katie. An unfamiliar woman had begun to talk.

"Well, she dudded know Katkajad," said the woman. Her lack of any accent declared her to be the lank-haired American. An accent would have improved her voice, though. It was nasal, as if she had a heavy cold, and it seemed as flat and lifeless as her hair.

"Lised to her," the American woman continued tonelessly. "Secretary ob state. Ad she dudded hab a clue what's about to habbed."

"Not'ing can happen wit' no money," said another man. "Time for working. What dese people here got to sell, in dis house?"

The next voice to speak was chillingly familiar: It was Trixie's. "There's silver in that drawer," she said, and Katie and David heard footsteps.

"David, they're taking our silver!"

But Trixie was still talking. "I think she's got some rings and necklaces and things upstairs, too," she added. "Wait—you can take it all at the same time."

With that a chair scraped back and Trixie's heavy tread moved across the kitchen floor.

"She's coming!" David leaped up, snatching Katie's arm and jerking her to her feet as well. Both of them were flooded with fear.

Like quicksilver both children slipped out the door. This big house! Their rooms were at the end of a long hall. If Trixie saw them moving from her room to their own she would know where they'd been. They must not be heard, either, and if they ran they surely would be.

They slipped frantically along the wall, willing their footsteps to be silent. Breathlessly they arrived in Katie's room just as Trixie emerged at the top of the stairs.

They dared not close Katie's door completely. Trixie would hear it click. So they left it slightly ajar, and through it observed her clomping down the hall and disappearing into the room they had just left. Silent moments passed, and they waited.

At length Trixie emerged. Mrs. Bowden's jewelry box sat open on her arm, and as she walked she poked through it with one fat finger. Their dad had bought their mom several beautiful things when Rover had been sold. Katie had been told that one day those things would be for her—for her and Theo. Now the children watched in silent indignation as Trixie carefully removed a ring and slipped it into her own pocket. That ring had an enormous glittering jewel of a brilliant purple color and it was their mother's favorite. Trixie snapped the box shut and, more briskly, proceeded downstairs.

"She's a thief," said Katie hotly when Trixie had gone.

"And she's robbing them, too—those guys downstairs," said David.

"What do you mean?"

"I mean they're supposed to sell this stuff, to make money for whatever they're doing in Katkajan. Remember what they said in the kitchen? Something's supposed to happen there, now that they've got Mom and Dad. They need cash."

"But she kept Mom's ring," said Katie, getting it. "She kept that for herself. You're right! She's even sleazier than they are!"

"Well, that's a little more money they won't have to make trouble with. So I guess that part's good," said David. "Not that it'll matter, though," he added gloomily. "Something tells me they'll still have enough."

They stayed in Katie's room all day. They could think of nowhere else to go.

As she always did, Katie had saved her Halloween candy, consuming it bit by tiny bit so that it lasted all year long. This was August, so there wasn't much left, and that was very stale. But they ate it that day, as neither could stand the thought of venturing to the kitchen for food. If only they had thought to take some when they were down there cleaning up!

Katie's window was at the front of the house so, half hidden by the curtain, they saw as well as heard the coming and going that went on all that long, long day. Over the hours so many cars arrived and left that they lost track of the number of people in the house. Everyone who came carried luggage. And many who left had the Bowdens' things in their arms; their mother's jewelry box and the felt-lined drawer containing their silver were the first to go.

Katie and David no longer even cared. Their mom and dad were gone, and Theo, too. What were jewelry and silver? But as the afternoon faded into evening the indignation they had thought was exhausted rose again. One of the strangers, grinning, emerged with a soccer ball and began experimentally kicking it on their front lawn.

"That's mine," said David defiantly.

The stranger called out in Katkajanian, lifting his face toward the house as he did so. His eyes were slightly crossed and his nose canted sharply to the left as if it had at one time been broken. These oddities had the effect of turning his grin into a leer. But despite the man's unpleasant appearance Katie and David heard answering calls from within the house and raucous voices moving toward the front door. The Katkajanians were organizing a game.

The nerve!

But it got even worse. Just as the door opened the children heard a startled cry, a stumble, and the yowl of a cat whose tail had just been trodden. They did not have to know Katkajanian to understand the loud exclamation that followed.

The next thing they saw from their perch at the window was poor Slank, not running but flying out the door. Cat-like, he righted himself in midair and hit the ground running. Before they could cry out his name, he had streaked across the front lawn, slipped beneath the surrounding shrubbery, and disappeared across the street. The man with the crooked nose howled with laughter.

"Oh! Oh, Slank—he's gone!"

"Did they kick him or throw him?" demanded David.

"Who cares? Did you see how he was moving? He'll be roadkill before dinner!"

As Katie spoke, David seemed to feel Slank's sleek, heavy weight again on his lap and to hear his throaty purring. Gone!

"*Now* look!" cried Katie.

Four more men had run down the steps to join the one on the lawn. A pickup game was beginning.

Katie turned away from the window. "I'm not going to *watch* them have fun with our stuff," she announced.

"My stuff," corrected David.

"Like it matters now! And anyway," she added, feeling suddenly quarrelsome, "whose candy have you been eating all afternoon?"

"I thought it didn't matter."

"It doesn't," Katie retorted. "I'm just making a point. I'm just remembering everything you said about me saving my candy while you ate yours in two days. Good thing I did!"

"Oh, excuse me! Sorry I didn't realize our parents would be kidnapped and we'd be held prisoner in our rooms and we'd need that candy to live on! What're we down to now?" he added, changing the subject.

Katie reached under the bed and withdrew the once-bulging sack. She upended it on the floor and they both surveyed the dwindling contents.

"We'd better divide it up," she said. "There's not a lot left."

"Eleven pieces," said David. "You can have six. I'm sick of candy anyway."

"Very generous."

But in the end they broke a chocolate bar in two and each stuffed their pockets with five and a half pieces of candy. It was funny how possible starvation made you want to share, and with your sibling, even. You'd think it would work the other way around.

■ ■ ■

Night fell and Katie and David each permitted themselves one piece of candy for dinner. They had never imagined that they could enjoy chocolate so little, or that it could leave them so hungry.

They agreed that David would sleep in Katie's room that night. At bedtime he would slip across the hall to his own room to get his pillow. They no longer feared that he would be noticed. It appeared that the hordes that had taken over their home had entirely forgotten them. Tomorrow they would even risk a raid on the kitchen for some real food.

But they had not been forgotten, and their sleeping arrangements would not, after all, be up to them. Before they had even begun to settle down they heard Trixie's heavy footsteps mounting the stairs once again, and moments later she flung open Katie's door.

She stood before them, hands on hips.

"Get up," she announced. "You're coming with me now."

"Where?" David asked.

"It's our bedtime," Katie protested.

"You got that right!" She grinned unpleasantly. "But that's not your bed. That bed's for guests."

Strangers in her bed! The thought made Katie sick.

"We'll go to my room," David said.

Trixie's brow lowered. "I said you come with me!"

They dared not refuse. As they passed David's room they saw through the open door that two Katkajanian men were already in it. One of them was sprawled on his back on David's bed, ankles crossed and boots on. He, too, grinned at David as the children passed.

Wild thoughts raced through Katie's mind as they followed Trixie silently downstairs. Could they escape out the front door? If they made a dash for it, would they be caught?

Watching Trixie's feet, David wondered briefly if he should trip her.

But they did neither of these things. Where was she taking them?

When they reached the first floor, Trixie led them toward the kitchen. Perhaps they would now be offered food. Perhaps she realized they had not eaten.

People were in the kitchen—many people. One was in the sunroom picking oranges—their oranges! But this was information Katie and David absorbed in a flash as they passed by, for Trixie did not take them into the kitchen. Instead she opened the door to the basement and led them downstairs.

There was a bedroom in the basement, a bedroom for guests. So the real "guests" were in their rooms and they were to sleep downstairs! It was a good thing their parents had arranged that room so comfortably.

But Katkajanian music warbled on the radio in the guest room and yet more strangers were inside it, putting down their things. Were they going to sleep on the sofa?

They would have no privacy at all! The strangers would see them all night and hear every word they spoke.

But the sofas were piled high with yet more sleeping bags and duffels. To the children's horror, Trixie led them to the farthest corner of the basement, where the furnace lurked behind a slatted door. She pulled this door open and gestured to the concrete floor within it.

There lay two thin blankets. Beside them were a bottle of water and a couple of sandwiches wrapped in plastic.

"You've got to be kidding!" The words burst from David's lips despite himself. He would not have believed he would have the nerve to object.

And Katie was livid. "There's no way we can sleep here!" she cried. She thought for an instant of her room upstairs—her pillow, her comforter, her books—and the vision of it overwhelmed her. She balled both of her hands into fists, stepped closer to Trixie, and stamped her foot. "You wouldn't—you wouldn't make a dog sleep here!" she shouted. "This is *our house!*"

But scarcely had the words escaped her lips than four glowering strangers stepped to Trixie's side. Five angry faces glared down at David and Katie. Slowly, the man nearest David folded his arms across his chest. His crossed eyes floated weirdly above a nose that canted left. No one spoke.

That was it. There was nothing they could do. David

took Katie's arm and, gently, drew her into the small concrete closet.

"We'll be fine," he said curtly, and without looking at anyone's face he closed the door.

"It could be worse," he said quietly when their captors had walked away. "It's not like it's wet or gross or anything. It's not even dark." He was right about that. A dim light entered through the slats. "And we're alone. Or sort of."

Katie scarcely heard him. She stood rooted to the spot, with her heart still pounding and her mind still racing. "It isn't fair, David. It isn't right."

But David was strangely calm. It had been five against two. Whether it was fair or right hadn't mattered. He sank to the floor, picked up his sandwich, and unwrapped it. In the faint light he pulled apart the pieces of bread and sniffed tentatively at the slightly acrid contents. Some sort of foreign paste was smeared inside.

But undoubtedly it was food. He was very hungry, and who could say when they would receive their next meal? He slapped his sandwich back together and took a bite. He didn't like it, but he could eat it. And after he ate it he could sleep. The floor was very hard, but he was very tired.

It was terribly noisy in the basement. Clearly the Katkajanians would be awake for a long time. But after a while David did lie down, and sometime later he was dimly aware that Katie had done the same.

"We have to get away, David," she whispered softly.

He did not answer.

"We have to escape from them," she insisted.

He wanted only to sleep, and again he made no reply.

"In the morning," she continued, aware now that she was speaking to herself, "in the morning we'll run away." And then—despite the noise and the slatted light and the concrete, despite her sorrow and her fear—she fell asleep.

BANISHED

But in the morning they were taken away.

At the crack of dawn—before it was fully light, before there were cars on the streets, before they had even woken up—Trixie and the crooked-nosed Katkajanian roughly and unceremoniously dragged open the door to their closet.

The basement was still dark. The house was silent and—but for them—asleep. Trixie carried a flashlight that she shone in their faces.

"Get up," she whispered.

The children, fogged by sleep, simply stared.

"Up," she repeated, now jerking the flashlight toward the stairs, as if to beckon them forward. "We're going for a little ride in the car."

They asked no questions. And fleetingly—through her sleepy confusion and her terrible fear—Katie noticed that neither did Trixie. At some point, Trixie had abandoned the irritating upward tilt that used to end her every sentence. There was no need to sugarcoat anything now.

The children stumbled to their feet and prepared to follow her. But Trixie, indignant, pointed back toward the floor where they had lain.

"Get that!" she barked, gesturing toward the plastic from their sandwiches, which had been flattened beneath their bodies. "You don't leave your trash for others to pick up!"

Clutching the wads of plastic and the empty water bottle, and stumbling with fear and fatigue, the children followed Trixie across the basement and up the stairs, with the other Katkajanian silently following them. Lighting a path with her flashlight Trixie led them across the kitchen and out the back door.

Their fear was intense but still, the fresh dark air was good after their night in the stuffy closet. At the first touch of it on their faces they were fully alert.

They were led through the side yard and across the dewy grass to the front of the house. There a car idled in the driveway, with its headlights off despite the still-starry sky. The colorless, lank-haired American was behind the wheel. Trixie slipped into the front seat beside her while the crooked-nosed Katkajanian opened the back door and pointed the children in. They slid across the cold seat, the man slid in after them, and the door was slammed shut. The American woman put the car into gear and they rolled down the driveway with the lights still off.

"Where are we going?" David's voice trembled audibly. Any attempt to pretend he was not petrified was hopeless.

But there was no reply.

They rolled through the familiar streets, away from their home, past the pool, and out of their new neighborhood. They rolled past their school.

The driver switched on the headlights at last as they slipped onto the freeway. They continued to cruise in total silence. And soon after that—too soon—Trixie was gesturing and pointing and they were exiting on a familiar ramp.

The ramp took them beneath a lonely overpass, and as they glided under it the lights once again went off. They emerged onto a bleak and well-known road.

Gone were the leafy branches that spread like a canopy over the streets in their new neighborhood. Gone were the neat lawns and the well-tended houses. On either side of them were wrecks and hovels, rubble and dirt.

Katie closed her eyes. It was their old neighborhood.

The children could have made the rest of the trip on their own, and with their eyes closed. They knew it that well. And their hearts, which they had thought could sink no further, dropped down, down, down with every turn of the wheel.

No Mom, thought Katie. No Dad, no Theo. No room, no house, no home.

They were back to where they had started, with less than when they had begun.

The car pulled to a stop in front of the old place and the driver cut the motor. The house had, if anything, sagged still further than when they had left it, hoping never to see it again. Vandals had punched holes in the front steps. They would have to pick their way to the door. Plywood had been nailed over the barred windows. Who had put that up, and when? Now there would be no light as well as no exit.

"We're home!" Trixie sang with a sudden trill of a laugh. Her loudness jarred them in the silent car. She shoved open her door and leaped out, all but dancing around to open theirs. "Out!" she snapped, low-voiced now in the open air.

It was funny how even the car, which had been a detestable prison moments before, felt like a refuge now. But they had no alternative. Reluctantly they slid from their seats and huddled together on the familiar pavement. Trixie tucked her flashlight beneath her arm and, from the capacious pockets of her camouflage suit, she withdrew a key. She began picking her way up the broken steps. The man with the crooked nose and the lank-haired woman emerged from the car. The woman carried a smallish brown paper bag bundled beneath her arm. Joining them, she gave David a shove to indicate he was to follow.

A flicker of movement to his left drew David's startled eye. A fat gray rat was slipping beneath the stairs. David shut his eyes and squeezed them tight.

Trixie turned the key in the lock. Katie noticed with surprise that when she did so, a new and unfamiliar deadbolt slid open on the outside of the door. The door creaked open, dislodging a clod of dust and dirt that fell onto Trixie's head. She muttered angrily in Katkajanian and brushed the filth from her face. Impatiently pushing aside cobwebs, she led the way in.

They followed. They had no choice.

The front door opened straight into the small front room. Once it had been their living room and they had done their best to keep it clean. Though it had not been so very long since they had lived there, they could see in the beam of Trixie's light that in their absence it had become filthy with spiders and dust.

The driver dropped her paper bag onto the floor. "Thad's sub food," she said in her flat voice, nudging it with her foot.

Trixie grunted in affirmation. "Water's in the sink," she added. "We'll check on you later. So you'd better be good."

Then, incredibly, she and her two helpers turned back toward the door. They were going to leave. That was it. That was all they planned to say.

Now Katie's voice shook, too, but not just her voice, and not from fear. Now it was her whole body. The outrage. The utter outrage.

"What are you doing to our mother and father?" she demanded loudly. "When are you letting them go?"

"And what about us?" added David. "How long are you planning to leave us here, in this—in this—"

Trixie wheeled around, hands on hips. "You think this is bad? You think this place is bad?" She stared at David, hard, as she spoke. "You haven't seen anything. If you aren't good, this is gonna get a lot worse."

Then she turned on Katie. "And do you want your mother and father? Do you want to see them again?"

A terrible, cold fear seemed to stop Katie's heart. She raised her clasped hands to her face in an involuntary appeal. "Are they alive?"

"Oh, they're alive," said Trixie. Katie felt as if her heart resumed beating at these words. Trixie was watching, and now she sneered. "That's very sweet," she said. "But listen up, cupcake: If you want to see your parents again, you *shut up*. You *don't. Tell. Anybody.*"

With that dreadful warning, she and her companions stepped out the door and shut it tight. Katie and David heard the key turn in the lock. They heard the creaking deadbolt slip into position, barring them in. Then their jailers' footsteps clomped down the front steps, the car doors slammed, the motor came to life, and their only hope of escape rolled away from the curb and was gone.

They were alone.

Fortunately, they were not left in total darkness. By the time Trixie and her friends drove away, the blackness outside had faded to gray. And while the windows of their ancient house were boarded over, the boards had been hastily and sloppily applied. Cracks between the panels of wood sent shafts of the rapidly brightening daylight across the floor.

But Katie and David were beyond appreciating this small piece of good luck. They felt that they had sunk as low as it was possible to sink.

And as bad as it was for both of them, David had a special and secret problem: rats. He was mortally afraid of them. When they had lived in this house—and how, he now wondered, had they ever lived here?—he had kept this shameful fact from Katie. She was his sister and they had few secrets from each other, but he had never wanted her to know this one. It was going to be hard to conceal it from her now.

Katie sank to the dusty floor. She crossed her arms on her raised knees and buried her face in them. "Sit," she said to her brother, her words coming muffled through her arms. "We're going to be here for a while."

"It's too dirty," he replied. No way was he sitting on that floor, where the rats could get him.

"They don't come out in the daylight," she replied. "We aren't going to see them till tonight. You may as well rest now."

So she did know. Embarrassed, David dropped to a crouch.

Katie lifted her face and gazed into his. She was very calm. "So what now?" she asked simply. "What do we do?"

David did not reply, so she continued. "The way I figure," she said, "there are two things. I mean, two things we have to do. For starters—"

"Katie."

"What?"

"Stop a minute—OK? I have to say something, and I only want to say it once. So you have to promise that after I do say it, we never talk about it again—all right?"

She was silent, curious.

"You have to promise or I won't—"

"OK! I promise."

David took a deep breath and his heart began to race. "I'm sorry," he said, trying to control his voice. "I'm sorry I got us into this. I know you didn't want them—you didn't want Mom and Dad to go."

For a moment she simply absorbed this. "OK," she said. "That's OK. David? I was trying to tell you, there are two things we have to do."

She didn't even seem to mind! Maybe he hadn't needed to apologize.

"The first thing," she was saying, "is that we have to get out of here, and before tonight."

Amen to that, thought David, remembering the rats.

"We can't sleep here," Katie continued, "and we don't want to be here tomorrow either. What if they come back? I never want to see Trixie again," she added feelingly. "So that's one. Two is that after we get out, we have to tell."

"But what about Mom and Dad, Kat? If we tell, they'll—"

"They'll what?" she demanded. "And what'll they do if we *don't* tell? If we don't tell, are they going to let them go?"

This had not occurred to him.

"Not telling—that's *their* idea. Those are *their* rules."

"Right," he said slowly, getting it. "We have to make our own rules, for us. But who do we tell? Because whoever it is, they have to handle this just right. As soon as we tell them they have to move fast. They have to get the Katkajanians before the Katkajanians can get Mom and Dad."

"Exactly. And even before that they have to believe us, and that means we have to tell the right person. I mean, if we tell the police, the first thing they'll do is go talk to Trixie. She actually is our nanny, remember? She has papers from the agency! And she'll laugh it off and say we just ran away, and they'll believe her. They always believe adults! And then they'll give us back to her and when the police are gone—"

"I get it," said David. "No police."

"We can't tell any strangers at all," continued Katie. "In fact, the way I see it, there's only one person we can tell."

"And that person is . . . ?"

"Uncle Alex."

David's jaw dropped. "Uncle *Alex*? Hermit Uncle Alex? Uncle Alex who we've never *met*?"

"Think, David! What's this all about, this kidnapping? Millions of people adopt babies—why take Mom and Dad? This is about Rover! They want Mom and Dad because of Rover! And who else in the world—besides Mom and

Dad, I mean—knows about that?"

"But isn't there something you're overlooking, Katie? We don't know where Uncle Alex lives!"

"That's not true! We know exactly where he lives. Mom and Dad have been telling us for years." She began reciting. "He lives on a mountain north of Melville, Vermont, just below the border with Canada. There's only one road that crosses Melville, and you take it straight through. You go half a mile past the first bridge out of town, then turn north into the woods by the big rock that was split by lightning."

"You climb, always going north," said David, taking over. Katie was right. They did know; they'd been hearing these directions all their lives.

He continued. "There are mountains ahead, and you keep the two big peaks in front of you, as if you were heading straight between them. But before you get there—"

"*Way* before you get there—"

"You come to the creek. And you follow it upstream, to the left. You just keep following the water and following the water—"

"And then you're there."

Both children were silent.

At length David spoke again, this time quite off topic. "If we found Uncle Alex, do you think he'd tell us what Rover is?"

"David, we have bigger problems than that!"

"Yeah, well, this one's always bugged me." And it had, too. And now that he was tired and depressed it was bugging him again. David sighed. "Just a thought," he said, moving on. "And you're right—we do have bigger problems. Like, how do we get ourselves nearly to Canada? Have you figured out that part, Kat? I mean, seeing as how we don't have any money."

Katie overlooked his sarcasm. "No," she admitted. "I don't know how we do that. Maybe we'll hitchhike or something."

"Great! We'd be very inconspicuous, a couple of twelve-year-olds with our thumbs out. The police would pick us up before we left the neighborhood."

"OK, so we won't hitchhike. We'll figure out something else. You can't expect me to think of everything."

"Anyway, we have a bigger problem," David continued gloomily. "We have to get out of here. And we're locked in, Kat."

"Probably," she admitted. "But I guess we should check anyway. Just in case."

Neither of them wanted to explore the house. Neither of them wanted to move an inch from where they had been put. Although they used to live there, the place now struck them as intensely creepy. It wasn't just the dust and the cobwebs and the silence; it was the darkness, too. Whoever had nailed the boards over the windows had done a much better job in the rest of the house than they had in the living room. There were almost no cracks between the pieces of wood in the other rooms, so beyond where they sat the place was nearly pitch-black.

But reluctantly they rose to their feet and rattled every door. With their bare hands they tried fruitlessly to turn the heavy screws that fastened the bars to every window.

It was hopeless. There was no way out.

Despondently they returned to the living room to wait out the long, miserable day.

They did not want to eat the Katkajanians' food. But they both felt the importance of saving the chocolate with which their pockets were stuffed, and at length hunger drove them to open the battered brown bag. It contained a dozen more of the same acrid sandwiches they had eaten the night before.

"Twelve of them!" Katie cried in dismay. "How long are they leaving us here?"

She had not wanted the Katkajanians to return, but now she feared they never would.

They each ate two sandwiches, telling themselves they'd better save the rest. Then they braced themselves for the long day and the coming night. The plan was that Katie was to sleep now, so that she could be up through the dark hours to scare away any rats that might emerge. After all, as she explained to David, she didn't like rats, but they both knew they bothered David worse than they bothered her.

It wasn't a great plan, but it was the best they could come up with. And as it turned out, the plan failed.

David had meant to stay awake. Certainly—certainly—he wanted Katie awake at night. But his body ached with weariness from his short night on the furnace room floor. And the light was very dim in this old house, and his mind and heart were heavy.

Weighed down by tedium and sorrow and worry, both children sank to the dusty floor and fell fast asleep.

Again David dreamed. He was in jail, in a lonely cell in a great stone prison. He wanted to get out but knew he could not.

Trixie was in the cell next door and she had a shovel. How he knew this he could not have said, but he could hear her digging. He heard the *skritch, skritch* of the shovel scraping through dirt and stone. He heard the rustle of the rubble she tossed aside.

She was digging a tunnel so that she could escape.

David didn't want Trixie to succeed. Through his dream confusion he felt the injustice of his being stuck while she got away. He called for the guard. The guard must stop her and take her terrible shovel.

Skritch, rustle. Skritch, rustle. Where was the guard? Why didn't he come?

He woke with a start to a resounding thud and a sharp squeal. "What!" David sat bolt upright on the floor of the old house. It was black as tar and he was terrified.

"Rats," said Katie's voice beside him in the dark. "It's rats."

"What was that noise?"

"My shoe—I threw my shoe at one."

"Katie, I can't see a thing!"

"Yeah, it's dark. I'm throwing at the sound. You can't sleep; we both need to stay awake. We need to make noise or we won't keep them away."

David leaped to his feet. Had there been a table he'd have leaped onto that. He was trapped in a lightless room with rats.

Katie had been crouching, removing her other shoe.

But now she stood beside him and began stamping her feet.

"David, make noise! We're bigger than they are."

But David was frozen with fear.

Katie stamped again, and now she jumped. She tried to shout, but her shouts felt puny in the dark and she could not get them out of her throat.

There was a long, bold skitter as something ran clean across the floor not three feet from where they stood.

David gasped. He felt panic rising in fumes around him, clouding his mind. Stay cool, he told himself. Stay cool. Don't give in to fear. He relaxed his clenched fists and drew in a deep breath, hoping it would calm him.

But he released that breath in a scream. There was something else in the room and it wasn't a rat.

The skittering to and fro had been replaced by bedlam. Another rat had raced across the floor even closer to them than the first, and this one had just been attacked. They could see nothing but they heard the thud that landed in the path of the darting rodent and the battle that was raging inches from their feet.

An anguished, half-strangled squeal mingled with David's scream and the besieged rat streaked from the room. Racing after it went something that yowled a high-pitched yowl.

A high-pitched and very familiar yowl. *Slank.*

"David, he's here!"

"It's got to be him!"

And sure enough, within seconds the soft, comfortable meow they knew so well came toward them across the blackened room and the sleek body of their cat was curling about their ankles. They scooped him into their arms, squeezing him tight and burying their faces in his warm, silky fur.

"He's come to save us," cried Katie, "to save us from the rats!"

"They sure are gone for now," answered David, as Slank's meows dropped a register into a deep, rumbling purr. He massaged the back of the cat's neck, rubbing him just the way he liked best.

"Oh, Slanky, you didn't get hit by a car!" David couldn't see Katie, but he could tell she was crying. "It took you days, but you came right back to your own house and you came inside and you saved us."

David's hand, which had continued to rub the cat, stopped short.

"Katie."

"What?" She was still nuzzling Slank's neck.

"Katie. He came *inside*."

"Right, David. That's where we are; maybe you noticed." She was not too upset to be sarcastic.

"Kat, think! He came *in*. He has no key, Kat!"

"Oh . . . *Oh!* "

"And how did he come in, Katie? Because however he

came *in*, he could go *out* the same way. And however *he* goes out—"

"The cat door! David, how did we miss that? How did we forget the cat door?"

"The only question is, will we fit?" David's voice was bright with excitement for the first time in days. "Wait!" he added.

But Katie had already dropped Slank and begun feeling her way toward the kitchen door where their father had cut a special hole for the cat, years and years ago.

It was strange how boldly they moved through the inky house, now that they knew where they were going. By the time David caught up with Katie, she was already there. She had sprawled across the filthy floor and was trying to slide through the little door headfirst.

"Wow," she said. "It's going to be really tight. And I'm smaller than you are."

"Take off the frame."

Both children began prying at the metal rim that was nailed around the edges of the opening, and to which a rubber flap was attached. Without it the hole would be at least two inches bigger, and that might make the difference.

They easily tore away the rubber and a faint, useful light came through the opening. But the metal was murderously difficult to remove in the total darkness of the kitchen, and with no tools.

"We need something to wedge under it; that's the problem," said David, shaking his now-bleeding fingertips.

"David, the drawers!"

"What?"

"Oh, please! We're in the kitchen! Didn't you used to live here? Check the drawers and cabinets. I'm sure we left some old stuff here!"

They had. It was a dirty business, because those drawers were now filthy with the droppings of mice and rats that had rampaged through them in the owners' absence. But by swallowing their distaste and feeling around, they found an old, bent spatula and, better still, a bottle opener. Armed with these tools they set back to work on the cat door and soon heard the welcome crack of nails wrenching free of old wood.

"That's going to do it!" said David, joyfully eyeing the new and larger hole in the pale light. He dropped onto his back and gripped the wooden edges of the door, preparing to slide out.

"Wait! My shoes. And the food."

"Yuck," said David, remembering the sandwiches.

"Don't be stupid!"

"You're right," he said. "Go get them, OK?"

"Come with me!"

Reluctantly he rose and returned with her to the detestable living room, where they found Slank sitting guard by the paper bag that was now all they owned in the world.

"Good Slank. You didn't let the rats get it." David stroked Slank's arching back while Katie tied her shoelaces.

"He saved our lives, David," said Katie, her voice quaking. "I wish we could take him. But," she added sadly, "I know he'd just come home again."

"We'll get him back someday," said David. "Bye," and though he wasn't the kissy type, he kissed the top of Slank's warm head. "Now, we're out of here."

And they were. With light steps and a rush of excitement, they raced back to the kitchen, dropped to the floor, and slid, easily now, through the hole in the door. When they leaped to their feet on the other side the night air washed over their flushed and dusty faces.

Night usually seems dark, because one generally enters it from a lighted place. But entering it now from their blackened prison was almost like stepping into day. The sky was a gorgeous wilderness of moon and sparkling stars and a fresh breeze was up.

They were free. David's wristwatch shone in the moonlight and he peered at it. It was ten thirty.

It was ten thirty p.m., they were free, and they had no idea how to get to the one place on earth where they could possibly go.

STOWAWAYS

It was amazing, Katie reflected a few minutes later, how quickly you could go from being thrilled to be free to being worried about what you'd do next.

Having no alternative, the children had set out walking. And no sooner did they do so than they remembered that they were in a blasted wasteland of ruined buildings and rubble-strewn empty lots.

A few buildings still showed signs of life. Lights shone in the occasional window and from somewhere they heard faint music. But the street where they walked was deserted—unless you counted the dangerous criminals who surely prowled the alleyways, or yet more of the fierce rats from which they had just worked so hard to escape.

And all of this surrounded them in every direction. So it didn't much matter which way they went.

Which didn't mean they couldn't have a fight about it.

"Katie," said David, "nice plan about finding Uncle Alex. That would be the uncle who lives about a million miles away. As I recall, this was the stage where we were going to figure something out."

A car rolled slowly past them. In its darkened interior they could dimly see a pair of young men eyeing them suspiciously. Katie and David caught their breath as the car braked slightly, but to their immense relief it only hesitated, then moved on.

Great. They looked too poor to rob. Katie resumed their conversation. "Like you have another idea," she said. "A better idea than Uncle Alex."

"That doesn't matter," he said. "Your plan can still be stupid, whether I have a better idea or not."

At this Katie stopped short and folded her arms across her chest.

"What?" said David.

"Go on! Go ahead. I don't have to walk with you."

"Give me a break."

"We don't have to stay together."

"OK. *Sorry*. Let's keep moving—this isn't a great place to stop," said David, looking around uneasily.

"And I don't have to think of everything, either," Katie continued, still not moving.

"You haven't thought of everything. I thought of the cat door, remember?"

"Well, now you can think of something else. And if you can't, don't be on my case about it."

"I said sorry! My bad."

Katie unfolded her arms and, with a sigh, resumed moving forward. "There's a gas station around the next corner," she said, remembering one of the few functioning businesses in that blighted neighborhood. "Let's go there."

"Because . . . ?"

"Because it has one of those little stores and they might let us use the bathroom. I want to wash my hands with soap." She was still thinking about the droppings in their old kitchen drawers.

"Katie, we don't want to be seen, remember? What are they going to think about a couple of kids showing up in the middle of the night, on foot, with no adults?"

"At that place? I hate to tell you, David. They're not going to care."

She was right. The man behind the thick glass shield gave them a curious look, but he said nothing. With a wordless nod he indicated the bathroom. "Think of something," Katie hissed in her brother's ear as she headed in. "Get an idea."

The bathroom door clicked shut behind her and David leaned with feigned casualness against it, looking out the window and trying to pretend that there was nothing odd about him hanging out in a gas station in the middle of the night.

While he stared, a massive tractor trailer turned ponderously off the street and rumbled, snorting, into the blaring light of the filling station. king foods, blared the logo from the side of the truck, amid gargantuan swirling photos of fruits, meats, and pastries.

David watched as, with much backing up and adjusting, the driver positioned his vehicle beside the diesel pump. Then the man cut the motor, leaped from his cab, and vanished on the far side of his truck to hook the gigantic rig up for fueling. This done, he reappeared, hitched up his jeans, and sauntered toward the small convenience mart where David waited for Katie.

David's heart began to pound and he shrank behind a cooler full of iced drinks. He willed Katie not to choose this moment to emerge from the bathroom. The clerk might not care what they were up to, but the driver was an unknown.

"Evenin'," said the driver to the clerk.

The surly clerk did not reply.

"How far to the state line from here?" the driver persisted.

"Which way you heading?" The clerk looked as if it pained him to speak.

"Headed north," the driver replied. "Toward Yonkers.

Soon's I get there I got to cut west. 'Bout how long's it gonna take me, from here?"

"Yonkers is four, four and a half hours," said the clerk.

"Pack of those," the driver said, slapping down a bill and gesturing toward a box of cigarettes. "Got a delivery for you," he added. "Be bringing it in, in a minute."

But David scarcely heard. His mind was humming. Katie had said to think of something and he had. North. The driver was headed north.

"Which way to the can?" the driver asked, and the clerk pointed toward the bathroom door. As the driver turned in that direction, his eyes swept the small space and landed on David.

He had been seen. It was all up. David stood, breathless, with his heart frozen in his chest.

For an instant the driver stared at David in astonishment. His brow lowered and David could practically hear the man's mind working. What was a lone kid doing in a place like this in the middle of the night?

Still frowning, the driver put his hand on the doorknob of the bathroom and turned it. He found it locked, and at this his face relaxed.

Of course. David's parent must be in that bathroom, right there. Now, reassured, the man nodded politely at David. "Evenin'," he began.

But at just that moment the clerk, glancing at a monitor before him, observed, "Your tank's full."

The driver grunted and turned back toward the exit. David's heart resumed beating as the man strode outside and disappeared yet again behind the massive vehicle. Katie slipped out of the bathroom. David seized her arm and pulled her behind a more distant rack that held magazines, snacks, and sundries.

"That was so close!" she whispered. "I almost walked out and then I heard him!"

"I know. And he actually saw me. He assumed you were my mom or dad. But did you hear what he said? Katie, he's going *north*."

She looked at him quizzically.

"North, Kat! Like us! We're going the same way!"

"So what? Are you going to ask him for a lift?"

They heard the clerk's chair swivel, and over the top of the rack they saw him craning his neck and peering at them curiously. Quickly David snatched a magazine, opened it, and pretended to read.

"No," he said under his breath after a moment. "We're not going to ask for a ride. We're just going to take one."

"Where, on the roof?" Katie was finding this conversation frustrating.

"Ever heard of stowaways?" her brother responded testily. "They sneak onto trains or ships and find a place to hide. When they get where they're going, they sneak off. We can stow away in the back of this truck."

"But he'd have to open it."

"Look out the window." David was facing the front of the shop, and over the top of the magazine rack he had a clear view of the pump where the truck was parked. Katie had been facing him and had seen nothing. But now she turned around and gasped.

The great doors at the back of the trailer were flung wide open and a ramp had been dropped to the pavement. The ramp led straight up and inside the glowing interior of the truck. It looked like the road to the Promised Land.

"But where's the driver?"

"Inside," said David.

"Little problem!"

"We have to wait for him to leave, that's all."

"And hope he leaves it open."

David was still clutching a magazine in front of his face. Katie seized one as well and, like her brother, stood staring tensely at pages she did not see, waiting and hoping and feeling as if by radar for any sign of movement at the truck.

CUT THE CALORIES AND KEEP THE YUM! chirped the headline on the page in front of her. Like I care; the thought flashed through her mind and was gone. Out of the corner of her eye she saw that the magazine David was "reading" was actually upside down.

She also observed, in silent amazement, that David's right hand was moving. Katie watched as it stealthily reached for the rack, where it removed from a wire prong two bubble packs containing flashlights and batteries.

David was stealing! Stealing was very wrong—as wrong as it got. But . . . like a high-powered computer, Katie's mind scrolled through the days ahead, imagining and anticipating what she and David would need to accomplish. Her eyes roved, flickering, over the rack before them and landed on a map labeled THE EASTERN STATES: PRIMARY AND SECONDARY ROADWAYS. Noiselessly she removed the map from its slot and slid it into her pocket.

Now she, too, had stolen. Wanting, somehow, to get her bearings, she glanced across at David's watch. It was five minutes before eleven. Heart pounding, Katie resumed staring at her magazine.

Then everything happened at once.

A loud sigh erupted from the clerk. He rose from his chair, stretched, and stepped through a door at the back of his booth. At the same instant, the truck driver emerged from the back of his truck, pushing a dolly on which he had balanced a couple of shrink-wrapped boxes. He descended the ramp with a clatter, wheeling the dolly, and headed across the pavement to the store where Katie and David hid with their magazines and purloined loot.

The driver shouldered the door open and entered the small store amid a gust of warm night air. He sighed with what looked like annoyance when he realized that the clerk had stepped away. Then he set down the dolly in front of the cashier's window, thumped across the floor to the bathroom, and shut himself into it, turning the lock with an audible click.

For an instant David looked at Katie and Katie looked at David.

"Now!" he mouthed.

Without a sound they slipped from behind the rack, out through the door, and across the wide open space to the truck. The gas station was brightly lit and the truck seemed very far away. If either the clerk or the driver emerged now—or even looked out the window—they would be seen and everything would be over. But they dared not run for fear of being heard.

They had reached the ramp that led into the truck. It rattled alarmingly as they darted up it.

"Hide!" cried Katie. Inside, an aisle ran down the center of the truck all the way to the back. On either side of the aisle—arranged in rows like the seats in a theater—were tall stacks of boxes and crates. Katie headed down the central aisle, ducked behind the third row of boxes, and dropped to a crouch. David followed. Quickly he noted that the boxes were fastened down and would not slide as they traveled—good.

"Dumb of him to leave the truck open in this neighborhood," whispered David.

Katie did not reply. She was trying not to breathe.

Whatever it was that the driver was delivering, it couldn't take more than a moment or two to make the drop. After that he'd be back.

Sure enough, there he was. They heard his heavy footsteps outside the truck. They listened as he wheeled the dolly back up the ramp and strapped it to the wall. Then he thudded back down the ramp, slid the ramp up, slammed the doors shut, scraped a bolt noisily into position, and clicked a lock.

At the same moment, the lights went out, but David and Katie didn't care. They were in.

Footsteps clomped to the front of the truck and the driver's door opened, and then it too slammed with a bang. With a jump the motor turned over and with a squeal the brake released. The great creature lurched into motion. Roaring, it lumbered out of the gas station, turned heavily onto the road, and slipped into the flowing stream of traffic. The children sat in pitch-darkness on a hard and rattling metal floor, but they could feel the vehicle swaying and gathering speed.

They were locked inside a moving truck. In another moment they would be on the highway and rolling north.

They could relax at last, but after so long a strain it would not be easy. Katie dropped her head onto her knees and tried to will her heart to stop pounding.

From beside her she heard her brother hiss *"Yes!"* and

felt rather than saw his fist pumping downward. "Kat!" David's voice was tight with excitement.

"What?"

"Kat, we did it! We did it! This is so *excellent*! I just heard the driver, then I got the idea, and it worked!"

"We hope."

"We *know*! It's working right now, Kat! Every single second we're a few feet closer to Uncle Alex!"

"Shhh! What if the driver can hear us?"

"He can't!"

"You don't know that! And you need to calm down. We still have plenty of problems."

"Oh, I'm so glad I'm with you. You really cheer me up, you know that?"

"You'd better pull out those flashlights you stole. We need to take a look at my map."

David was furious, but she could hear him fumbling in his pockets and then biting at the hard plastic that encased the flashlight. "Here—give me one," she ordered. He thrust a hard, heavy package in her direction and she began to feel around the rim of it for an opening.

"Good thing it comes with batteries," she said, beginning to feel a little sorry that she'd been so negative.

But David did not answer. She didn't just get to make up. Not just like *that*.

■ ■ ■

It was some time before their flashlights were ready to use. Hard as it was to unpack them—when they couldn't see a thing—it was harder still to load them with batteries. For one thing, as soon as the flashlights came loose from their plastic, all four batteries spilled onto the floor and promptly rolled away. They had to crawl after them, feeling around on the floor in the dark. As soon as they found two they tried to load up one light so they could look for the others. But they couldn't tell positive from negative, and kept getting confused about which ends they'd already tried to position in which directions. By the time they finally generated a thin beam of light they were sweating, dusty, exhausted, and once again thoroughly furious with each other.

But the light itself was a great relief. They quickly found the remaining batteries and assembled the second flashlight much more rapidly than the first. For a few moments they simply sat, basking in the luxury of their newly made lights and trying to recover their tempers. But then . . .

"We shouldn't use up the batteries," Katie remembered, flicking the switch on hers. "Let's just check out the map, then we'll turn both of them off."

"Why do you keep saying we need the map?" queried David, reluctantly conceding that she was right about not wasting the lights they had labored so hard to assemble. "We're not the ones driving."

"Because he's not going to take us all the way to Uncle Alex, is he?" responded Katie. "He's only going to Yonkers. Then he's going west—you told me so yourself. So we have to switch to another truck in Yonkers, and we'd better pick one that's going the right way."

"I get it." David's voice was gloomy. How were they supposed to do that? This stowaway thing had been amazingly easy the first time, but that didn't mean they could pull it off twice.

"What time is it?" continued Katie, all business.

David peered at his watch. "Eleven thirty."

"Good. We got in here just after eleven, so that means right about now"—she snapped open her map and pointed at one precise spot—"I figure we're probably here."

David hunched over Katie's finger, which was positioned about halfway between Washington DC and Baltimore, Maryland, on Interstate 95. For a moment her eyes wandered north. "There," she said, and—moving her finger north and slightly east—she deposited it squarely on Interstate 91. "That's the road we want. I-91 goes straight up through New York State to the border with Vermont—see? And it goes through Yonkers. So after we get off, we just have to find a truck that's headed for I-91 north."

"But Yonkers is big," said David, dismay in his voice. "Just because we're in Yonkers doesn't mean we'll be anywhere near I-91."

"I told you we still had problems," she retorted with gloomy satisfaction, beginning to fold up the map. "But at least now we know what our problems are."

"I can tell you *my* problem," said David, looking worried. "Or it isn't a problem yet, but I think it's going to be. At some point I'm going to have to go to the bathroom."

"Well, you can't do it here," cried Katie, alarmed. "It stinks enough as it is."

She was right about that. It was summer, after all. The temperature in the truck must be hovering around ninety degrees, and the air was dusty, humid, and dank. Turning their traveling car into a toilet would not improve matters.

"Well, I'm not that desperate," replied David, miffed. "I can wait. Thanks for your support, though," he added sarcastically.

"We'll be getting out very soon," urged Katie.

"Let's not talk about it," said David. "What we need to do now is get some food."

Both of them were very hungry. It had been daylight when they last ate, and in their haste to board the truck they had left the bag containing the remaining sandwiches on the floor at the gas station. They had both been nibbling on chocolate until they were sick of it, and anyway, there was little of that left.

Fortunately, they now found themselves in a truck full of groceries. So David was right. This was an opportunity they could not pass up.

They soon discovered, though, that turning packaged groceries into food was very hard to do. For one thing, everything was stacked so high and sealed so well that it would not be easy to get through to the contents of any box. And for another, it turned out that relatively few groceries amounted to anything they'd actually want to eat.

Once again both flashlights were on as they cruised the aisles of their rolling grocery store, searching for foods that did not need cooking and looked as if they could plausibly be extracted from their packages.

"'All-Purpose Flour,'" read David, shining his light on the side of a shrink-wrapped crate and running his hands over the plastic that enclosed it. "'Two-Ply Paper Towels.' 'Powdered Dishwasher Detergent.'"

"Shhh!" said Katie from the other side of the truck. Why did David never remember to keep it down? She peered yet more closely at the label before her. Canned soups. Those would be hopeless. Salad dressing. Who would have thought there'd be nothing to eat in a truck full of food?

Katie heard a barfing noise from David. "What?" she asked.

"Dog biscuits."

"Actually—"

"I'm not that desperate!"

Sighing, Katie turned down the next aisle, waving her flashlight listlessly at the boxes that lined it. Her heart leaped. "David!"

He scurried to her side, and triumphantly she pointed her light squarely at the middlemost box in the wall of cartons on her left.

THE CHEESY SNACK! announced the only side of the box that they could see.

"Sweet!" said David, pouncing on the carton.

"What are they?" whispered Katie.

"I don't care," he answered. "Let's get 'em open."

They quickly decided that it would be easier to tear a hole in the side of the box and pull out the snacks— whatever they were—than to pull the box out of its stack and open it the right way. But "easier" wasn't the same as "easy."

Cardboard, it turned out, was nearly as unbreakable as wood. So instead of punching through the box, they had to tear off the tape that sealed the carton around the edges and open it at the seam. This resulted in numerous paper cuts and broken nails. And as if their bruised and bleeding fingertips were not aggravation enough, they had to wage the whole struggle in a tight, narrow space, with flashlights wedged under their arms, in a hot, unventilated, moving truck.

Sweat rolled in rivulets down Katie's sides, and her

cuticles stung as she jammed her dirty fingers into the gap they were painfully trying to open along the side of the box.

"David," she gasped, "we don't need snacks; we need drinks."

"That's next," he grunted.

With a wrench the side of the box came free, exposing a wall of blue and orange cracker boxes.

"Yes!" Both children lunged. Their flashlights clattered to the floor, flinging wild beams everywhere as they pulled out armfuls of boxes and retreated with their booty to the wide center aisle of the truck.

David dropped to the floor and ripped the top off of one of the boxes, letting the others tumble in a heap about him. He was just tearing at the foil packet inside when Katie suddenly said, "David! Don't."

He stopped, staring up at her in bewilderment. "What?" he said. "I'm starving, Kat!"

"What time is it?" she demanded.

He looked at his watch, his irritation increasing. "It's twelve twenty. It's after midnight, Katie! I think we last ate at, what? Six? I'm incredibly hungry!"

"I know; I am too. But listen, David. We've been in this truck for an hour and fifteen minutes. It took us *over an hour*—OK, some of that time was for the flashlights—it took us about an hour to get these crackers."

"So?" Defiant, David ripped the foil, but he did not eat.

"So it could take us at least that long to find something to drink."

"Get to the point!"

"I am, if you'd just listen! David, we have to find drinks! Who knows what'll be in our next truck? The next truck could be carrying . . . lightbulbs, I don't know; or furniture, or toilets—"

"Don't say that!"

Katie simply stared.

"Don't say 'toilet'! Katie, I can't drink anything!"

"Oh, I forgot. Sorry . . . although in that case," she continued, "you shouldn't eat crackers at all. Look at the box. They're going to make you even thirstier than you already are."

The box was emblazoned with a banner that screamed: THE CHEESIEST EVER! David chucked it across the aisle, defeated and miserable. She was right, of course.

"Why'd you have to say 'toilet'?" he repeated, disconsolate. "Now I feel even worse."

"Sorry," she said again. "But we do have to look for drinks and we'd better find them before we start eating 'The Cheesy Snack.'"

David glared at her back as she plunged yet again down one of the narrow canyons between the walls of cartons. But before long she heard him sigh and rise to his feet to join her search.

This time they looked for a very, very long while.

Eventually they had read and rejected every label at eye level. That left boxes they could only examine by crouching uncomfortably in the dust, or, worse, by climbing. "How are we going to unpack these drinks if they turn out to be up near the ceiling?" Katie demanded as she clung to the crevices in her cardboard wall, peering at a very high label.

David did not answer. Soon after, though, she heard him utter a muffled cry.

"What?" With the back of her hand, Katie wiped the sweat that poured down into her eyes. Her face was gritty with dust.

"I said, *got it*!" shouted David. He had long ago stopped worrying whether the driver would hear him.

David had found juice boxes. They were packed, as Katie had feared, at the very top of a towering wall of boxes. And they were obviously intended for very young children. Even their crate had cartoon characters all over it.

But by this time they would practically have drunk mouthwash. And as luck would have it, the position of the box turned out to be an advantage. "Geronimo!" called David, and shoved it to the floor. It was heavy with liquid and fell with a thud. The box's cardboard seams split on impact, and it took only a moment's work for Katie and David to rip it wide open, exposing the gaudy, cellophane-wrapped flats of juice within.

"Thank you, thank you!" cried Katie, tearing one open. With trembling, exhausted fingers she peeled the wrapper from one tiny straw and jabbed it into the box. Her exertions had left her so weak that she could barely pierce the foil. But as soon as she did so, she inhaled the contents in a single slurp. The juice was sweet and sticky and as hot as she was, but it was liquid and it was delicious.

She grabbed a second box. "You're torturing me," said her brother bitterly, watching her.

"Just start filling your pockets," she said, scuttling down the aisle to where they'd left the crackers. "But wait!"

"What now?"

"Let's just pick this stuff up," said Katie. "Because he might stop. And if we leave it in the middle of the aisle, he'll freak the minute he opens the door, and then he'll find us."

This was a good point. They filled their pockets to bulging with drinks and snacks and shoved aside the goods they'd unpacked as inconspicuously as possible.

Then they turned off their flashlights to save batteries, sat down in the aisle, and waited.

One o'clock became one thirty. One thirty became two o'clock.

David, unable to bear it, peed in the back left corner of the truck. The stench embarrassed him and added to their troubles. He waited for Katie to say something mean, but to his surprise she said nothing about it. She knew he'd had no choice. Besides, if this continued for much longer, she would be in the same position.

David drained three juices boxes, practically in a single swallow.

Two o'clock became two thirty and two thirty became three, and still they rumbled forward.

"Kat," said David eventually.

"Mmm." Katie was leaning against a wall of boxes with her knees up and her arms tight around them. It was plain from her voice that she was growing drowsy.

"Kat, should we have some kind of plan? For Yonkers, I mean."

"Plan?" Katie must be very drowsy indeed, not to perk up at that word. Usually she had a plan for everything. Katie was the kind of girl who diagrammed her homework.

"Yes, plan," he said irritably. "Like, when this thing stops, how do we get out of here without being seen? And where do we go after that? What if there's no other truck? What if we're in the middle of nowhere?"

"We can't plan it, David," she said. "Because of all that—of what you just said. We don't know enough. We have to take our chances—that's all. Now"—she broke off in a yawn—"now leave me alone. I'm really tired."

And she rested her chin on her knees and closed her eyes.

But David stared into the dark. So they were both worried about Yonkers. Great! He could feel the road rumbling beneath them, and that part was good. It was excellent to be covering so much ground. But eventually the truck would stop, and the back would open, and then all bets would be off.

He shifted uncomfortably. It was dark and very hot. But eventually, that rumbling road had the hypnotic effect that continuous motion always does, and like his sister, he slept.

THE NET

"Back!"

They awoke with a start to the sound of a voice seemingly right beside their ears.

Both children sat bolt upright. Their truck had stopped moving and now it began inching backward, emitting a monotonous beep.

"Keep it comin'," the voice continued. "Back . . . back . . ."

It was still coal black inside the truck, but they did not need a light to know that wherever it was they had been heading, they had now arrived. Someone was maneuvering their driver into a parking space.

"Stop!" called whoever it was. "You're good!"

It was weird to be so close to this voice and yet so invisible to its owner. They were separated by only a thin sheet of metal and could hear him as if he were right there.

"Hide!" Katie whispered. They had fallen asleep in the main center aisle of the truck. Now they hustled toward the back, struggling to hurry and be silent at the same time. David dove into the last row on the right and Katie slid in behind him. No sooner were they in position than the driver cut the motor and they heard the wheeze of the giant brakes locking the vehicle into place.

After so many hours with the roar of the motor filling their ears, the silence seemed deafening. To move anywhere on the rattling metal floor had just become impossible. Whether or not they had chosen the best spot to hide, they would now have to stay where they were.

It stank in the rear of the truck and the smell reminded Katie of all that had happened the night before. By now she needed a bathroom too.

They could hear the driver call, "Which way to the dock?"

"Around to the right," replied the man on the ground. And then they heard the driver get out and walk away. There was nothing to do but wait until he came back.

In the meantime, they were surrounded by a terrifying number and variety of voices. Men and a few women, too, were calling out to one another and on either side they could hear the noisy panting of other great trucks idling. The fumes of diesel oil were nauseating.

Katie and David dared not speak to each other, but separately they concentrated on these sounds and smells, searching with their ears and noses for information about where they might be. In the distant background they seemed to hear car doors slamming and occasionally the piercing voices of children. Beneath it all was the roar of a highway, very close by. From the sound of things, they were at some kind of roadside rest stop and had taken their place in a long row of trucks.

Then—too abruptly—they heard their own driver's voice once again, and very nearby. He had returned. They heard him fumble with the latch on the truck's rear doors and slip the bolt loose.

So this was it. Quickly David switched on his flashlight and shined it at his watch. It was 3:35 in the morning. They had been locked in this truck for more than four hours. Dark and smelly and uncomfortable though the truck was, it had become their refuge, and now they were about to leave it. The metal wall that had shielded them from wondering eyes and strangers' hands was about to be thrown open.

It was a moment of great, great danger.

Click. The latch released and the doors at the rear of the truck swung open. Though it was still night, the rest stop was brightly lit and the great lamps instantly chased the sheltering darkness from the narrow rows of boxes where David and Katie were hiding.

With a clatter, the ramp dropped from the truck to the pavement below. Heavy, booted feet climbed up and in. They heard the driver unstrap the dolly from the wall and lower it, rattling, to the floor. They heard the rustling of papers, as if he had paused to flip through a clipboard.

The driver of their truck was getting ready to unload.

David and Katie were tense with attention and thinking fast, and they both came rapidly to the same conclusions: The driver was in the truck, and that was bad. On the other hand, he appeared to be alone, and that was good. Only one man stood between them and safety. When they got past him, they would be in the clear.

All they needed was about thirty seconds. That's how long it would take for them to escape. But for those thirty seconds, they needed this man to go away.

And to go away now, thought Katie, whose mind was turning like a motor. Because in about one more minute, she thought, he'll figure out what he's here to get. Any minute now he'll start looking for the boxes he needs. With any luck, they won't be in the back row, where we are. With any luck, he won't find the mess we made with the crackers and the drinks. With any luck, he won't notice it *stinks* in here—no way, she thought with despair, no way he won't notice *that*.

Hurry, thought David, whose mind was running through the same course as his sister's. Let's load up that dolly and roll it away. And dude, *don't breathe.*

Smack. The unseen man slapped his clipboard down on top of a box. "Hokay," he muttered, and they heard him stretching. "*Ho*-kay." Slowly, ponderously, he ambled down the center aisle toward the back of the truck.

No. David and Katie tried to flatten themselves into their corner. There were long pauses between each of the man's steps. Katie feared that her heart would pound its way out of her chest.

"Whoa!" In the middle of the truck, the man abruptly stopped short. "What the—"

He had found the broken box of snacks! Now he would certainly search the truck. David shot an agonized look at Katie.

"What the heck is this?" They could hear the man stoop to examine the broken bits of box and the scattered crackers. "Somebody been in here?" Purposefully now, he strode toward the back of the truck, inspecting every aisle for additional damage. "Dang!" he cried, finding the broken carton of drinks.

Closer the man came, and ever closer. Now he was only one aisle away from where David and Katie crouched tightly in the very back of the truck. Now they could hear the indignant huffing of his breath. They braced themselves for his face around the corner, his cry of astonishment.

But it did not come.

Instead—from the other side of the very last wall of boxes that separated him from them—they heard him snort in sudden disgust.

"Whew!" exclaimed the man. "Stinks in here! Stinks like all *heck!*"

Abruptly, he turned on his heel and strode back toward the open door of the truck. They heard him push past the dolly, stomp down the ramp, pivot, and head straight for his cab.

Their ears told them what happened next, as clearly as if they had seen it with their eyes. They heard the door of the cab opening, the man hopping in, and the door slamming shut.

They did not wait to hear his angry voice on the phone.

In less time than it would have taken to say it, David and Katie leaped to their feet and streaked down the truck's center aisle. They paused for a split second at the ramp and then, knowing it would rattle, jumped from the back to the ground. It was farther than they'd thought, and David tumbled when he landed, slightly twisting his ankle.

But no twisted ankle on earth could have stopped him at that moment. David took a quick, wild look around him. The King Foods truck had parked in a row of big rigs that were lined up alongside one another like the keys on a piano, with narrow aisles between them. Now David headed down the nearest of these aisles, slipping between their own truck and the enormous vehicle next to it.

"Not that way!" whispered Katie urgently, panicked that their driver would see them through his passenger-side window. Instead, she struck out across the backs of the trucks, moving tailpipe to tailpipe down the row.

She heard David following. Good. Now, with every muscle in her body longing to run, Katie willed herself to walk. They had needed a miracle and, incredibly, they had gotten one. Their driver had left the truck. They had escaped unseen. Undoubtedly, the driver was calling the police at this very moment. Within minutes, a search would be on for the unknown stowaways who had trashed the King Foods truck.

Running, they would stick out like sore thumbs. Walking would be torture under these conditions, but walking was their only hope.

They reached the end of the row of trucks. At their left, a gigantic parking lot was lit as bright as day by great floodlights. Gazing across this open space, they could now take their first good look at the spot where their trip as stowaways had taken them.

They had been right. It was an enormous all-purpose rest area near the junction of several massive highways. In the glare of the lights they could see that beyond the long row of trucks where they had disembarked was a huge gas station backed by a busy glass-fronted market.

Past that was—unsurprisingly—a King Foods. And away across the sprawling parking lot was a visitors' center, where scores of people streamed in and out.

This visitors' center would be their salvation. Right now, a crowd of people was a place to hide.

"Hungry?" asked Katie. She did not whisper but spoke at a normal volume with pretended casualness. "C'mon, let's meet Dad at the food court." And just as if no one in the world were hunting for her, she sauntered across the wide-open space in the full view of anyone and everyone.

David followed. And a few moments later, they melted into the crowd and flowed through the double glass doors into the visitors' center.

WELCOME TO YONKERS! read a sign above the front door. PLEASE HELP US KEEP OUR REST STATION CLEAN.

They were in. The air-conditioning was as frosty as a tall cold drink and the shops and restaurants were *normal*. Never had normal looked so good.

"Yes," said David quietly, pumping his fist. But no one heard and no one cared. They were home free.

Or so they thought.

The visitors' center housed a food court and various small shops. But with stiff legs Katie and David headed straight for the restrooms.

Katie had never been so glad to see sinks and toilets and paper towels. She was very dirty, and it was surprisingly comforting to wash. Despite her desire not to call attention to herself, she spent an astonishingly long time simply staring at her face in the mirror. She met her own eyes as if they were those of a stranger and she felt exceedingly weird.

At long last she emerged and rejoined her brother. She found David with his face to the corner of a shop window.

"I never thought I'd be so glad to see a toilet," she said.

But David did not reply. He was staring hard at a display of . . . earrings?

"David!" she said. "What are you looking at?"

"Shhh!" he hissed. Face to the ground, he headed rapidly for the exit.

"And where are you going?" Katie hurried after him, scrambling to keep up. "David, I want to look around." She felt relieved to be in a crowd of families and glad to be moving her legs. She didn't want to get right back into another truck.

He paused for only an instant to reply. "I've been seen," he said quietly. "Let's go."

Looking down, they melted into the crowd and streamed with it out of the building and into the parking lot. David was striding ahead of Katie toward the gas station, and she half trotted to keep up. Lining the wall of the station was a row of vending machines. Still saying nothing, David made a beeline for a soda machine and stopped in front of it. He stared as if contemplating what to buy.

"Who? Who on earth saw you?"

"The driver. Our driver. The King Foods guy. He was in the bathroom."

"But he doesn't know you!"

"He saw me, remember?"

Dismay flooded over Katie. Of course. The driver had gotten a look at David at the gas station back in Washington, before they hopped a ride on his truck.

"He was in the men's room," David continued, now pretending to push a couple of buttons. "I was washing up at the sink and he came in."

"Did he recognize you?"

"Yes."

"David!"

"But he couldn't place me. He just stared for a minute looking confused, like he was trying to figure out where he knew me from. I acted like I didn't notice—like nothing was wrong. I just dried my hands on my shirt and walked out."

"The minute he does place you, he'll know there's something wrong." Katie was thinking fast. "No way it could be a coincidence, us being here."

"Totally no way."

Katie was still thinking. "If he figures it out—if he remembers where he saw you—he's going to know it was you in his truck. He is *so* going to know."

"Correct."

"Then they'll be combing this place, looking for us. We have to leave now!"

"Right. But to leave we have to find a truck."

"Could we just—"

"Shhh!"

Katie followed the direction of David's gaze as he shushed her. On their left, just beyond the vending machines, a man had planted himself against the wall. He fished a cell phone out of his pocket, thumbed in a number, and crammed the device up close to his face. His back was turned to David and Katie, but David was right—he was close enough to overhear them.

"I don't want a soda," said Katie in a louder voice. "I'd rather get something to eat." She put her hand in her bulging pocket, as if she were jiggling change instead of juice boxes and crackers.

"Not me. I'm thirsty," said David, copying her stagy voice.

"Yo! It's me." The man to their left spoke into his phone. "Yonkers," he added after a moment, apparently in reply to a question he'd just been asked.

Staring at his back out of the side of her eyes, Katie noticed something that made her heart leap. She nudged David surreptitiously and when he met her eyes she mouthed, *"His jacket."*

David glanced with pretended indifference at the man's jacket. It was styled like a truck driver's. Then he glanced at the logo scrawled across the back. mega burger, it read.

Mega Burger! This guy must drive a Mega Burger truck! David and Katie both loved Mega Burger. They would definitely need more food, and riding in a burger truck would be even better than riding in a grocery truck. Both children strained to overhear the man's conversation. He'd said where he was; now perhaps he would say where he was going.

I-91, thought Katie. I-91 north, please.

But the driver appeared to be stuck in a long talk about something quite irrelevant.

"Na, I no hear not'ing," he said in accented and very annoyed English. Another long silence followed and he hunched yet more tightly over his phone.

"Can't do dis now," he protested, his voice rising slightly. "You want I lose dis job? Dis good for anyt'ing if I lose dis? I got a good route—it take me da right way. So first I make delivery. Den we see what we can do."

Like we care, thought David. But Katie felt very differently. A creeping unease was crawling up her spine.

"Yeah, she here wit' me," he said after another long pause. "Nort'. We go nort' up 91."

Down by his side, where the man couldn't see, David made a quick thumbs-up and jabbed excitedly at Katie's ribs.

But Katie's mind was shifting and turning. There was something about this that she did not like. What was it?

"Dis mornin'. We dere dis mornin', at dat old house."

That old house. Something was wrong. Really, really wrong. In a single explosive realization she put it together: *The accent. Katkajan.*

Katie went rigid as a spasm of fear swept over her. And just as it did, the man's voice rose in sudden anger.

"Dey gone, dat's what!" Then—remembering—he lowered his voice. "Dey get away 'dose kids," he whispered. "Bot' of dem. T'rough a leetle hole. So we goin' nort' to da uncle, to look." And with those words he shifted his body, throwing his profile into view. His nose canted slightly to the left.

Horrified, Katie turned to David. One glance told her there was no need to say anything.

Act normal; act normal. David turned his back to the man and—slowly—began strolling along the wall away from the vending machines. Katie followed, also willing herself to walk as if nothing were wrong. But while her body sauntered, her mind raced and swirled.

Where on earth could they go? They had to leave this gas station, but for where? Back at the visitors' center the King Foods man might be hunting for them, right this very moment. The King Foods store would certainly not do. It was as if a net were tightening around them.

They reached the corner and David threw Katie a look over his shoulder. His face was tight with the strain of his casual smile and his eyes telegraphed his question: Which way from here?

She widened her own eyes and tilted her head slightly to the left. They would head back to the trucks. They had no other choice. Wordlessly David veered in that direction, leading them across the brightly lit sea of gas pumps.

She knew it was a bad choice, but she could see no alternative and she followed. Then she collided into David's back with a bump. He had halted dead in his tracks.

David pivoted and again their eyes met. His were two deep pools of blackest panic. She looked over his shoulder and saw why. Over by the trucks were the flashing blue lights of two police cruisers. The King Foods truck was open and from across the pavement excited voices could be heard within it.

The net was closing.

Katie turned on her heel and headed toward the glass front of the station's convenience market. Again she knew it was a terrible choice—the lights, the people, the likelihood that the Katkajanian would go there next. Her blood drummed in her temples as she shouldered her way inside. The thrumming in her head was so loud that she could barely hear the hum of voices all around them. David was behind her, and instinctively both of them headed for the bathrooms. They would lock themselves in and wait until the coast was clear. They would wait until it was all over. They would wait until the police broke down the doors.

But the doors of both bathrooms were already locked.

Magazines. A rack of bright covers stood between the bathrooms and the rest of the store. Katie reached out blindly and lifted a heavy, glossy volume to her face. She would hide within it while waiting for the bathroom door to open. Hunching, she buried her head in its pages. Beside her David was doing the same.

And then the net fell.

"Susad! Steved!" A heavy fist landed on Katie's right shoulder and another landed on David's left. *No.* Katie tried to sink still deeper into her magazine, hiding her eyes from the lank hair, the colorless face, that familiar voice.

"Oh, darligs!" cried the woman in loud, artificial tones that clashed bizarrely with her flat, nasal twang. "I foud you! Sweetie!" she sang out. "They're *here*!" As the woman's nails dug into David's shoulder, another hand—a man's this time—grasped his upper arm. Fingers twined around David's biceps like cords of iron.

As the man with the crooked nose grabbed David, the lank-haired woman wrapped her fingers tightly around Katie's hair, in the back where no one could see.

"What a relief!" she cried. "We were worried sick! You mused ever rud away agaid!"

These—these *kidnappers* were pretending to be their parents. So that was their story! With a grunt David attempted to wrench his arm free. The grip that held it tightened like a vise.

"You no run away no more," said the man in a stern, fatherly tone. "You no make you mother cry like that. We talk about this at home." His crossed eyes wandered weirdly around the small store as he began pressing David toward the door.

Katie looked at David and David looked at Katie. Each read the anguish in the other's face. The net had closed. It had snapped shut, and they were in it.

LIES

The two children were marched to the door with one fist wrapped around David's arm, five fingers twisted tightly in Katie's hair, and their captors grinning like doting parents behind them. But the commotion raised by the lank-haired woman and the crooked-nosed man had drawn notice. People were looking.

Maybe this meant help. Desperate, Katie met the eyes of a curious woman. There she saw only sternness and rebuke. Of course. That woman would not help her. Katie was a runaway.

Reaching over David's head with his free arm, Crooked Nose shoved the door open and pressed David through it. Katie and her captor began to follow when suddenly the cashier called out.

"You gonna pay for that?"

The lank-haired woman, surprised, glanced down at a magazine that was clutched in her free hand. She must have been reading it when she discovered Katie and David. She had forgotten that she still had it.

"Whoops," she said. "Here." Lank Hair thrust Katie at Crooked Nose. "This'll ody take a secod."

Crooked Nose's brows lowered as he seized Katie's arm. "Forget it!" he growled. Katie winced, but stole a glance at Lank Hair's magazine as the woman cut across to the register. What could be so important?

A FIRMER FANNY FOR A FANTASTIC YOU! blared the cover. Beneath the caption was a picture of a loopily grinning lady with her bikinied backside to the camera.

There was no time to ponder the absurdity of this. Lank Hair was in line and Crooked Nose was shepherding both children out the door and into the night.

The grip on Katie's arm was brutal. While maintaining his lurid, fatherly smile for the benefit of any onlookers, Nose half dragged the children around the side of the building to wait for Hair. In the relative quiet by the gas station's far wall he pushed both of them roughly against the brick and leaned over them, his acrid breath on their faces.

"Where you runnin' to?" he demanded. "You go to dat uncle? Dat where you go?"

Katie could not think. The pain in her arm was too great.

"Where he at? He in New Hampshire, right? What town?"

This, at least, was good. Nose had the wrong state.

But David spoke up. "You cretin," he said contemptuously. "It's Vermont. A week on my parents' computer and you couldn't figure that out?"

Katie was dismayed. Why had he told? But Nose grinned in satisfaction. "Vermont," he said with a sneer. "Ha! Dat a nice try! What town in New Hampshire?"

Despite everything Katie felt a surge of admiration. How had her brother thought of this so fast? Nose would assume that David was lying. Because he had said Vermont, that was now the last place the Katkajanians would look for Uncle Alex.

But Nose was still hammering David about New Hampshire. "What town?" he again demanded.

"You'll never know," said her brother, giving his arm an angry jerk where Nose was gripping it. "You'll never—"

But David stopped, midsentence and openmouthed. He stared, stunned, over Nose's shoulder. Coming at them from around the corner he saw Hair, with her magazine tucked in a plastic bag and alarm on her face. And right behind her was a pair of enormous policemen dressed in blue, their massive chests glittering with badges and buckles and their holsters bulging with apparently real guns.

They looked like a blue wall, and they did not look happy.

David's mouth closed, his words unspoken. Now what?

Voices and static crackled out of the first policeman's walkie-talkie. David and Katie could make out none of it, but without looking down the cop pushed a button on his hip and replied, "Yup."

A pause followed. All six of them stood in frozen silence as the policeman stared straight ahead, listening to the gibberish that continued to issue from his hip.

"Got 'em. Boy, girl. With an adult female, adult male."

That must mean them. Them and Hair and Nose.

There was another pause and more gibberish from the policeman's hip. Then: "We came into the station and asked the clerk had he seen any kids, travelin' alone. Guy pointed me straight at this lady who was buyin' a magazine. Said she had 'em."

The cop was listening to yet more staticky conversation. This time Katie and David managed to make out a few words.

"Bring 'im over for ID," crackled the voice on the other end.

Huh?

But the policeman understood. "Ten-four!" he said, and again he pushed the button and the sound clicked off.

For a moment both halves of the blue wall stared down at the kids. Then the walkie-talkie cop turned to Nose. Walkie-Talkie was an African American officer with a middle-aged face, penetrating eyes, and a deeply skeptical expression.

"Hands offa those kids and up against the wall," he said impassively. He looked to be about six foot three. Nose instantly dropped his hold on Katie and David and, raising both arms, put his palms flat against the wall of the gas station. As his head sank between his hands he threw David a private look of intense fury.

The other cop had freckles and a youngish expression and was, if anything, even taller. He jerked his head toward Hair. "You too," he said. Despite her confusion Katie noticed that Freckles seemed to be imitating Walkie-Talkie. He must be a new policeman, she thought, though he's so enormous. New—that was good. He'd be easier.

Hair followed Nose to the wall and leaned against it with both palms, as he had done. Walkie-Talkie turned to Freckles and raised his eyebrows, and Freckles stepped over to the two captives and began patting their sides.

The policemen were frisking Nose and Hair! How much did they know?

And how much did Katie and David *want* them to know? They had always thought of the police as their friends. But that was before they had been left with a nanny to whom they must not be sent back. That was before Katkajanian kidnappers had seized their parents. That was before the truth was a story no one would believe.

Now Katie watched as Walkie-Talkie, hands on his hips, looked down at David. The cop was about to ask a question, and it was obvious from David's panicky face that he didn't have a clue what to say. But suddenly Katie did.

Her mouth seemed to open by itself. "Mom!" she cried, her voice quivering in distress as she turned to Nose and Hair. "Mom and Dad—are you OK?"

Five heads swiveled in her direction. Five faces stared blankly into hers, but the one she met was her brother's. Katie's eyes locked on David's as she spoke and she poured her secret message through her gaze: Follow my lead. I know what to do.

"Steven," she pleaded, remembering the name Hair had given David. "They can't do this to Mom and Dad! It's over, Steven. We have to go home now."

Katie willed a small, pathetic break into her voice. She must appear to be heartbroken, as if at the end of a wonderful dream. She turned to Walkie-Talkie. "It wasn't supposed to turn out like this!" she begged. "We just meant—"

"What's your name, sister?" Walkie-Talkie fished a pad and pencil from his pocket, and waved at Hair and Nose to drop their hands. Hair still looked very flustered but a wary relief was spreading over Nose's face.

"Susan—Susan Anderson," said Katie. Right away Walkie-Talkie gave her a look and she instantly wished she had chosen a last name that sounded less fake. But she barreled forward. "This is my brother, Steven. And we—"

But Katie's story was interrupted. A police car was swinging toward them from around the back of the gas station, blue lights flashing. It braked a few feet from Freckles, and another enormous cop emerged heavily from the front seat. The back door opened as well and out stepped a familiar figure wearing a cap and jacket with the King Foods logo. The driver of their erstwhile home, the King Foods truck, stared at Katie and David.

"This him?" said Walkie-Talkie, looking inquiringly at the driver and gesturing toward David.

"That's the one," said the driver. But Walkie-Talkie was again talking to David. "You been ridin' in his truck?"

David threw a begging look at Katie. "Don't be lookin' at your sister, son," said Walkie-Talkie sternly. "I'm askin' you."

"Ye—yes," said David tentatively. He had no idea what Katie was doing, pretending to be Susan and calling those creeps Mom and Dad.

Katie chimed right in. "We both were," she pleaded. "We didn't know, though. We didn't know it would turn out like this! We just . . . We just wanted to know if it would work." She cast down her eyes, as if ashamed.

"We were being stowaways," said David, following blindly. "We just wanted to see."

"Mom?" Katie turned to Hair. "Mom, I'm really sorry." Katie spoke carefully, praying that Hair and Nose and David would hear the message behind her words. "We were awful, but we know it's over. We know we have to be good. We know"—for this part she looked straight into Nose's eyes—"we know you're in charge."

Nose visibly relaxed and a smug smile snaked across his face. And Hair spoke. "Thad's OK, sweetie," she said. "You're safe. Thad's the maid thig."

Freckles was trying to suppress a smile. Despite his bulk this second cop seemed barely old enough to drive.

Walkie-Talkie, on the other hand, still looked skeptical. He turned back to the King Foods man.

"You want to press charges?" he asked.

"I'll have to speak to my dispatcher," said King Foods.

"Okay." Walkie-Talkie stashed his pad in his pocket. "We're gonna have to talk this over. There's a substation right over at the visitors' center. Everybody's gonna need to sit down for some questions."

"Officer, we need to take dese cheeldren home!" Nose slapped a fatherly hand on David's shoulder. David wanted to barf.

"Some questions," repeated Walkie-Talkie. "Now you"—this was for King Foods, who nodded—"you walk on over and meet us there. And you four—Anderson's your name?" Neither Nose nor Hair replied. "Into the car."

As they climbed in, Katie realized with despair that there would be no opportunity to explain her plan to David. She just had to hope he would figure it out.

They had only one chance of getting away: They must convince all four of their captors that they didn't want to escape. The police had to believe they were with their parents. Nose and Hair had to believe they had given up. Only when everyone was certain that Katie and David had nowhere to go would the children no longer be watched.

The police substation was indeed in the visitors' center, but it was in the back with its own separate entrance. It was quieter here, away from the endless river of families streaming in and out of the food court. Inside was a lobby lined with dirty plastic chairs and presided over by a battered and vacant receptionist's desk. A door behind the desk led to a small cluster of windowless rooms.

Katie and David, with Hair and Nose, were taken to one of these rooms and left to wait around a long table. Freckles remained to watch over them while Walkie-Talkie spoke with King Foods in the room next door.

David looked around. Even with Walkie-Talkie gone he didn't like the odds. To escape they'd have to get out of this room, down the short corridor, and then through the lobby. That meant there were at least three doors between them and freedom. Three doors and three adults.

He sighed and tried to pay attention to what Freckles was saying. It was all small talk. It turned out the young cop was a baseball nut. He knew they had boarded the truck in Washington DC, so he was rambling cheerfully on about the Nationals. David appreciated the good intentions, but he wished the guy would be quiet so he could study the layout of this place.

Katie was worried too, but not because she was planning a run for the exits. Hair and Nose had been asked to produce their driver's licenses, and Walkie-Talkie was plainly unhappy that neither adult was named Anderson. Katie's whole strategy depended on everyone thinking they were one big happy family.

The door opened and Walkie-Talkie returned to the room alone. He stood at the head of their table, arms folded across his massive chest.

"The King Foods Corporation's not gonna press charges," he said.

"Good! Then we go," said Nose, rising.

"Not so fast," said Walkie-Talkie. "I got a few more questions before I release these children to your custody."

At this, Nose's unruffled expression began to crack. "You no can keep my cheeldren from me!" he said sharply. "You got no cause for dat!"

"They hab to go hobe," protested Hair. "They deed sobe rest!"

But Walkie-Talkie was unmoved. "Officer Sanders, will you take these kids to the lobby, please?" he said.

Katie rose to follow, her concern deepening. But David's heart leaped as they passed out the door and back to the lobby. The way he saw it, they had just gone from three adults to one. He turned to look at their lone remaining captor and grinned up at the young man's frank and friendly face. Sanders. So that was Freckles's name.

He's big, David thought, but he's way too nice. We can take him.

Katie had deposited herself dejectedly on a rickety chair in the lobby. David dropped lightly beside her, flicking a candy wrapper off his seat before he did so. Sanders had stationed himself at the receptionist's desk and a quick sideways glance revealed that he was staring at them with a look of compassion.

Oh, yeah. His "parents" were being interrogated. David hastily rearranged his expression along serious lines and turned a worried face to their jailer.

"How 'bout the Wizards?" the cop asked, looking genuinely sorry for him. "You like basketball?"

David did, and for a while that gave them something to talk about. But forty-five minutes and many professional sports later, neither David nor Katie wanted to talk about anything. The hour was growing late, they were tired and hungry, and it had become obvious that while Sanders was certainly very nice, he wasn't going away. They were close enough to the exit to taste it and, compared to before, they were very lightly guarded. But if they couldn't make a break for it pretty soon, the others would emerge from the back and this opportunity would slip through their fingers.

Then—from somewhere deep in the pocket of his pants—Sanders's cell phone rang.

The big cop hitched his body to the side and fished out the small, trilling object. He peered at the screen that displayed the number of the caller and his eyes lit up. He clutched the device close to his face and cupped his hand around the mouthpiece for privacy.

It wasn't quite private enough. Both of them heard his low, eager voice. "Hi, sugar," said Sanders.

David looked at Katie and Katie looked at David. Both had precisely the same thought. This was a development. This—*this*—was an opportunity.

They could not hear everything, but very soon they heard enough to know that all was not well between Sanders and his sugar. The cop was hunched tightly over his phone and his murmurings into it acquired a troubled and urgent quality.

"Honey," they heard him saying in tones of gentle remonstrance. "Honey, you know that's not true!" Sanders's eyes flicked upward over the top of his phone and met the children's gazes. Nice though he was, his brow lowered coldly and he stared down at the desktop. Sugar continued to talk. He continued to listen.

"No, baby." Sanders's voice, which he had labored to keep low, was rising and there was a pleading note in it. "No, that's not what I meant!" Again he glanced upward and again he saw the children. This time he turned his body impatiently away, seeking escape from their eyes.

Sanders was pouring every ounce of his gigantic self into the tiny sliver of a phone that he clutched to his massive head. Their three other captors were still locked away in the back room. No more than a tissue hung between Katie and David and the highway to Vermont.

But the lobby was a single large square and the only door that led to freedom stood smack in front of the desk where the cop sat. A wave of despair washed over Katie. They were so close but so utterly, utterly trapped.

"Officer Sanders?"

David rose and loped over to the desk where Sanders sat. Katie's hopes stirred. Maybe her brother had a plan.

Sanders, flustered, looked up from his call. His face was flushed from his struggle with Sugar.

"Officer Sanders?" said David, who was now standing right before him. "I'm really hungry."

It was brilliant. There was no food in the lobby. To get any, Sanders would have to leave. David was a genius.

Sanders put his hand over the receiver. "Won't be too

long now," he replied. A tight smile appeared as he did so. "They'll be out pretty soon."

"We haven't eaten anything for hours!"

From across the lobby Katie chimed in. "And we're thirsty, too!"

Sanders's smile grew a little more desperate. "It'll only be—" He broke off as a torrent of words that even the children could hear erupted from inside his phone. Beads of sweat appeared on Sanders's forehead.

David spoke again. "We're *starv*—"

Sanders raised his hand, cutting him off. Then without allowing the phone to budge from his ear, he reached deep into his pocket and removed his wallet. Katie and David watched as, one-handed, he unfolded it and extracted a five-dollar bill.

He wouldn't. It couldn't possibly be that easy. He wasn't really going to *give them money and send them away*.

Still glued to the phone, Sanders held out the five, met David's eyes, and mouthed: "*For the food court. Come right back.*"

"Mmm-hmm," he murmured into the phone. "Me too, baby."

Katie rose and turned for the door, trying to act casual and trying to quiet her pounding heart. But where was David?

From behind her she heard his voice. "No!" he repeated loudly. "We're *really* hungry!"

A surge of anger flooded over Katie at this totally unnecessary risk. Incredibly, though, it paid off. The cop glowered, but he fished out a second five and handed it to David without a word.

"Thanks!"

Now both children bounded for the exit. Katie shouldered open the wide glass door and they pushed through it into the warm and humid night air. Every cell in her body wanted to run but she knew they were still in Sanders's line of sight.

The children turned left—casually, casually—as if they were heading around the building toward the main entrance and the food court. But within just a few paces they had cleared the window and then they knew they could no longer be seen.

"Man!" David exploded in glee. "Can you believe that?"

"Shhh! David, what do we do now?"

"Love makes men *stupid*."

"David, focus! We have, like, about sixty seconds before they're after us and that's if we're lucky. We need a truck or a place to hide or—"

"I'm buying food."

"What!"

"I'm hungry!"

"That's crazy!"

"I'm very hungry and I just got us ten dollars, no thanks to you."

"I—I—you're on your own."

"What's that supposed to mean?"

"I'm not going with you."

"What—"

She was as good as her word. Katie turned on her heel and struck out across the parking lot toward the gas station.

It was a miracle that they had gotten away. If they got caught again they would be held under lock and key. She didn't intend to let that happen—not to her. If David followed her, fine. If not—well, she wasn't looking back to find out.

But as Katie approached the now familiar station the old panic began again. Why had she decided to go this way? She would immediately be recognized. But then, she couldn't go to the visitors' center either. That was where they would look for her the minute they discovered Sanders had let them go. And she could not go near the trucks. Every driver there would surely be talking about the recent excitement over the stowaways.

It was after five thirty a.m., and day was breaking. They had been all too visible by artificial light. Daylight would not help. Again Katie felt the net closing in. Only moments before it had released them, yet already it threatened to engulf them once more.

Katie's desperate eyes roamed from left to right, searching. Just ahead of her at the gas pumps, a man was attempting to fill up a small, battered white truck and swearing as he did so.

"It won't take my card!" he cried, to no one in particular. In exasperation he dropped the nozzle and stalked past her, headed for the cashier.

Katie looked at the side of the truck. It was painted all over with apples and across the top ran the words: fresh to you . . . from the green mountain state.

The Green Mountain State. That was Vermont!

Katie did not really want to leave her brother behind. Though she had been very angry, she earnestly hoped he was watching her and would follow her lead. But this was her chance and she meant to take it. She walked straight to the truck, opened the back door, and climbed in.

Follow me, she thought, willing David to read her mind. Don't be mad. Please, please be watching. Please, please follow.

He did. Stunned by her willingness to walk away, David had not gone to the food court after all. An instant later he slipped in after her and Katie closed the door and clicked it shut, sealing them inside.

This had been their boldest move yet. They had climbed into this truck under the full glare of the lights and with people all around. Both children stood motionless inside the door, afraid to breathe. Together they listened for the shouts of outrage, the angry footsteps. They heard nothing.

Then the man returned, still muttering. From behind their metal walls they listened as he reinserted the nozzle into the tank. They heard the swoosh of the fuel as it flowed in, filling it.

In the meantime, though, some kind of commotion seemed to have broken out in the direction of the visitors' center. From behind the sheltering walls of the truck Katie and David heard one—no, two—sirens speeding that way. Through the cracks of the door they faintly saw flashes of blue light from the bars atop the police cruisers.

Those lights and sirens—those were for them. Their escape had been discovered.

Hurry, hurry. And in fact the man was done. He removed the nozzle, sealed the tank with the cap, hopped into his cab, and started the motor. With a jerk that sent them tumbling to the floor, he pulled away from the gas station and onward toward the open road.

"We don't know where he's going," David protested, worry in his voice. "He's *from* Vermont. That doesn't mean he's going *to* Vermont."

"Yes, he is," said Katie, her pulse at last slowing down. "Look," she added, fishing out her flashlight and turning it on. She shone the thin beam around the interior of the small truck.

"See? It's empty." The sweet perfume of apples flooded the truck, and rattling crates and boxes were piled everywhere, but she was right; there was no fruit in any of them. An unzipped duffel bag containing a jumble of worn laundry lay tossed in a corner. "He's *made* his deliveries. He's *been* to New York. Now he's going home."

There was a long silence as David took this in. Then a wide smile spread across his face.

"Yes!" Again David whispered his victory cry and pumped his fist in noiseless jubilation.

"Not yet!" said Katie.

"That was, like, out of a movie or something," said David, still basking.

"It's not over," she cautioned.

"No, but man, back there? Katie, we did it!" he said. "They caught us, but we got away. We've gotten away twice," he amplified, remembering with pleasure their earlier escape through the cat door. That had been his idea too, if memory served.

"We lost 'em," he continued. "We got off track, but now we're right back to where we were. We're on our way to Vermont, like we should be."

"Yeees, but . . ."

"But what?" This was very annoying, this "but" so soon after such a triumph.

"But we're not just back to where we were. It's worse now," Katie said.

"Because . . . ?"

"Because now we know they're looking for us. The Katkajanians, I mean. And of course, now the police are too."

It was always so depressing to listen to Katie. "Um, New Hampshire?" said David. "We're OK, Kat, thanks to me. As soon as the cops let those two clowns go—the guy with the funky nose and the woman with the bad hair— they'll be headed for the wrong state."

"For a while, but not for long."

"You just don't want to admit it. You won't admit it because that New Hampshire thing was mine—I thought of that."

"Give me a break, David." She sighed. "Look, the New Hampshire idea was good—it was very good. And it's going to keep them off our trail for a couple of days. But then they'll figure it out and when they do, they'll be after us again. And then . . ."

"And then what?"

"And then they'll be really, really mad."

NORTH

"We're definitely on 91," Katie repeated impatiently. They had been over this many, many times. "If you're going to Vermont from Yonkers, that's your only route. Our problem is, where on 91 will he stop?"

They were seated on the rattling, bouncing metal floor of the apple truck, peering at their map in the glow of a flashlight. "We know Uncle Alex is just outside Melville, right?" she continued. "And according to this map we can *walk* to Melville from 91. But it's a long highway. So it only works if we get out at the right part."

"Let me see that." David reached for the map.

They had been in the truck for almost five hours. For much of that time they had been trying to guess where they were and how they might slip out somewhere close to their destination. The driver of their truck had stopped a couple of times along their route—for breakfast and coffee, they'd assumed. Each stop caused them to dash behind the empty crates in a panic that he might open the back. Each stop caused them to estimate their rate of speed, check the number of hours they'd been traveling, and take a wild guess about where on the map they might be.

They figured they were not yet close enough to try to leave the truck. But that was a guess, and they were not sure they were right.

"I am so incredibly sick of these crackers," said Katie, looking with disgust at the blue-and-orange box into which she was thrusting her hand. Never would she have imagined that she could be so hungry and so disgusted by a cheese cracker, both at the same time.

Wordlessly, David took the box and helped himself to a handful as well.

"But we should stop eating them," she added, watching him. "We're almost out and we don't have anything else."

"We have ten bucks," said David. "Thanks to me."

"That won't get us very far if we have to walk fifty miles," she replied. And she patted her pockets, checking them. Her few belongings were all carefully stashed. When you have no idea where you are or when your driver will open the door, it is important to be ready to jump at any time.

David clicked on the other flashlight and its faint beam lit up the dark interior of the truck. As Katie watched, he scooted over to the duffel bag that lay by the wall, tucked his light under his chin, and began to rummage through it.

Katie sat up.

"David Bowden! What on earth are you doing?"

"I'm seeing if there's any money in here." His voice came out funny because the flashlight prevented him from moving his jaws.

"Because . . . ?"

"Because if there is, we're going to need it. You said so yourself. Ten's not enough."

"You're *stealing*? Just like that? You're just going to—"

"Hello?" David transferred the flashlight to his hand and turned to look at her. "What's that in your pockets, Katie? We've been stealing ever since we left home."

"That's not the same!"

"Why? Just because it's from a store or a truck? Stealing's stealing, Kat"—he made little quote marks in the air with his fingers—"news flash."

"It is not. This is much worse."

"Why?"

Katie glared but did not respond.

"Give me one reason why it's worse, Katie." David sighed heavily. "It isn't worse," he said, answering his own question. "It isn't even *wrong*. None of it is. We're in an emergency. Look."

He rummaged again in the duffel and pulled out a small white card. "I have the guy's card. It has his address on it. When we get to Uncle Alex's we can send the money back. That's more than we can do for King Foods. I don't think we can repay them, so if you want to get *technical*, that was actually wor—"

"What money? Did you find any?"

"I found four dollars."

"Oh! That is so—" But Katie's words were cut off as the truck braked sharply and took a tight curve upward and to the right. She braced her hands on the floor to avoid toppling over.

"Exit ramp," said David tensely.

"No kidding." The abruptness of the exit had left Katie slightly carsick.

"Hide," her brother ordered. As they had done at previous stops, David rose to a low and unsteady crouch and crept toward the rear of the truck, where he ducked behind a jumble of empty apple crates in case the driver decided to open the back. Hastily Katie followed him and lowered her body next to his in the cramped space.

And there they waited. But this time the truck did not stop. It was no longer on the interstate but it rumbled on and on over bouncing, ill-paved roads that turned and swooped, this way and that. After a very long while they could feel it turning onto what seemed to be slower and quieter roads.

It felt like a neighborhood. Was the driver going home?

Now they slowed way down, swerved sharply to the left, and rolled over a short bump. They crunched over a gravel bed that felt ominously like the driveway of someone's house. Then suddenly—finally—they stopped. The motor went dead, and with a soft squeal of the pedal the driver set the brake.

For an instant it was absolutely silent. And then they heard a sound they had never expected but instantly feared: a dog.

The dog was only a few yards away, and the moment the motor was cut it began to bark in great excitement. The animal's rapid, light footfalls pelted toward them and it threw itself at the side of the truck, just outside the very spot where they were sitting. The metal walls that encased them banged and rattled wildly with the impact of the creature's body on the other side.

The driver's door flew open. The man spoke. "Hush! Hush up, now!" They heard him leap lightly to the ground, and the barking gave way to glad whimpering as the dog greeted his friend.

"Katie! I think we're at his house!" David spoke directly into his sister's ear and in the lowest possible voice, but the dog's sensitive ears heard him and it resumed its hysterical barking.

"I said *hush*!" There was a light smacking sound and

the jingle of a chain as the man jerked the dog's collar. The animal subsided, whining. "What's got into you?"

And then they heard the driver's footsteps. He was headed for the back of the truck.

The duffel, thought David with a stab of fear. He's home now. He'll be taking out his stuff.

The dog, thought Katie. It's already heard us. When he opens the back it's going to jump *in*.

Both children buried their faces in their hands. The door flew open and the midmorning light flooded into the truck. The dog instantly went berserk. With a ferocious, deep-throated yelp it leaped into the truck. Not only would they be discovered, they would be mauled. A scream rose inside Katie's throat.

But before her scream could escape, the driver, cursing hoarsely, seized the animal's collar and jerked it hard. A second jerk pulled the creature back to the ground.

"Chester, knock it off!" With his one free hand the driver reached into the truck and scooped out his duffel. Then he slammed the door shut, causing the dog again to bark frantically.

"Man!" the driver exclaimed. "Musta been a squirrel in there yesterday. Can't go nuts like that, every time you catch a whiffa squirrel!" And he walked off, dragging Chester after him. Both children listened tensely as the man's mutterings and the animal's yips and whimpers retreated across the yard. Far away they heard a screen door open.

Make him go inside, Katie prayed. Put the dog in the house.

He did. Off in the distance, with a final yelp, the door closed on the truck driver and Chester.

"Let's get out of here."

In less time than it would take to say it, the children unlatched the truck door, jumped to the ground, and slipped into the shrubbery that lined the driveway. Glancing over his shoulder David saw the big, rough form of Chester appear in the living-room window, barking as if his life were on the line.

But the dog was too late. The Bowden children had reached the safety of the street and were gone.

Where were they?

It was steeply hilly and it felt like mountain country. The air itself was different—colder and drier—and the plants and trees were not the same as the ones they knew.

But where were they? From the apple farmer's business card, they knew they were in Hawthorne, Vermont. But they did not know what road they were on, and there did not seem to be any street signs.

They were lost, Katie reflected, and to make matters worse, they were conspicuous. She gazed at her brother. He was a mess. The shrubbery through which they had escaped while fleeing from Chester hadn't helped. Twigs and debris were caught in his hair. But beneath all that he was showing the effects of the past two nights. No, three, she thought, remembering. Before the night in the dusty old house, with the rats, they had slept on the floor back at home.

Since then they had caught only snatches of rest on the floors of the two trucks. They had washed only once, at the rest stop in Yonkers, and they had barely eaten. Not surprisingly, David's eyes were sunken, his face and body were smeared with grime, and his clothes were rumpled and filthy.

Katie knew how hungry her brother was, because her own hunger was becoming a serious problem. And he stank, too. "What?" he said, seeing her face.

153

"Nothing," she replied. "It's just that I realized I probably look as bad as you do. That's all."

He surveyed her critically. "Worse," he said matter-of-factly.

Having no alternative they simply wandered. David was ahead by a few paces, but Katie could tell that their aimlessness was bothering him, too. Still, she was outraged when she saw him stop in front of a bulging mailbox at the edge of someone's lawn and begin riffling through the contents.

"David!" Her whisper came out as a furious hiss. It was bad enough that he had brazenly stolen four dollars. Now he was stealing mail, too?

"Appleton Lane," he announced, shoving the mail back in and walking on.

She scuttled to catch up. "What?" she asked.

"We're on Appleton Lane."

"Oh." He had checked the address. The anger eased out of Katie. "That was smart," she admitted somewhat reluctantly.

Sitting on a low curb at the edge of someone's lawn, they broke out their map to search for Hawthorne, Vermont. They took care to unfold it only to the size of a magazine. Two ragged kids on a curb, studying a map, would certainly raise eyebrows.

"With the Hawthorne part, we're in luck," said David with relief in his voice. "Look. Hawthorne's here"—he jabbed his finger at the page—"and Melville's—"

"Here." Katie found it first. "Melville's here. It's close." She began to feel excited. The two dots representing Hawthorne and Melville were really quite near each other. "We're actually almost there—*wow*." But Katie checked her own enthusiasm.

"We're not done, though," she added. "Close on the map can mean a long way on the ground. We could have a long walk ahead of us."

"Right." David returned to the map. "But before we can figure that out, we need to know where in Hawthorne we are. And we don't. I mean, knowing it's Appleton Lane is nice, but it doesn't actually help, since the only

Hawthorne road that's on this map is Route 24. It's too little a town." He clutched the fraying edges of the map, eyes roaming.

Then he rose to his feet, jammed the map into his pocket, and dusted his hands on his shorts. "Route 24's what we need to find," he said. "And *coincidentally*, that's the road that goes to Melville, too. But of course we have no idea where it is."

It was after one o'clock in the afternoon, and they were desperate.

It had been almost eleven a.m. when they emerged from the apple truck in Chester's yard. They had been wandering ever since, but although they had exhausted themselves, they had still not found Route 24.

Worse still, they were attracting attention. After almost an hour of trying, they had succeeded in making their way out of the neighborhood where they had landed and into Hawthorne's small downtown, where its stores and banks and gas stations were clustered. Since then, however, things had gone badly. Maddeningly, though they tried to avoid it, they kept returning to the same spots over and over again.

They'd find themselves at a crossroads and randomly pick one of their two choices. When that failed, they'd have to retrace their steps to try the other. Sometimes they'd try roads that looked like they went in new directions, only to find that they had doubled back to someplace they'd already been.

This had one important advantage: There were three public water fountains that they passed over and over again, and from which they drank every time. Their endlessly circular route was terribly dangerous, though. Hawthorne wasn't a big town and at some point someone was bound to notice two unfamiliar kids in dirty clothes walking the same streets over and over again like homeless people.

But they were loath to ask how to get to a road that everybody local was sure to know. As David said, they might as well wear sandwich boards reading strangers.

Eventually, the inevitable happened. They crossed the street in front of Hawthorne's biggest grocery store, where they'd already been three or four times. A car stopped to let them pass, and as it did so a head craned out the window to peer at them. Katie turned to look and her eyes made contact with the driver's. With a chill of fear, she recognized a face she had already seen at least twice that morning.

Katie looked casually away, being careful not to let her recognition register on her face. Under her breath she spoke urgently to her brother. "She's noticed us. No"— Katie seized David's hand to stop him from turning his head—"don't look. But that woman in the car has noticed us. David, what are we going to do?"

They arrived at the other side of the street and David turned resolutely toward the left, determined to behave as if he had a direction and a purpose. Behind them the intersection was clear. There was no traffic to block her way, but the woman in the car did not pass through it. She hung there with her motor idling. She was watching them.

What David did then was simply brilliant: brilliantly conceived and brilliantly executed. A few yards away a boy stood expectantly on the corner, wearing a baseball uniform and carrying a glove. He looked as if he were waiting to be picked up for practice, and he looked about eight.

He was not too young to talk to, but just young enough to be a little bit cowed by a boy and girl of twelve. He was perfect.

"Dude, how're you doing?" David sang out to the boy and strode up to him as easily as if he'd known him all his life. He held up his hand for a high five.

Katie saw the child's expression flicker uncertainly between do-I-know-you and happy-to-see-you. Then shyly—amazingly—the boy raised his arm and allowed David to slap his hand.

"Who're you playing?" David asked. He rested his hands on his knees and bent down slightly so his face was level with the younger boy's.

"Tigers," came the soft reply.

Behind them, the car that had been hovering moved on, apparently satisfied. Katie resumed breathing.

"Well," David was continuing, "go kill 'em. Listen, can you tell us how to get to Route 24? Which way do we walk from here?"

"Sure," said the boy, with evident relief. So that was what these unknown kids wanted. He began to point. "See that—"

"Naw," said David gently, "don't point it. Just tell us. Which way?" If anybody was looking, he didn't want to be seen getting directions.

Fortunately, what the kid had to tell them wasn't complicated and they repeated it until they had it.

A car was slowing at the curb; stopping. His ride!

"How far?" asked David, already starting to move off.

The boy shrugged. "Couple miles, I guess," he said, and reached for the car door.

"Who was that?" The piercing notes of another child's voice floated into the street as the car door opened. But David and Katie had already turned the corner and were gone.

The boy had sent them in the right direction, but he had been totally wrong about how far they had to go. It took them an hour and a half to reach Route 24. By the time they got there, it was midafternoon and blazing hot.

"That kid was right on the money," said David cheerfully

as they emerged at long last at a fast-moving road split by a double-yellow line.

He was feeling good, thought Katie, because his idea had worked. She, on the other hand, was tired, sweaty, and once again, hungry. "He underestimated the distance just a little," she retorted.

"Chill, Katie. We're there. It took longer than we thought—OK. But we made it."

"We didn't 'make it.' We aren't 'there.' 'There' is Melville. This is Route 24. We're still a long way from Melville—we don't even know how far away we are. David, I'm worried about the rest of our trip. I don't see how we're supposed to keep going."

"Because . . . ?"

"It must be ninety degrees, David!"

"We'll rest for a while, and walk at night."

"Without food?"

Wordlessly, he reached into his pocket and handed her his last box of crackers

"David, be reasonable!"

"We'll steal more food—or buy it." Between the ten dollars from Sanders and the driver's four, he was feeling rich.

"What if it's thirty miles? What if it's fifty?"

With this Katie hit a nerve, and she knew it. It could be either, or it could be twelve or it could be seventy. Their map had a key and, technically, they knew how to use it.

But it was very hard to translate a tiny curved line on a piece of battered paper into actual distance, and they were both aware that a small error in doing so could mean many miles of hot pavement.

As her brother hesitated, Katie pressed her advantage. She was in a miserable mood and she wanted him to feel as discouraged as she did. "How many miles can we walk in a day?" she demanded. "Ten? Fifteen? We have no idea. It's not going to work, David."

"I'd like to point out that you picked this route."

"That's not fair."

"'We can walk to Melville from 91!'" he mimicked cruelly.

In a rage, Katie swung out her arm and hit him. He grabbed her wrist with one hand and her hair with the other. She opened her mouth to shout.

But it was one thing to fight at home in their own house, with their parents standing by to break it up. It was another to fight by the side of the road in a strange place, where all they had was each other. At the same moment both of them seemed to realize how stupid they were being, and just as quickly as their fight had begun it stopped.

For an instant Katie felt tears welling in her eyes. She really, really missed her mom and dad.

"So what do you have in mind?" asked David, subdued.

"Another truck," said Katie.

The thought was loathsome. "No," he replied. "No more trucks."

She didn't argue. She was suddenly exhausted. She didn't want another truck either. It was great how far you could go when you had one, but the effort and the fear—she couldn't go through that one more time.

She needed to rest. Turning away from her brother, Katie waded into the tall grass at the side of the road where she would not be seen. Finding a small hollow, she dropped to the ground. "Let's not do anything right now," she said through the grassy screen around her.

And they didn't. The sun passed slowly across the sky and the cars passed swiftly along the road. David watched the traffic whiz by. Katie watched the insects pursue their busy lives in the miniature world before her. There were scores of them, and they had homes, comrades, and purposes. For at least an hour as she and her brother sat, she almost envied them.

Katie's mind must have wandered far afield, because it returned with a start. Her brother had whistled.

He hadn't whistled for her, either. If he'd wanted to get her attention, a low hoot would have worked, but he'd made a sound that was loud and long and shrill. She peeked through the tall blades of grass. He was standing right by the edge of the road and frantically hailing an approaching car.

What on earth . . . ?

The car slowed and with a spray of gravel it braked to a stop just a few feet in front of David. It was a taxi.

They had fourteen dollars, and it appeared that David had just hailed a cab to take them to Melville. But unless she wanted to argue with him in front of the driver, it was not possible to do anything but play along.

Quickly Katie scrambled up and dusted off her shorts. David was already talking to the driver. She reached his side just in time to hear him offer a price.

"Ten dollars," said David. Ah, so he was saving some money to buy food.

"Sorry, kid," replied the driver. "You're going to need three, four times that much. Cost you thirty or forty dollars to get to Melville from here."

David's face fell. "Oh," he said awkwardly.

"Tell you what, though," said the driver, eyeing them. "I can get you ten dollars closer than where you are. Hop in."

Any misgivings they might have had about spending so much of their money to cover only part of their distance vanished as soon as they entered the air-conditioned taxi. The cab was the lap of luxury. They were sitting on upholstered seats and except for their brief stop in the police station, it had been forever since they'd sat on anything but metal or concrete or dirt. And then, to be able to look out the windows and see the landscape fly by as they were whisked along at sixty miles per hour . . .

It was only a regular taxi, but it felt like a rolling hotel as it dipped and swerved through the hilly country. Both of them knew they mustn't let their faces betray their awe. In the rearview mirror the driver was peering at them. He was a burly man with thinning hair and a ruddy, fleshy face, and his small, sharp eyes were unmistakably curious. David's guard began to rise.

"Hey," the man asked. "Where you kids from?"

Both of them saw instantly that they should have worked out a story. Now, having no choice, David thought on his feet. "Hawthorne," he said artlessly.

"Whatcha doin' in Melville?"

"Friend of ours is there."

"Maybe I know him. What's his name?"

"Alex." David's failure to supply a last name hung conspicuously in the silent car, but he did not want to say any more. The children had no idea whether the people in Melville knew about their uncle Alex or what they thought of him if they did. Now was not the time to find out.

"You were plannin' to walk that far?" asked the driver after a pause.

"Mom and Dad told us to walk, but we can ride. It's my money."

"They told you to *walk*?"

Man. That had been a mistake. He had gotten nervous, that was all. He had wanted to mention parents. He hadn't wanted the driver to suspect that they were on their own.

But one little mistake like that—one small slip of the tongue—could sink them.

Alarmed, David did not reply. He turned his face out the window and they rode in silence. But Katie could see that in his rearview mirror their driver continued to scrutinize them.

David was so busy reproaching himself for his stupidity—*Mom and Dad told us to walk!*—that he didn't even notice how the taxi was eating up the miles. Minute after minute passed in agonized silence and still they flew up and down the winding hills of Route 24.

Katie realized this first, and with a start. "Where are we?" she asked abruptly, snapping out of her anxious daze. "How far have we gone?" She seized the back of the driver's seat and pulled herself forward, searching for the meter that would tell them how many dollars' worth they had traveled.

The mileage counter read 000 and their fare showed as $000.00. The meter was turned off.

"We only have ten dollars!" she cried, frightened. Where was he taking them?

"I know that," said the driver calmly. "Don't worry. I can take you all the way there, and it won't cost you more 'n ten. I'm going to Melville anyways, see? Picking up an old lady there, called for a ride. Easier to take you all the way there than to stop an' put you out."

David and Katie shared a quick, uneasy glance.

"Are you sure?" Katie asked.

"Thanks," added David stiffly, his mind frantically working. All the way to Melville for ten dollars! They'd be there! But something about this did not feel right. Maybe they were being kidnapped.

Apparently not. Moments later they passed a road sign reading melville: 23 miles. And a little while after that came a sign advertising a Melville realtor, then one for a Melville diner, and then they were there. They were pulling into town. They had arrived.

It was clear at a glance that this was an even tinier place than Hawthorne and that Route 24 was the road about which they'd been told, the one that went right through it. Their driver did not ask them where they wanted to get out. Instead, he rolled straight into the center of town. Then he pulled to a stop by what looked like the town square, set his brake, cut his motor, and shifted his bulky frame completely around in his seat to look both of them straight in the eyes.

David had the money ready. "Thank—"

"Now, you listen here," said the driver, cutting him off. "You just listen to me."

David and Katie sat back, stunned.

"That was a load of baloney you fed me, back there on the road. I know when I'm bein' lied to. You two are a mess. Neither of you's seen any mom or dad for a week."

"That's not—"

"Don't interrupt me."

David fell silent.

"Sum'pm's going on with you two—sum'pm's wrong. I don't know what it is, but I don't like it. Now. You want to tell me the truth, or what?"

Neither of them said a word. They simply stared, terrified. The cabbie's eyes were narrow and penetrating. A long silence hung in the car.

The driver broke it. He sighed and turned back around to gaze once more out the windshield. "I ought to turn you in," he said heavily. "I really ought to."

Katie and David stared at the back of his head and the rolls of flesh on his neck. Should they make a run for it? Katie's mind frantically scrolled. She glanced out the window. The wide-open square, the little town—they'd never make it.

"Tell you what I'm going to do," said the driver, breaking into their thoughts. Slowly, his enormous hand reached for his glove compartment. A spasm of terror seized both children. They had come so far. Could it really end here, on the last leg of their long journey?

But it did not end. Instead, the man opened the hatch and lifted out a stack of small printed cards fastened with a rubber band. With his thick, fleshy fingers he extracted one and held it out to David.

"This here's my card—you take it," he ordered. After a

slight hesitation David did. The driver lifted a fat finger and shook it at them. "If you need help with anything," he said, "if anything happens to you that you don't like—you call me. My name's Mike; you can see it right there.

"I'm not gonna get you in any trouble. I don't want to know what you did. You need any help at all, you call me. Understand?"

David, dumbfounded, said nothing.

"Thank you," replied Katie in a low voice. Her heart was still drumming in her chest.

"I got kids myself," the driver continued. "Course they're all grown now, but once a parent, always a parent. And I don't like to see people your age in trouble. So you put that card in your pocket. No"—David had returned to his senses and was holding out his cash—"I'm not gonna take your money. I got a feeling you might need it."

"Really, it's—"

"Put it away. Now, anything else you want to say to me? No? Then out of the car."

"Thank you. Thank you very much, Mike," said David, and he scrambled for the handle and tumbled out the door. Katie was right behind him. The taxi pulled forward, swiveled backward, and in a spray of gravel and a cloud of fumes pivoted around to head back up Route 24, the same way they'd come.

David and Katie stood blinking, watching it go.

"He's going back toward Hawthorne," said David, bewildered.

"So much for the old lady in Melville," said Katie.

Worried and depressed, they wandered the streets of Melville.

They knew they should be happy. They had made it, after all. It was just after four o'clock and they had arrived—in air-conditioned comfort, for free—at a place from which they really could walk to their uncle's house.

So they should be happy, but they were not. They could not decide whether to strike out to find their uncle, or try to find food instead.

After three days without proper meals, their need for food had finally become urgent. For the first time since they had left home, they had nothing to eat. Apart from their map and their flashlights, their pockets were empty.

They had fourteen dollars, but since that business with Mike they were afraid to use their money even to satisfy their hunger. Mike had noticed they were in trouble but had let them go. A cashier or a waitress might not.

"You know what's happening," said Katie after they had strolled around for nearly an hour, kicking this matter to and fro in half whispers. "Because we can't decide what to do, we're getting the worst of both worlds. We're not getting anything to eat and we're making ourselves conspicuous anyway. We need a plan, David!"

"Fine," said her brother. "Let's go back to that diner and get sandwiches. With fries," he added hungrily. The smell outside the diner had just about drilled a hole in him.

"But they'll ask questions! And what'll we say?"

"OK! So let's just leave, then. Let's forget about eating and head out to Uncle Alex's." The diner called, but fear called from the opposite direction.

"But what if we have to walk a really long way? We'll faint, David!"

He threw up his hands.

"Besides," added Katie with affected casualness, "we don't know Uncle Alex."

Here was a new one. David stopped walking and his eyebrows lifted. "Meaning . . . ?"

"Meaning we don't know him. Like, now that we're getting close I'm just thinking about that, that's all." Still her brother stared, and she stumbled on.

"You have to admit it's unusual," she said, "him being a hermit and all. I mean, what kind of person does that?"

"I dunno. A person who had a really bad fight with his girlfriend a really long time ago. That's what Mom and Dad told us, anyway. Does it matter?"

"I don't know. Maybe. Though by the way, if we do find him? We're not going to ask."

"Give me a little credit."

"And what if it turns out he's weird?" Katie continued, not replying. "What if he's—what if he's *not nice*? What if he won't help?"

"Now you say it."

"I know. I know! It's just that now that we're getting closer I'm realizing—"

"That he's a total unknown."

"Right! Who doesn't like to be around people. And here we are, dumping ourselves right on top of him. Two kids, with a really big, really important problem."

So they wandered, neither deciding to eat nor deciding not to; neither fleeing to their uncle nor abandoning the plan. Five o'clock became five thirty and five thirty became six. It was summer, they were in the north, and the days were long. But even so, they knew that night would come. And their hunger tightened like a screw and their spirits sank.

They were beginning to pass people they'd already seen once or even twice before, and they were beginning to draw looks. They knew it, but they felt so low in body and mind that they almost did not care.

Then they rounded the wrong corner. Spying a quiet, leafy block lined with neat wooden houses where they had not yet been, they turned onto it with slow footsteps. Katie let her fingers trail along the top of the low picket fence surrounding the first house.

Then her heart was slammed into her throat. An enormous dog—head low, fangs bared, and jaws slavering—tore snarling across the front lawn straight for them.

The creature threw itself at the flimsy fence in a frenzy of barking. A hoarse scream burst from Katie's lips and she stumbled backward, falling against her brother and nearly knocking him down.

The instant the dog hit the fence it jerked sharply back. Now the children could see that it was tethered to a long chain that would not let it off the property. But the damage had been done. Perhaps at another time they would have laughed off a scare like this one, but not today—not on top of all their other troubles.

So they freaked. Clutching each other they turned on their heels and fled, and when they reached Route 24 they didn't stop. They ripped around the corner and kept running, up the sidewalk to the end of the block, across the street, and up the next block as well. By the time they paused to catch their breath, they had decided what to do.

They'd had enough of Melville. They were hungry and they were scared, but it was time to move on. Whoever he might turn out to be and whatever he might turn out to do and regardless of what awaited them along the way, it was time to find their uncle Alex.

LIKE AN ECHO
FOR THE EYES

"It *sounded* close; that's the problem," said Katie wearily. "It's the way the directions *sounded*."

"Right," said David. "That plus a little machine called a car. When Mom and Dad did this, they always drove."

They were both right, and they knew it. But it didn't really matter. Nothing changed the fact that the trail to Alex's, which they had always assumed you picked up right outside of town, was not right outside of town.

They were supposed to remain on the road through Melville until about half a mile past the first bridge. Then they were supposed to find the rock that had been split by lightning, turn off the road, and head up the mountain. After that it was easy: Left at the creek and you're there.

It sounded like nothing. But that first bridge! It was now

almost seven in the evening and they still hadn't passed it. Soon it would be dark. In fact, in this hilly country the sun had already slipped behind a rocky peak, throwing them into shadow.

They continued to walk, and their road began taking them more and more steeply uphill. Until this point, David had not really put it together that because their uncle lived on a mountain, they would be climbing, and that climbing was hard. His huffing breath and trudging feet fell into a rhythm, and he tried to concentrate on that instead of thinking about his stomach. Step—*unh*—step—*unh*—step . . .

They would eat when they got to Alex's, David told himself. Assuming they found him, that is. And assuming he fed them, and assuming their arrival didn't make him mad, and assuming he didn't turn out to be just too weird for them to get anywhere near him.

Step—*unh*—step—*unh*—step . . . For as Katie had pointed out back in Melville, being a hermit, there was a fairly high probability that Uncle Alex would be as weird as a . . . as weird as a . . . as a—"What's that noise?" David demanded, cutting off his own thoughts.

"Water." Katie's head was down and she kept her answer short. She, too, had found a rhythm that she didn't want to break.

"Water! It is! Katie, where there's water there might be a bridge!"

"Not very smart, are we, David?"

He was too relieved to take offense. Just knowing the bridge was ahead of them put fresh energy into his step, even as his nerves buzzed with something that could be excitement or could be fear. They *were* close. They were very, very close after all.

The water beneath the bridge was bright and cold and so good that it almost felt like food. David crouched on a flat rock by the stream, his cupped hands full of the icy stuff. He had never tasted such water before. He splashed some over his face and it felt great. Their success with this part of their journey had restored his sense that things were working out and, David-like, he had entirely regained his good humor. He stretched out on his back and closed his eyes.

Katie, on the other hand, was concerned. She had never really worried about the bridge. She'd known they would find it. But that rock! There were rocks everywhere. Split by lightning—what would that look like?

"It's getting dark, you know," she said.

"Right. Cooler," David commented, his eyes still closed.

She didn't reply, and he sighed. She was going to go nuclear again, just when he was starting to feel OK.

David opened his eyes and sat up. "We have flashlights, Kat. And they should last us to Uncle Alex's. We've been pretty good about the batteries."

"Little, tiny flashlights. We have little, tiny lights that throw little, tiny beams. There are thousands of boulders, David! We can't be looking with little flashlights for lightning cracks in thousands of boulders! And after we find it—if we find it—then what?"

"We climb through the woods."

"Which way? Straight between the two peaks, right? Are you going to find *them* with your flashlight?"

"It's ten after seven. We have another *hour* of daylight. An hour and a *half*, maybe."

But Katie stood, dried her hands on her shorts, and started clambering back up over the rocks. For a few long moments David continued to lie still. Then, resentfully, he rose to follow her.

But Katie had set a driving pace and by the time he caught up, she had stopped walking. She was sitting by the side of the road. Her back rested against a massive boulder, round like a ball but taller and wider than a house.

The boulder's soft, sloping sides were covered with mosses and lichen, and shrubbery sprouted from crevices in its crumbly surface. It looked as if it had sat on that spot since the glaciers receded a couple of ice ages ago. But inches from Katie's right arm the rock was sliced wide open. A great slab of it had fallen away, revealing two perfectly straight, perfectly flat cut surfaces. It looked as if a knife had been taken to a ball of cheese.

David gazed at the slashed stone. "Lightning," he said briefly.

Then his eyes roved to the side of the rock and he saw it. Had he not been looking for it he would certainly have missed it. It didn't look like trails do in pictures. It wasn't at all like the trails he had walked with his family, when he and Katie and their parents had gone exploring in the park or the country on weekends, back in their other lifetime. It was so faint, it almost could not be called a trail at all.

But curving around the fallen piece of rock—suggested by a bent branch, signaled in a smooth patch of earth—was the barest, faintest suggestion that someone had walked there before.

There could be no question who that walker was.

"I guess this means he's real," said David. Katie did not ask who he meant.

They had thought the light would fade gradually away. They had thought they would have time to prepare for the total darkness—to tighten their shoelaces one last time, to check David's watch, to orient themselves with one final look toward the peaks that were their only guide.

But that was not how it happened. Darkness dropped like a curtain. One moment they were squinting for the faint traces of their path, and the next they were in utter blackness. Beneath the thick cover of the trees there was not even moonlight to guide them.

"We should never have headed into the woods when it was almost night," said Katie when they realized what had happened. "Now we'll have to wait. We'll have to stop, and sit, and walk again when the sun's up."

"I'm not 'sitting' anywhere," said David. In the dark, his voice made the angry little quote marks that his fingers could not. "And we 'headed into the woods' because we wanted to get where we were going. I'm hungry, Kat, and I'm thirsty, too. I'm not waiting while all of that gets worse."

"You're going to walk all night?"

"I'll rest at Uncle Alex's, after I've eaten. I won't rest in a thornbush"—angrily, he dragged a bramble from his hair—"when I'm starving."

"We'll get lost. The sun will come up and we'll look around and we'll have no idea where we are."

"We'll figure it out. We have flashlights. It's not that complicated." David snapped on his light and Katie caught a glimpse of his scratched and weary face before he turned it on the bushes in front of him. "There!" he announced angrily, waving the beam at a barely discernable gap between two shrubs. "See that hole? That's it—that's the way." And he ducked, shouldering his way in.

"Oh—that's *ridiculous*! That—that is *such a bad idea*!"

But David did not stop. So with deep misgivings Katie followed him.

Neither of them knew just how long they labored up the hill, but they knew hours passed. Worse yet, neither of them believed they were headed the right way.

Within minutes, they forgot where the peaks lay. After that they tried aiming uphill, on the theory that they were supposed to be climbing. But there wasn't just one way up. From some spots the ground would seem to rise around them in all four directions, and in others it seemed to drop down.

Continuing to walk under these conditions was absolutely wrong, and by now they both knew it. But somehow they could not stop. They just kept hoping that each new footstep would correct the last bad one. Back over there—they had surely done that part wrong. But surely now they were doing it right. And so they wore themselves out, walking in a circle for all they knew, and beating at the bushes with sticks as if they could beat away the knowledge that they had traveled all this way just to find themselves alone on an unknown mountain in the middle of the night, friendless, hungry, lost, and on a fool's errand.

Then the moment came when they could beat away these thoughts no more. It happened when their flashlights, having glowed faithfully through thick and thin, finally faded, quivered, and went out. David's went first. Katie's was not far behind it.

"We shouldn't have turned both of them on at once," David said, amazed that they had been so dumb. "If we'd used them one at a time they might have lasted until morning."

"What difference does it make?" Katie dashed hers to the ground and sank to the earth cross-legged. Without their small lights, the night was staggeringly black. She was consumed by despair. "David? Just tell me one thing, David. Why are we here?"

He did not reply, so she went on.

"I know why we're here," she said. "And I know it was my idea, but it wasn't my fault. We didn't have any choices." For some reason it was terribly important—now, when they were down to zero—to know there was nothing they could have done differently. Katie concentrated, thinking back. "We could have starved to death in the old house with the rats, or we could have come here, where maybe we'll starve on this mountain."

"The mountain's better," said David. "Even if we do starve, I'd a thousand times rather be here than where those people—those Katkajanians—might have come back and gotten us again. If I'm going to die," he added grimly, "I'm just going to *die*, that's all. I'm not letting those freaks kill me and I'm *not* letting them watch."

But Katie wasn't really listening. "And I guess we could have told the police," she said, still thinking. "But they'd have gone straight to our house to talk to Trixie, and they might have believed her, and then Mom and Dad and Theo would have been killed."

"That's really why, you know," said David.

"Why what?"

"Why we're here. You were asking? We're here because of Mom and Dad and Theo. We're here because we weren't ready to write them off. We wanted to try to save them. We were hoping we could fix it, get everything back—you know."

"Was that dumb?"

"I don't know. I don't think so," he said, reflecting.

"I guess I don't think so either," she agreed. "I mean, I think it made sense then—it made sense to try, so we did. But you know what? I think at this point, we'd probably better figure out what we're going to do if we fail."

With this, a long silence fell between them. And into this silence, sounds began to creep: the sounds of the night. It was still very dark, but their eyes had adjusted just enough for them to see vague shapes and shadows in the faint moonlight. A soft, fitful breeze rustled the leaves overhead and a mosquito whined in Katie's ear. She slapped at it, missing. Cicadas whirred in the distance and somewhere a branch snapped as something pounced in the underbrush. From far away, the low notes of flowing water warbled softly beneath it all.

David sat with closed eyes. He knew he should be thinking of a plan, but his mind was simply too exhausted to do anything but float. For a few moments it floated on the soft music of the water. His mind rode on the water as if on a carpet, a beautiful floating carpet. Must be a creek, from the sound of it, a sparkling, rippling creek like a carpet unfurling through the wood—

A creek. He sat bolt upright. "Katie, that's a creek—listen. Don't you hear it?"

"Yes, and I'm thirsty too, David. But I'm not going anywhere right now. Not even for a—"

"I'm not talking about drinking! Think a minute. What were we looking for, walking up that hill? Where were we supposed to turn?"

"The creek. Oh! Oh, David. Do you think that's it?"

But he was already scrambling to his feet. "It has to be. And we can hear it, Katie. We won't need our flashlights; we can follow our ears." He looked wildly around in the direction of the sound, then plunged into the surrounding underbrush.

"David, wait!" But once again she got up and followed.

It had been maddening to try to make out a nearly invisible trail with two tiny flashlights. Nonetheless, it was even worse to chase a fitful, dancing, and distant sound through an obstacle course in near total blackness. Sometimes they thought the sound was actually getting fainter and once, despairingly, they lost it altogether. But after a long while—it was impossible to say how long—the rippling and burbling of the water began to grow stronger.

Either they were getting closer, or they were now so hungry and tired that they were hallucinating. In a confused way Katie realized this was possible. She had never before known such hunger. She felt as if an iron fist were balled up in her stomach, and she knew the pain and weakness it caused were playing strange tricks on her mind. She began to feel as if her parents could see and hear her. And then she found herself staring at her mother's face. Worse yet, she didn't mind. She could not stop gazing at it: dark and oval-shaped, with the deep black eyes beneath the black hair, the warm, slow smile. It presented itself to Katie's exhausted mind as vividly as if her mom were right there, and it helped.

Katie's stomach twisted in agony. Without even thinking she stripped a fistful of leaves off a passing branch, shoved it into her mouth, and bit down. The bitter taste made her gag and spit, shattering the vision of her mother's face.

She could have been poisoned!

"Katie!"

As David's voice broke through her thoughts, she heard the water once again. This time there was no question that it had grown louder.

"I think this is it! I think we're just about there!"

The bushes around them were now ferns—Katie could feel their long fronds—and the sound of the water was very near. She suddenly realized that she was desperately thirsty. David was plunging down a slope; she could hear him beneath her. Then she heard a new sound in the water. She heard splashing. He was there.

The water was fabulous. It filled their empty stomachs, even if only briefly, and refreshed their weary faces.

Left at the creek: Those had been their instructions. Left at the creek and then you're there. With barely a pause they set out in the direction of their uncle's home and forged onward, driven now by their desperate need for food.

Her mom was back. Again Katie saw her face. This time she knew it was a hallucination, and she guessed that meant she was going crazy, but she didn't even mind. The face seemed to hover in the air above the creek, or sometimes to watch her from the other bank. It helped Katie feel that they were not alone.

There were no trees above the water and the moonlight that had barely penetrated the forest shone full upon them through the now open air. Katie could see David's gaze roaming everywhere through the new brightness as he trudged forward, searching for a sign, any sign, of their uncle Alex.

"You follow the water and you're there." That was how their parents had always said you did it, and in the end that was how it was. Katie and David did not know what they were looking for—a hut? A cave? What did hermits live in, after all? But they both saw it at the same time

183

and they recognized it at once. It was on the other side of the creek and it was a house: a small, neat house made of wood. A well-tended garden enclosed by a fence lay beside it. Curtains were drawn across its two windows, but light shone from behind them. Light poured, too, from the front door, which stood wide open.

And in the doorway—looking right at them—was a man as familiar to their eyes as an echo is to the ears. He was not a stranger. He seemed to be someone they had seen before and loved for a long, long time. He was of medium height and slim, but in that first moment neither Katie nor David noticed any of that. They saw nothing but the dark oval of his face and the deep eyes that gazed at them in wonderment from beneath his black hair.

It was as if their mother's face, which Katie had seen with her mind's eye, had suddenly turned real. She was not afraid anymore. A path of flat stones ran straight across the creek to the little house. Wordlessly she stepped across them toward the man in the doorway. David was right behind her, and then they were in his arms.

But the shock of recognition was not over. Another still more dazzling one was to follow, the instant their blinking eyes adjusted to the warm light within their uncle's home. All around them on every wall were photographs—dozens and dozens of photographs—of them. There were David and Katie, moments after their births. There they were as toddlers, and there was a picture of them just a few months ago in the new house. Their parents were there too. They were there as a young couple just married, and then holding their twin babies, and smiling with their children, and with their arms around Alex.

But the real Uncle Alex was right there before them, and he was busy. From a small cupboard on the wall he was lifting down plates and mugs and a loaf of bread. Their stomachs twisted yet again as he cut the bread into thick slices and spread it with butter.

Nothing had ever been as vivid as those pictures and that bread. Neither Katie nor David had ever seen anything so striking or tasted anything so intensely. So absorbed were they in these sensations that neither of them noticed how Alex somehow fixed their beds. But all at once, the beds were there. Then they fell into them and fell asleep, as entirely and suddenly as if they had fallen off a cliff.

IN THE DARK

It was nearly evening of the next day when they awoke. But that was hardly surprising, as they had not arrived at their uncle's house until almost dawn.

So when at last they opened their eyes, it was to the aroma of dinner, bubbling in a pot over an open fire in Alex's front yard. Not wanting to wake them, he had cooked outside. But they could not sleep through that smell: the smell of the first hot food that had been fixed for them since the pizza they had eaten the night before their mom and dad had left for Katkajan, a lifetime ago.

The savory odor cut through David's stomach like a knife, causing him to sit up sharply on his mat on the floor. His blinking eyes met his uncle's smile, which was framed in the window.

"I thought it'd wake you if I cranked this up," Alex said, gesturing at the window, which he had just propped open with a stick. He was outside minding the meal, but he bent over to rest his elbows on the sill. "Based on how hungry you were last night."

Katie was awake too. "What is it?" she asked urgently. "That smell, I mean." She had been given the bed, and now without further ceremony she swung her feet to the floor.

"A little something from the garden," said their uncle. "And there's a fish roasting too. I caught it just about an hour ago. Healthful and delicious, like everything here," he added proudly. "It's from the good, clean mountain earth."

But then concern furrowed Alex's brow and his smile faded. "I did hate to wake you when you're so tired," he said. "But I have a feeling that my very welcome guests have a story to tell me, and I think it's time I heard what it was."

Of course he let them eat first. They were ravenous, and neither of them had ever tasted anything like the flaky white fish that steamed beneath its slightly charred skin, or the thick, flavorful soup. Sighing, Katie and David mopped up the last drops with more of their uncle's rich, chewy bread.

They ate at his small table, with the doors and windows

open and the cool, early-evening air floating through. The mountaintop smelled amazing, and there were no sounds at all but birdsong and the trickling of the creek. After their long days and nights on the road, amid the dust and grit and stink of truck stops and highways, David found he was as hungry for the clean and peaceful setting as he was for the food. Maybe Alex wasn't weird after all, living in a place like this.

Certainly their uncle didn't seem weird. Katie tried not to stare at all his things, but she couldn't help noticing how nice his tiny house was. It was so neat and clever. Everything he needed was there, and it all fit in so ingeniously.

And it was great to be clean. Alex had given them clothes of his own to sleep in and while they had slept, he had washed their shorts and T-shirts. Then hungry as they were, he had insisted that they bathe before sitting down to eat in them. They loved the shower he had rigged up behind his house. Sweet water from his well was pumped into a tank that rested high up on tall stilts. The water was warmed by a flame, and when it flowed down over her Katie thought she had never felt anything so lovely. She couldn't stop sniffing her arms, just to marvel at their fresh smell.

Their uncle waited patiently while they ate. But when they had finished, over mugs of sweet, minty tea they told him their story. They didn't tell it very smoothly. They interrupted each other and left out a lot of parts, and everything seemed to get said in fits and starts. But even so it was a huge relief to spill it out. And in a way, they only truly grasped what had happened to them when they saw the horror on Alex's face.

They stumbled a little at the end, when they told him how they had climbed the mountain to his house. "We stopped walking for a while," David said, suddenly not knowing how much to share. "It was hard without the lights and we were afraid—we weren't sure—well, we didn't know if you'd be glad to see us," he finished lamely.

He had barely caught himself. He'd almost said "We were afraid of what you'd be like."

Their uncle reddened and swallowed. Apparently David had not caught himself in time. Alex seemed to have figured out what he had really meant.

"We're not worried anymore," added Katie hastily.

Their uncle nodded seriously. "It was perfectly reasonable for you to wonder," he said a little stiffly. "You'd been through a lot and you didn't know me at all. And most people don't live by themselves, the way I do. You were probably afraid I was some kind of freak."

Katie was mortified. "No, we weren't!" she cried.

Unexpectedly, though, David grinned and looked his uncle straight in the eye. "Yep," he said, "we were. Uncle Alex, we were afraid you were *dangerous*."

"*David!*"

But David's candor seemed to relax their uncle, who

now grinned back. Katie, who found all this frankness irritating, glared at her brother and pressed forward.

"What we were really worried about," she said, "was that maybe we'd just been dumb. I mean, we started to worry that even if you *were* nice—and of course, you *are*"— again she glared at David—"you might not be able to help. Even though you know about Rover and everything, we thought maybe there wouldn't be anything you could do to save Mom and Dad and Theo."

Alex rose to his feet and began striding back and forth across the small room. Katie and David watched him in silence. He seemed lost in thought.

Then he abruptly stopped his restless pacing. He hitched over a stool and sat down between them, planting his elbows on the tabletop and his chin in his hands. "Kids," he said, frowning, "what you've been through is horrible—beyond words. For children to have to endure this—at your age—I don't know how you made it through. And I really, really want to give it a happy ending, where you get back everything you've lost. But I know you want the truth, so I'm going to tell you right now that it might not be possible."

Remorse flooded his face as he saw their dismay. "That doesn't mean I'm not going to try," he corrected hastily. "There is one thing I can do."

The blood had drained from their limbs and now it began, tentatively, to return.

"I can't say whether it will work," continued their uncle. "But I can give it a shot, and I will. And you definitely did the right thing coming here," he added. "If this doesn't do it—what I'm going to try—then probably nothing could." He paused. "We're going to have to take a trip."

"Where?" asked Katie.

"*You?*" asked David, incredulous.

This time Katie blushed to the roots of her hair at her brother's rudeness. But once again, Alex didn't seem to take offense. He grinned another crooked grin.

"Of course," he said. "Travelin' man."

"Not," said David. Alex just looked blankly at him, so he amplified. "You're not. Not a travelin' man."

"*David!*"

Their uncle grew very grave. "It's OK, Katie. It's true that I'm not usually a traveler. I travel to Melville for supplies, but apart from that I haven't left this mountain in almost fifteen years. But try to remember: Your mom and dad and Theo are my family too."

"But where are we going?" asked Katie.

"Washington."

At this Katie looked alarmed. "Washington DC? But there are Katkajanians all over Washington! They could be looking for us in Washington—that's where Trixie is!" Her uncle had named the last place on earth where she wanted to be. "That's where we just came from! We can't go—"

Firmly, Alex cut her off. "If we didn't have to, we wouldn't," he said. "But there's someone I must see—someone to whom I must speak. And that person is in Washington DC." Rising distractedly, he produced a large, flat washing pan and began to stack their plates and cups inside it.

"Do we have to go with you?" asked Katie, getting up to help. She felt that she could see Nose and Hair, and hear Trixie's harsh, splintery laugh.

"I'm afraid you do—both of you," said Alex. "I don't want either of you staying here alone."

"We can take care of ourselves!"

"Yes, Katie, of course you can," he replied. "But that's not it. Those two thugs who grabbed you will eventually figure out where I live."

This was too close to what they already knew to ignore. The blessed sensation of protection that they had both been savoring since they walked through their uncle's door vanished like smoke. The sighing of the wind in the trees and the trickling of the creek, which had been the sweet music of safety, became veils that concealed creeping footsteps and approaching danger.

"So we'll all need to go," repeated Alex, "and first thing in the morning."

"Maybe we should leave now," said David. Katie had been right. Nose and Hair would only waste so much time in New Hampshire.

"No," said Alex firmly. "Right now it's almost dark. We'll travel in the morning." He gazed at their ashen faces, and woe creased his forehead. "I've scared you," he said miserably. "I'm so new to all this. I have so little experience with children. Please forgive me. Sit down," he added, abruptly changing his plan. "We'll wash these later—or rather, I will after you've gone to sleep, which you'll be doing again, very soon. But first I want to talk about Katkajan."

And he did. They all pulled their stools outside, where the evening sky deepened from blue to indigo to black as the stars grew bright above and the fireflies glimmered below. While night fell, Katie and David's uncle told them about the faraway place where their sister had been born and their parents had vanished.

It seemed that Alex had lived in Katkajan, years ago when he was young. He had loved the place and the people. Katkajan was a free country then, but already a growing insurgent movement threatened its peaceful government. When Alex had returned home and he and the Bowdens had developed Rover, he'd particularly hoped their invention would help Katkajan, along with the people there whom he admired so much.

"So I don't like to see you hating Katkajan, Katie," said her uncle. "It isn't a bad country—there are no bad countries. There are only bad people, and most Katkajanians are good. I'm sure most of them would help your parents if they had the chance."

193

"Is that your plan?" asked Katie. "Are you going to get the good Katkajanians to help?"

"No—I'll be trying something different," said her uncle.

"But what?" Katie persisted.

"We can discuss that later," he replied. "You've been under a terrible strain. Right now you need your rest."

Katie was about to say that she was not too tired, but David cut her off.

"Uncle Alex," David said, "this all reminds me—all this talk about Katkajan and stuff. About Rover—what is it anyway? I mean, what does it do?"

Katie heard this question with interest. Rover had always been off-limits, but David did have a point, asking about it now. Things had changed, after all.

Apparently they had not changed enough. Alex's face shut like a book at the mention of Rover. "David," he said, and his voice was kind but firm, "I can certainly understand why you would want to ask. But I'm afraid that information is only available on a need-to-know basis. That means that only those who need to know can be told. And right now you have no such need. Fortunately," he added.

"Well, will you use it? To help find Mom and Dad and Theo?"

"We'll see," said their uncle. "But first we have to get to Washington."

Katie and David exchanged glances. They were glad

that Alex was helping. It was a huge relief, just being with him. But as for Rover, they were not at all sure that they didn't need to know.

Alex, though, was moving on. He frowned. "I rarely wish that I had a car, but I have to admit that tonight I do."

"We have a car," said Katie.

Alex looked confused. "Of course you do. Maybe even two cars, at home. But we'll need one here," he said. "In Vermont."

"It is here. David, where's that little card?"

David gave her his I'm-being-patient-with-a-mentally-challenged-person look. "Katie?" he asked, eyebrows up. "I have no idea what you're talking about?"

She glowered. "The card from the taxi guy. We came here in a taxi," she explained, turning to Uncle Alex. "I guess we didn't tell you that part. And the driver gave us his card."

"A taxi?" asked Alex. "I thought you said you rode in trucks."

"Mostly it was trucks," said David. "We just took a taxi part of the way. It was my idea," he added, feeling suddenly proud. Pretty cool idea, come to think of it.

"The driver was very nice," said Katie. "He could tell something was wrong and he said we should call him if we ever needed anything. So I'm sure he would take us to Washington."

"Washington's a long way to go in a cab," said Alex dubiously.

"Here it is," said David, who had been fishing in his pocket. He produced a battered rectangle of white cardboard and looked around for a phone. "Mike. I'll call him. What do I say?" he asked, suddenly not knowing.

"Depends," said his uncle. "What did you already tell him?"

"A bunch of lies," admitted David. "But we never told him we were looking for you, if that's what you mean. Or not exactly, anyway."

"Tell him now," said Alex decidedly. He rose and continued talking as he bent to lift his stool. "Tell the driver you found your uncle who lives on the mountain. It's OK," he added in response to their questioning looks. "I'm a hermit, but I'm not a secret. They know about me down in Melville.

"If this Mike was worried about you, then at first he might not be happy that you're with me. He might not like it that we want to go so far. But we don't actually have to convince him to take us—not tonight, anyway. We just have to get him to talk to us. So tell him I'm the one you were looking for. And tell him now that you've found me, we want to go get your parents."

"Which is true," put in Katie.

"Right. But don't tell him anything else. And we'll have to watch what we say when we're in his car. No one must know what's really going on. Not even Mike." Alex stood, stretched, and then swung his stool indoors.

"Got it," said David. "Um, how about a phone?" he added, holding up the card.

Alex stepped smartly over to a shelf above his bed, lifted down a box, and removed a small, sleek cell phone. He held it out to David, grinning. "Thought I didn't have one, didn't you?" he asked.

David grinned back. "No comment," he said, flipping it open.

Katie was very tired. She scarcely listened as David dialed and he and their uncle arranged to meet Mike for a conversation the next day. Mike hadn't said yes to the trip, but he hadn't hung up on them either. Good.

Nice as it was outside, Katie simply felt better indoors and she breathed easier once her uncle locked the door. Ever since his warning, shadowy figures had seemed to watch her from the darkened woods, and the flickering of the fireflies seemed like reflections from their bright, hidden eyes. The cool air was refreshing, but she reached up to close the window, wanting it, too, to be sealed and locked.

As she raised her arms, the short sleeve of her T-shirt slid back on her left shoulder and the corner of her eye seemed to catch its slithering motion. She gasped and slammed the window shut, her heart pounding in fear.

David and Alex turned in alarm to see her pale, staring face.

"I saw something. It must have been just my sleeve," Katie said miserably.

"Are you sure?" demanded David.

"I think it was," she said. Because if it wasn't, then what she had just seen was the quick, stealthy movement of someone in the woods.

Their uncle strode to the door and threw it open. "Who's there?" he barked.

Not so much as a twig snapped in response. For a moment Alex simply listened to the silence and stillness that met his gruff call. But then—and without taking his eyes off the woods—he reached for a cupboard that hung by the door. Pulling it open, he drew out a pistol. Gripping the weapon in both hands, he cocked it.

The unmistakable sound of a firearm clicking into shooting position ricocheted through the silent woods.

Neither David nor Katie so much as breathed. They had never been so close to a gun before.

Alex closed and locked the door. When he turned around to face them, his expression was grim.

"Neither of you is to touch this gun," he said.

"No problem," said David. As if they would.

"I'm a man of peace," continued Alex, looking unhappy.

"Understood!" said David.

"I cherish the quiet of my mountain."

"We believe you!" said David.

"But sometimes, when you live alone, you need a weapon."

"Uncle Alex," said Katie, jumping in, "we're not arguing!"

Alex sighed. "Everything looks good out there," he said. "What did you see, Katie?"

"Probably just my own arm," she confessed, embarrassed that she had reacted as she did. "I'm pretty sure I didn't see anything. Sorry I yelled."

Alex looked relieved. "You're tired," he said. "And everything you've been through has made you jumpy. It's time for bed."

Wearily Katie laid herself down. She was beyond tired. She was so tired, she was broken.

No sooner did Katie's head touch the pillow than she felt it begin to swirl, spinning her down, down, downward. But despite her weariness—just before she slipped into unconsciousness—she distinctly heard the click of the cupboard as her uncle opened it and put the pistol away. And she also heard the fastening of the window latch as he locked it for the night and carefully turned it tight.

TRAVELIN' MAN

That was not the last they were to see of their uncle's gun. Early the next morning, just before they left the little house on the mountaintop, Alex again opened the cupboard, then slipped the weapon into his pocket.

He thought that Katie and David did not see this, but they did. They exchanged a look, but neither of them said a word.

The rest of their preparations went quickly and smoothly. Alex produced a backpack into which he put his phone, a bottle of water, some homemade bread, and a fat hunk of Vermont cheese. The children added their map, which was now badly bedraggled, and their flashlights, which would need new batteries. And then Alex brought indoors the things he usually kept out, turned the key in the lock, and led the way.

Katie and David followed their uncle along the bank of the stream, heading down the same path by which they had arrived two days before. The morning was clear and cold. Sun shone where they walked by the water, but daylight had not yet chased the shadows from the woods. They could see only a short distance into the forest on either side of them.

It was deeply still in there, and the darkened woods were silent.

Katie gratefully savored the warm sunshine on her shoulders and averted her eyes from the blackness on either side of them.

Alex appeared to be absorbed in thought, and they tramped along in silence.

David was the first to break it. "Um, Uncle Alex?" he asked.

"Mmm?" said Alex.

"Do you have money and stuff like that?"

"David!" Katie exclaimed. Talk about a mood-breaker. Really, her brother had no manners.

"I mean, for the taxi. Because, like, the last time this guy drove us we didn't have enough to pay him."

"That's incredibly rude!"

"It's OK, Katie," said her uncle. "If you're going to live

as strangely as I do, you have to expect questions. And the answer is yes. I have money from Rover, just the way your parents do. And the first place we're going to ask your taxi to take us is to my bank in Melville. Katie, it isn't necessary to scuff the leaves that way. Let's try to enjoy the silence of a mountain morning."

"I'm not scuffing," said Katie.

"Well, David, then. Please pick up your feet."

"Right," said David absentmindedly. "That's good about the money, Uncle Alex. It's a good thing you're so normal."

"*David!* Oh my *God*!"

"'Cause we only have fourteen dollars! That's all I meant, Kat!"

"Oh my *God*. I don't *know* you!"

But Alex did not seem to care. "David," he said. "I'm sorry to interrupt you. But would you please stop that rustling noise?"

"I'm not. It's Katie."

"I am not scuffing!"

"Well, whatever it is you're doing, please stop. It isn't necessary to make noise everywhere we go. I think that city children sometimes forget—"

"Uncle Alex."

Something in David's voice stopped Alex in mid-sentence and he whipped around to face his niece and nephew. They were not rustling. In fact, they were not walking at all. They were standing stock-still, with faces white as death. And from the woods to their left came a steady, stealthy dry noise, like the scuffing of old leaves.

Neither Katie nor David could have predicted that the sound of one small pistol would be so loud. It was so loud that it was as if they hadn't even heard it. It was rather that they felt it in their chests.

Alex had pointed the muzzle at the sky, and the bullet went straight up and disappeared. Birds they hadn't even known were there shrieked and fled in a whirl of noise and feathers. For a long moment, the boom hung in the air, echoing off the surrounding mountains. And to their left, an unseen something bounded away through the underbrush.

They all listened to its retreating footsteps until they could hear them no more. The stillness that followed was complete.

At last Alex spoke. His face was ashen, but his voice was firm. "Katie, David," he said. "I'd like both of you to know that that was a deer."

"Um, right," said David.

"David, I have lived on this mountain for fifteen years," Alex said. "I know a buck when I hear one. Are we ready to go on now?"

"Sure," said Katie.

"I'll bring up the rear this time." Alex waved the pistol. "There will be no further need for this. I'll be putting it away now. Kids, proceed."

They did. But they managed to meet each other's eyes,

and their raised brows signaled that they were thinking the same thought.

A deer?

As they rounded the twists and turns of the creek, Katie and David could see the sunlight flash off the bright metal object that their uncle continued to grip in his hand.

The sun was fully up—and Alex's gun was finally stashed away—by the time they reached the road. The creepiness of their walk faded in the brightness of the day and the normalcy of pavement and cars.

The plan was to meet Mike at the bridge. He had arrived before them and had found a spot to park. As soon as he saw them trudging toward him down the road he stepped out of his cab and leaned against the side, his massive arms folded, watching.

"He doesn't look very friendly," said David while they were still out of earshot.

"I imagine he wants to take a look at me," said Alex. "It's a little unusual to take a taxi from Vermont to Washington DC. And from what you say, he's concerned about you. He probably wants to make sure I'm really your uncle."

"What do we do?" asked Katie. It would be awful if Mike tried to separate them.

"Don't do anything," said Alex mildly. "He's just being responsible. I'm sure I'd feel exactly the way he does, if I were him."

Nobody said another word until they reached the cab. Then Alex and Mike shook hands. "I appreciate you coming out to talk to us," said their uncle.

Mike gave him a steely look but did not reply. Instead, he turned to David.

"How're you doin', kid?"

"Good. Thanks."

He turned to Katie. "You?"

"I'm fine, thank you."

"You two kids want to go to Washington with this man?" Mike demanded with a penetrating stare.

They assured him that they did, and he sighed heavily. His sharp eyes peered for a long while at Alex, then at David, then back to Alex.

Then, unexpectedly, Mike's features relaxed. He unfolded his arms, stood up straight, and clapped Alex on the shoulder. "Well," he said, looking Alex straight in the eye, "one thing's for sure—no, two things. One, those kids are a lot cleaner. They're lookin' better. And two, he looks just like you." With a jerk of his head Mike indicated David. "You got that same face. Let's talk about this trip. Where're you folks wantin' to go?"

Alex opened the door of the cab and indicated with a glance that Katie and David were to get in. As they did they heard him say, "First to the Bank of the North, in Melville." And then the door closed. Hearing nothing, for some time they watched the two men talk.

At length Mike and Alex shook hands, and then Alex got in the back with the children. "We're on," he said, looking relieved. "It'll be a long ride—about ten hours." He glanced at his watch. "It's a little after nine right now. We'll get there at dusk if we're lucky. But Mike's a good guy." He chuckled. "To tell you the truth, I think he just wants to keep an eye on me."

Now Mike, who had been walking around to the driver's side, opened his door and lowered himself behind the wheel. The whole car sank as he did so. "OK!" he announced cheerfully. "First stop, Melville. Next stop: Washington DC."

Mike turned the key and the motor sprang to life. He backed the cab into position, swung out into the road, and they were off, rolling smoothly down the same route the children had walked just two days before. David looked at Katie and Katie looked at David, and each knew they were thinking the same thing: cars. It's amazing how fast you can move when you drive.

Melville was just waking up when they arrived in town. The sun sparkled on the town square where Mike had left them two days earlier and gleamed on the brass fittings of the Bank of the North. David couldn't help noticing how relaxing it was not to worry whether anyone was looking at them.

"I'll just be a minute," said Alex, hopping briskly out of the cab, which Mike had parked in an open spot. David and Katie watched their uncle sprint up the bank's white marble steps and disappear through the heavy wooden doors.

Mike turned heavily around in his seat and for a moment they worried that he was going to question them. But instead he smiled. "Now," he said, "what kind of radio do you kids like?" And for the next few minutes they busied themselves reviewing the on-air options in Vermont.

Then the door was opening and their uncle was returning. He patted the pocket of his jeans reassuringly. "All set," he said and handed an envelope to Mike, who removed a metal box from under the passenger seat and locked the money inside.

Both men asked Katie and David about bathrooms and both kids shook their heads. Mike hitched his thick arm along the back of the seat and screwed his head around, squinting over his shoulder at the road behind him before backing out of his space.

Katie sighed for an instant, just savoring the blessedness of being in a regular place where people had ordinary concerns. Over in front of the market the grocer was sweeping the sidewalk. He was getting ready to open up. The post office was being painted. A black SUV with a crooked fender was pulling out beside them; the driver was probably thinking about getting that fender fixed. It was normal. It was nice.

Then they swung into the road and in no time at all

they were past the square, rolling out of town, and headed south toward Washington.

It was great to be in a regular car with two adults. The dank and smelly trucks in which they had ridden on their way north seemed like a distant memory on this sunny and comfortable trip south. Mike, who had been so taciturn on their first ride with him, turned out to be a cheerful and voluble talker. And gradually the uneasiness Katie and David had felt ever since Yonkers began to seem silly and faded away.

So it took a while for Katie to realize that their uncle, sitting at her right, was not sharing in the happy mood the rest of them were enjoying. Glancing up at his solemn face she realized that what was luxuriously normal to them must feel very strange to him. She stared until he turned and met her eyes.

"Thank you," she said awkwardly. "For all this, I mean." As soon as the words were out she realized that she should have said them sooner.

David looked over, surprised. "Oh yeah," he said. "Yeah, thanks. I guess this is pretty weird for you, huh? Being out here and everything."

Alex had stiffened in surprise at Katie's words, but now his startled face softened in grateful pleasure. For a minute he blinked, not replying. Both children earnestly hoped he wouldn't cry.

"There's no need for either of you to thank me," he

said at last, feelingly. "And yes, it's a little weird. It's very weird," he corrected, "but not bad."

Glancing in the rearview mirror David could see Mike staring at them.

"You two run away from home?" he queried sharply. "Is that it?" None of them replied, so Mike continued. "Well, it's a good thing he's taking you back. I know things can get rough with parents and kids, but running away is never the answer. Got kids myself. Say"—Mike turned to Alex—"how come you're livin' on that mountain, anyway? You like bein' all by yourself?"

Katie was indignant. She liked Mike, but this was rude. Even David—who was not exactly Mr. Tact—had known not to ask Alex about his solitary way of life.

David, though, just eyed their uncle curiously. It was true that he hadn't asked, but he certainly wanted to know.

"I was . . . ," began Alex stiffly. "I live there because— well, before I lived there, I was . . . I was attached to someone. To a lady."

Now Katie and David both eyed their uncle. This was *quite* interesting.

"I wanted to marry her," Alex continued, "but she . . . she . . ."

"Another guy," finished Mike. "Dude, that's rough."

"Certainly not!" Alex retorted.

Go Alex, thought David, pleased by this display of backbone.

"Beg pardon?" said Mike.

"There was no one else," continued Alex, stammering. "But she—she had a bright future ahead of her and—and a crowded and busy one. And I'm—I don't like a fast life," he finished lamely.

No kidding, thought David.

"So she—she—" And here Alex faltered. Mike jumped in to help.

"So," he offered, "I'm guessing she went her way and you went yours."

"Yes," said Alex, relieved.

"Rough, dude. Rough. Like I said. But it looks like you got a good setup anyways. How're you fixed? You pretty comfortable up there?"

Katie and David were amazed. Mike, who didn't know Alex at all, had managed to ask a question that they, his niece and nephew, wouldn't have touched with tongs. What's more, he'd gotten an answer.

And now Alex positively brightened. With obvious pride, he began to explain how he managed in his small house.

They all had questions about this and Alex, warming to his topic, answered every one. Then Mike talked about Vermont, where he had been born and raised, and Alex told how things had been when *he* was growing up.

Then David and Katie wanted to know what their mom

had been like when she was a kid, and what Alex had thought of their dad when they'd first met. And the miles disappeared beneath the wheels of the swiftly flying taxi.

None of them wanted to stop for proper meals, so when the bread and cheese were gone, Katie and David and Mike began looking for drive-through restaurants.

"Drive-through food," said Alex sternly. "I accept the need for such a thing on a day like today, when we're in a very big hurry. But I hope you children aren't eating that junk all the time. It's very heavily processed. And if you can't even take a couple of minutes to sit down and eat like human beings, then you have to ask yourself—"

"Mega Burger!" Mike announced, interrupting. "Beg pardon, Alex. But there we go, kids. Next exit."

Katie and David looked at each other. They had always loved Mega Burger, but seeing Nose in a Mega Burger jacket had kind of killed their appetite for it.

"No, thanks," said Katie.

Their uncle looked very proud.

Mike looked curiously into his rearview mirror. "Sum'pm wrong with Mega Burger?" he demanded.

"It's a long story," said Katie.

"Taquito Frito is better," said David.

"Well, OK," said Mike. "But those burgers are right here and I'm hungry now." He gunned it past the exit.

"Taquit—"Alex just sighed and looked out the window.

211

They did find a Taquito Frito, but as Mike had predicted, it took a while to get there. By the time they did everyone was hungry. Katie, David, and Mike selected enormous combos featuring delectable fried tacos stuffed with savory fillings, and cheese-slathered sides of spicy rice and creamy beans. To wash down this feast everyone ordered tall, icy drinks, sweet with syrup. Alex, however, studied the menu with pain in his eyes and ultimately selected a salad and a cup of coffee.

"Salad!" said Mike. "Didn't even know they sold those here. Well, suit yourself." And he placed their orders from the driver's window.

Money changed hands and a heavenly aroma was borne in through the window in crisp, white bags. Mike idled the car briefly while he distributed the paper-wrapped packets and foam containers, and everyone inserted their drinks, hissing fizzily, into the cab's various cup holders. Then the car again sped forward, this time in silence as everyone happily chewed.

David's taquitos were divine. He popped the last crisp bite into his mouth and, sighing, brushed the crumbs from his chest with greasy fingers. They had eaten well at their uncle Alex's, but after their days of hunger he still relished a square meal.

"Want one, Uncle Alex?" asked Katie. "Did you ever have them before? They're really good." And she offered him one of the four fried, rolled tacos that rested on the wax paper spread across her lap. Her face was so beseeching—and then, too, the aroma was so compelling—that with a sad smile her uncle accepted one.

"Poor Uncle Alex," said David happily. "First we drag you onto a highway for the first time in fifteen years. Then we make you eat taquitos."

"Fifteen years—that how long you been up there? Man," said Mike between sips of his soda. "Didn't know it'd been that long. How'd you make out in that big snow we had, 'bout eleven years back?"

"Do you have any more of those?" said Alex, swallowing his last bite of taquito.

Everyone shouted with laughter. "It's fantastic," Alex said sheepishly. "I've never tasted anything so good."

And their wheels ate yet more miles as Alex ate another taquito from Katie's stash.

The bathroom, of course, followed the lunch stop as night follows day.

"May as well gas up, too," said Mike, pulling into a filling station. "But let's make it a quick one. Don't want to be finding a bed in Washington too late at night."

David and Katie went first to the restrooms while Mike filled up the cab and Alex studied their map. But their uncle was waiting for them when they emerged, and he had good news.

"We've come farther than I thought," he said. "I was

afraid this was taking longer than it should, but we're right on schedule. Go ahead and stretch your legs and I'll see you back at the car in a moment."

Though they were safe now, Katie still felt a tug of fear as they wandered into the glass-fronted shop where the station attendant sat in his booth. She'd had too many bad experiences in these places lately. "I wonder if I'll ever feel the same way about gas stations again," she said to David. "I mean, after all the scary things that have happened to us."

"I wonder if Uncle Alex would let us have some of these," said David by way of reply. His eye was roving over a case of candy bars.

214

"David, you know he hates unhealthy food. I don't think we should ask him. Don't even look," said Katie, turning her eyes steadfastly out the window.

"He probably wouldn't—"

"David—look!"

"I thought you just said *don't* loo—"

"No—outside! Look—isn't that the same car we saw in Vermont?" Just on the other side of the glass, filling up at the nearest pump, was a black SUV with a crooked fender. "We saw that car back in Melville. Don't you remember?"

"There are a lot of those cars, Katie."

"No. I remember the fender. It was beside us when we left the bank."

David studied the front of the car. "That's amazing,"

he said. "It's a pretty incredible coincidence. How many miles do you figure it's been?"

But Katie's face was ashen. "It's not a coincidence, David! That car is following us!"

"Oh . . ." Now David went pale. "Do you think—" He craned his neck, but whoever was filling up the car was hidden behind the vehicle's bulky body and could not be seen.

"We can't let Mike know," continued Katie, her mind working fast. "We have to tell Uncle Alex before he gets back to where Mike is. No—don't go past that guy!" She snatched the back of David's T-shirt as he moved toward the exit. "What if he pulls you into his car?"

"But there goes Uncle Alex," said David, pointing as their uncle walked from the restroom to the taxi, where Mike was just screwing in the gas cap.

"Wait here. Maybe he'll come get us."

But it was Mike who came to get them.

"Time's up, kids," he called, half opening the door of the shop and calling in.

"Wait!" cried Katie as he turned to leave ahead of them. She did not want to walk past the SUV by herself.

"'Tsa matter?" asked Mike in a puzzled but not unkind voice. "I'm not gonna leave here without you."

They ducked through the door under Mike's big arm and scurried back to the cab. Katie couldn't look, but David stole a glance around the SUV as they passed it. Too late.

Whoever had been pumping had gotten back in the car and was bent over behind the wheel as if rummaging in the glove compartment. Shadowy bodies lurked in the backseat but every face was completely invisible.

"Ready?" called Alex as David and Katie returned to the taxi. His warm smile shone on them. Mike was right there, and they could say nothing. They would have to find a way to speak without words. As she bent to climb into the car Katie turned her back to the driver's seat, tugged quickly at her uncle's arm, and flashed him a face of pure alarm.

His smile froze. With the slightest possible flick of her head and eyes Katie gestured to the black car, then slid across to her seat.

Casually, as if he were merely stretching, Alex craned his head to the left and stole a quick glance at the SUV before sliding in after her. The black car had pulled away from the pump and was loitering at the side of the station, motor running. The driver's face was concealed behind an enormous map, and the back windows were obscured by a thick, dark glass. The crooked fender hung sloping down the front. The SUV appeared to be waiting for them.

"Everybody ready?" Mike sang out. "*Heeeere* we go!" He pulled toward the exit, merged into the oncoming traffic, and headed for the on-ramp.

The black SUV was right behind them.

RUN LIKE HECK

The hardest part was not the relentless presence of the SUV. In a way, that part was actually easy. It simply did not leave them. It hugged their every movement like a shadow. They wondered, in fact, how they had missed it before. They wondered how Mike could miss it now.

Nor was it particularly hard not to be able to talk about what they were all thinking. None of them knew, after all, what they would have said.

The hardest part, rather, was concealing the change in their mood from Mike. For a while they tried to maintain the cheerful banter that had caused the first part of their journey to pass so speedily. But the cold fear in each of their hearts made this impossible.

"I'm kind of tired," said Katie apologetically after about fifteen minutes of futile effort. "I might just try to rest."

"That's a good idea," urged her uncle, getting it. "You should probably do the same, David." And after that they rode in silence.

The hours passed. New York seemed ages behind them and the green highway signs overhead began to count down the miles to Baltimore. Then right around dinnertime Baltimore too flashed past and the sky began to dim as they flew south toward Washington DC. Katie's stomach tightened. They were approaching home and were now driving through territory that was somewhat familiar to her and David. How strange it was to be here under these conditions.

"Where to in Washington, Passenger?" Mike's gruff and kindly voice broke the long silence. Katie felt another pang of remorse that they had all gone so unaccountably quiet on him. She hoped his feelings weren't hurt.

Alex flipped open the map and searched through a panel with a detailed picture of the Washington DC streets. Katie's heart sank when she saw it. She no longer wanted to reach their destination. With that car slithering along beside them she was terrified to emerge from the warm safety of their taxi.

"C Street," said Alex finally.

Katie looked at David and knew he was wondering the

same thing. There were government offices on C Street. Which one were they going to?

"You'll want to go north around the Beltway," Alex continued. "I'll tell you the way from there. I doubt we'll hit traffic this late," he added, muttering worriedly to himself. "Rush hour's probably over by now."

Wasn't it good to miss rush hour? Katie wondered why her uncle sounded concerned.

Closer and closer they flew, and the road that had been somewhat familiar became very familiar. First the Beltway was approaching; then they were on the well-known parkway that encircled the city of Washington. With a pang of regret, Katie and David watched as they sped past the exit that led to their own lost home. Their uncle had certainly been right; there was no traffic.

The sky, which had been gradually fading, was now a clear but deep blue and a very few stars had pricked through the darkness. Then Alex was guiding Mike to an exit and they were soaring around the curve of it and gliding in toward the city. Their ugly black shadow followed them as if it were attached by a string.

The streetlamps were on in the city, and lights gleamed everywhere. Alex seized David's wrist and looked anxiously at his watch.

Suddenly Katie understood. They were heading downtown. They were on their way to a government office. If they got there too late, whoever it was that they were trying to find would have gone home. With a spasm of fear she imagined what would happen to them if they were met with a locked door, with that black car hot on their heels.

Now Alex was hitched forward in his seat and directing Mike through the city streets in a low, steady voice. It was well after eight o'clock. Pedestrians hurried along the emptying sidewalks in the fading light, and through the glass windows of the restaurants, faces clustered over candles that glimmered on tabletops.

They were surely too late.

Their taxi rolled smoothly down the nearly vacant avenues, and the black SUV rolled behind them. And then they hit traffic.

It happened on a side street. Alex had pointed Mike toward a right turn, and as soon as the cab rounded the corner it stopped short. The block ahead was wall-to-wall cars.

Everyone gasped.

"Sum'pm's wrong here," said Mike, concentrating.

"It's too late in the day for this," said Alex. "There must be an accident or something." For a moment or two the cab sat motionless, with a pickup truck three feet ahead of it and the black SUV three feet behind. Mike turned his eyes to his rearview mirror and stared right at the big, dark car.

If he could look, then they could too. The children

craned their necks around. As they did so the windows of the SUV began gliding ominously downward. Despite herself Katie caught her breath.

"OK," said Mike, "that's about enough of that. Everybody, hold on." Gripping the gearshift he shoved the lever into reverse. Then with another quick glance in his rearview mirror he hit the gas and slammed the taxi backward, ramming the crooked fender behind him and knocking it to the pavement with a clatter.

"Been wantin' to do that for quite a while now," he said calmly. Then Mike slid the gearshift back into drive, cut his wheels sharply to the left, and executed a tight, expert U-turn that peeled him out of the line of cars in which he had been stuck and pointed him straight back out of the jammed street. Reaching the corner, he turned neatly back onto the empty avenue on which they had been driving moments before.

"We can turn right on the next block," he said levelly. His passengers were openmouthed with awe.

But as they zoomed toward their next right turn they heard tires squealing behind them. The black SUV—its fender gone, its front end deeply dented, and its cover blown—was now in hot and open pursuit.

They did not turn right on the next block. Before they even reached it they could see that it was just as jammed with cars as the one they'd left. And so was the next. As they sped toward the block after that, an enormously long city bus cut between them and the SUV, offering them a moment in which to think. But they knew this reprieve was only temporary.

"How many blocks that way d'you need to get?" asked Mike shortly, jerking his head to the right.

"About four," said Alex.

"Run," Mike ordered. He flipped a switch to his left, unlocking the taxi doors. "Just get out and run like heck. And God bless."

For a split second everyone was still. Then Alex threw open the door and leaped out, with Katie and David behind him. Somewhere a light changed and the city bus that had lodged itself between them and the SUV began roaring slowly forward, clearing the way for their pursuers to follow them.

They were on foot now, but what about Mike? Kicking the door shut behind him, David screamed at their driver. *"Go!"*

And that was good-bye.

Alex clutched Katie's wrist in one hand and David's in another. Thus dragged they fled for the side street. It was as narrow as a canyon between the tall buildings on either side of it, and they were desperate to reach the shelter of its walls before the bus cleared the intersection and the occupants of the SUV managed to see where they were going.

They didn't make it. Halfway down the block Katie

looked over her shoulder and saw three figures in dark clothes coming toward them.

The three were not running. The drivers of the cars that jammed the crowded side street would have noticed had they torn out after a fleeing man pulling two frightened children. But it did not matter. They were following and they were fast. Katie and David and their uncle were cornered and they would be caught.

"There they are!" gasped Katie. "They're right behind us!"

"Where are we going?" asked David, panting. "How far?"

"Straight across," said Alex.

They had just reached the corner. Now they saw before them not another sheltering block, but a wide-open space of lawns and trees crisscrossed by lanes of fast-moving cars on either edge. Far away on the other side loomed a massive gray stone building in which a very few windows still twinkled with light. That was undoubtedly their destination. But to reach it they would have to cross the first road, sprint across the spacious and exposed lawn, and then cross the second road as well.

When Alex had told Mike they had four blocks to go, he had not mentioned that three of them would be like this.

"No *way*!" There was panic in David's voice. His head darted left and right, searching for a break in the traffic that barred their path. Both lanes zipped and zoomed with whizzing cars. "This is impossible!"

"We're crossing with the light," said Alex with unexpected firmness. He still had an iron grip on each child's wrist.

"We'll be caught!" cried Katie.

"You haven't come all this way to be killed by a car," retorted her uncle. "Besides—"

"Just walk!" commanded Katie. And she wrenched her arm free, set her jaw, and strode straight into the teeth of the oncoming traffic.

Horns blared and one car skidded to the left as its driver slammed on the brakes. So stunned were her brother and her uncle that for a moment they forgot to follow her. But then a driver leaned out of his window and shook his fist at Katie. "Whaddya think you're doing!" the driver yelled.

This seemed to shake sense into David and Alex. Instantly they scrambled after her. *Going to die; going to die right now*, thought David. They caught up to Katie in the middle of the road and—seizing her arms—propelled her to the opposite curb. At the very moment they arrived, their pursuers reached the corner they had just left. But there they were stuck; the traffic had closed like water over the gap that Katie and David and Alex had made in it.

David looked back. Three enraged and frustrated faces appeared in flashing glimpses between the swift-moving cars. They would not be held back for long. "Run!" shouted Alex, again taking hold of his niece's and nephew's wrists.

Half dragged, half running they tore over the grass, driven by fear and no longer daring to look behind.

One more road lay ahead. They had only to cross it, mount the imposing stone steps before the building's great glass doors, and walk inside.

One more road. This time there was a crosswalk and a traffic light too. But the light was red and the rush of oncoming cars was a roaring river. Jaywalking here would be like strolling across a superhighway. It was completely out of the question.

As if to signal as much to Katie, Alex twined his fingers around her wrist in a grip she could not possibly break. In the bright light of the intersection they waited. And in total silence the black-clad figures emerged from the darkness of the lawn behind them and they were surrounded.

Of course it was them. Nose stood beside Katie. Hair stood beside David, and behind their uncle they recognized the thick, squat form of Trixie herself. Something Trixie clutched in her fist gleamed in the light of the streetlamp. It was half concealed in the sleeve of her coat, but from the corner of his eye David could see what it was. It was the muzzle of a gun.

No one said a word. In this very public place their three pursuers dared not risk a struggle, and Trixie dared not fire that gun. But all six of them knew it was there.

Then the traffic light began to flash its Walk sign. Katie, David, and Alex stepped off the curb and headed across the street. The three thugs walked with them, clustered around them like three black shadows.

Thank God for the lights, thought David. Thank God for the cars.

Please, God, thought Katie. What will we do if we can't find the person we came here for? What will we do if we have to walk back out of this building and face these people again, with all of us knowing we failed? Please, please, God, we must not have a gunfight, here in the middle of the city.

They were climbing the steps and the great doors were in front of them. Don't be locked, thought David. Don't be closed. Alex grasped the massive steel bar that spanned the door and pulled it toward him. It moved in his hand. The building was open!

Alex held the door as Katie and David passed through. But just as he himself entered—just as the door swung closed between them and their three pursuers—Trixie spoke.

"We'll be waiting?" she said in her familiar honey-slicked voice. "We'll be right here when you come out."

With those words, she and her companions vanished into the night.

They were in at last, in the cavernous glass-fronted lobby of the gray stone building toward which they had been traveling for so many exhausting miles throughout the long, hard day. Katie's knees all but buckled from the pressure and the relief and the terrible remaining uncertainty.

Where, precisely, had they arrived? David nudged his sister. Their eyes met and he mouthed, *"Look at the wall."* She looked up. There across the wall before them—in letters as high as she was tall—were emblazoned the words:

UNITED STATES DEPARTMENT OF STATE

Above that was the Great Seal of the United States of America, with its fiery eagle clutching an olive branch in one talon and a cluster of arrows in the other. And arrayed below it were flags: dozens and dozens of flags, representing seemingly every country in the world.

"The State Department," said Katie quietly. "We're at the State Department."

Now Alex was striding across the gleaming marble floor toward the guard who sat behind a wide desk of polished wood. Katie and David hurried after him. The desk was as long as a city bus and the face of the guard behind it was very stern. But their uncle stood squarely before the guard and looked him straight in the eye.

"I'm here to see the secretary," he said.

The Secretary of State? Uncle Alex?

"Do you have an appointment?" asked the guard. He turned to his computer and clicked on a screen. "I don't show anything for her right now."

"No," said Alex boldly. "I don't have an appointment,

but it won't matter. Would you please just tell her that Alex is in the lobby."

Alex is in the lobby?

They saw it now, and it was brilliant. This was the plan that had taken them from the mountains of Vermont to Washington DC. It was a bluff, and a nervy one: a piece of pure genius. If Alex said he knew the secretary of state, then maybe, just maybe, she would be curious enough to let them in.

Who would have thought that their reclusive uncle could be so bold? Katie and David quickly composed their faces. They must play along, as if they saw the secretary all the time.

But would it work? The guard was taking in Alex's clothes. For the first time the children noticed how badly worn they were, and how many years out-of-date. The guard was eyeing Alex's hair, too; it looked as if he had cut it himself with a jackknife. He probably had.

Alex must have seen the skepticism in the guard's face, because now his chin lifted. He looked the man straight in the eye, and when he spoke again, he did so calmly and with great authority.

"The secretary is here, I take it," he said. "She hasn't gone home for the day? Then would you please tell her that Alex is here, and that he needs to see her. Please tell her," he said coolly, "that it's urgent."

WHAT'S THE MATTER
WITH UNCLE ALEX?

Urgent. The guard hesitated for another moment. But then he tucked the receiver of his phone between his shoulder and his chin and he punched in a number. As the line rang he looked back to Alex and spoke in a voice that was low and very cold. "You'd better hope she sees you, pal. Because if she doesn't, I'm calling the cops. Over there," he said, waving them away to a bench along the opposite wall. "Sit. I'll let you know."

With as much dignity as they could muster, and with footsteps that sounded too loud, they walked back across the great hall and sat themselves down on the bench. The guard's eyes drilled holes in their backs as they walked.

"What if she says no?" There was a trace of panic in

David's whisper. "Man, Uncle Alex! The secretary of state!" This was practically like asking to see the president.

"She won't say no," said Alex calmly. "If he tells her what I told him to, she will see us."

"How do you know that?" demanded David.

"And what if he doesn't tell her?" asked Katie. "What if he chased us away just so he could call the police? We can't go back out there!"

"Kids," said their uncle, "this is my best hand, and I've just played it."

Great.

There was a loud click from across the lobby. The guard had hung up the phone and now he stepped down from behind his desk. Slowly he sauntered across the floor to where they sat. Katie's eyes were riveted to his hip, where a gun hung low in a leather holster. His hand rested on top of it and it bumped against his leg with every step.

The guard stopped before the bench and stared down at them with ill-concealed dislike. "OK," he said reluctantly. "You can head on up. Seventh floor." And he gestured loosely toward a metal detector at the far end of the lobby. "Step through the machine, and the elevator's to the left."

"She's going to see us?" David blurted this out.

"'At's what she said. Don't ask me why," said the guard, turning away.

Success. Katie and David met each other's eyes and barely restrained themselves from whooping out loud.

Katie turned to her uncle in jubilation. "Uncle Alex!" she whispered. "You did—"

But her cry of triumph broke off, unspoken. Alex did not look jubilant at all. A flush had flooded his face and he rose unsteadily to his feet.

What on earth could be wrong?

Their uncle had just accomplished something amazing. He had done many amazing things, in fact—amazing for him, anyway. He had left his home in the woods and taken to the highway for the first time in practically forever. He had traveled almost six hundred miles in a single day—she had seen the map. He had eaten fast food and liked it, even. He had outrun three thugs in black suits and outsmarted a hostile guard. And he had just talked their way in to see one of the highest-ranking officials in the U.S. government.

And best of all, thanks to their uncle they now had a chance to save their mom and dad and Theo. The secretary couldn't say no. When she'd heard their story—and she would now definitely hear their story—she couldn't refuse to help.

So why did Alex look nervous now? The secretary *couldn't* refuse to help them—could she?

"This way!" said their uncle. His voice was brisk, but he still looked flustered and distracted. "We'll just step through this machine." And without even thinking, he headed straight for the metal detector.

No. Katie reached out and seized her uncle's arm,

jerking him to a stop. Metal detectors were supposed to look for weapons, right? If, after all this, the guards discovered what Alex had in his pocket . . .

Her uncle's eyes skittered nervously and the guard looked at him with frank suspicion. Even though the guard had invited them in to see the secretary, his hand still rested on his holster. Katie turned so that only Alex could see her face and mouthed, *"Your gun."*

Alex clapped his hand to his head. It was clear that he had completely forgotten.

"Yes," he said out loud. "My niece reminds me." He looked the guard in the eye and, without hesitating, he reached into his pocket and withdrew his pistol. Gripping it with the handle forward so that he was not pointing it, he offered it to the guard. "You'll want to hold on to this while we're upstairs," he said.

The guard's eyes popped. For an awful moment Katie and David feared that he might withdraw the permission he had just granted. The expression on Alex's face wasn't helping. He looked like his thoughts were a thousand miles away. What had come over him? In this urgent situation, Alex suddenly looked nutty.

For a long moment the guard simply stared at him. It was the stare of a predator at a small, loathsome animal that it considers too disgusting to eat. Then he turned to call across the lobby to the guard stationed at the metal detector.

"Pat 'em down!" the main guard barked. And he walked back to his desk, bearing Alex's gun with him.

Through the metal detector they filed. Afterward all three of them were individually searched with a metal-detecting wand and patted down by hand. Alex was still in outer space, and he had to be asked twice to put his backpack on the conveyor belt. The deep suspicion on the face of the attendant turned to deeper disgust when the pack was found to contain only stale bread crusts and the rind of an old cheese.

"Left, Uncle Alex!" David seized his uncle's arm and tugged him in the proper direction. "Elevator's to the left!"

"That's where I was going," said Alex peevishly, turning around to follow his nephew. Then he ran his hand nervously through his hair. "Where's the bathroom?" he asked unhappily, muttering to himself. "Ought to check a mirror. Should have brought a comb."

Behind his uncle's back, David raised his eyebrows inquisitively at Katie. What *was* the deal with him? She shrugged, but inwardly her concern was deepening. Having gotten them this far, Alex must not choose this crucial moment to fall apart.

I'll do the talking, thought Katie. If he can't explain what happened, I will. Mentally she began composing what she would say.

The elevator arrived with a bright *ping*, and wordlessly they all stepped inside it. Alex reached out for the button marked 5 and David quickly redirected his finger to the 7. "I know what I'm doing," snapped Alex.

"Sure—sorry," said David soothingly. Now his eyebrows telegraphed wild alarm at his sister. Their uncle didn't even notice. He was elsewhere.

The car rumbled upward and then jolted gently to a stop, causing Alex to stumble slightly. He probably hasn't been on one of these for years, Katie realized. To their surprise, the doors slid open to reveal a small gilded lobby dominated by a massive mahogany door. Outside the door an armed and uniformed guard stood at attention.

None of them had expected this formality in an office building. Now they were all disconcerted.

"Mr. Alex?" said the guard respectfully.

Still inside the elevator, Alex nodded dumbly. As he did so the doors started to close. The guard stepped forward quickly and reached out to stop them. Politely he appeared not to notice their confusion. "Right this way," he said pleasantly. "Madam Secretary will see you now."

After everything that had gone before it, in the end it was this courtesy that reduced all of them to jelly. Like robots with quivering knees they walked out of the elevator. With a flourish the guard pulled open the great door and stepped aside for them to pass through. They could not turn back now.

With Alex in the middle and Katie and David on either side of him, they stepped into a cavernous and magnificent room. And far away on the distant side of it—behind a vast desk like a dark ship, and beneath a towering, ornately carved ceiling—a small, pale, thin woman in a blue suit rose to her feet.

She lifted her hands anxiously to her hair, smoothing it. Just like Uncle Alex, thought Katie fleetingly.

And what about Alex? Standing between Katie and David and gazing at the secretary with suddenly rapt eyes, he raised his hands to his heart.

"Darling?" he asked. He sounded as if he were choking.

"Oh, sweetheart," the secretary replied. "Sweetheart, it's been so long."

Somehow, Katie and David were ushered from the room. Despite the emergency that had brought them there, they did not resist this. It was pretty obvious that, for a few moments at least, their uncle and the secretary of state needed to be alone.

They found themselves back in the gilded lobby, sitting on a pair of gilded chairs, with the mahogany door firmly closed.

A uniformed attendant came and offered them sodas. They accepted, grateful for the cold refreshment.

"Well," said David between greedy sips, "that explains a lot."

"I can't believe I never figured it *out*," said Katie, aggravated. Her uncle had had a girlfriend. Of course.

"This may take a while," said David. "He hasn't seen her since—how long has it been? A couple decades?"

"And Mom and Dad always liked her when we saw her on the news and stuff. They always said she was really good! Why didn't I get it?"

"Katie, one of these days you're going to have to lighten up. Like, because Mom and Dad liked the secretary of state, you should have figured out that she was Uncle Alex's girlfriend? Relax. This is very, very good for us." David was elated. Definitely, *definitely* this lady would help.

"I don't know," said Katie worriedly. "Remember that they did break up. They broke up so badly that he became a hermit for fifteen years."

"Fifteen. Right. I forgot," said David cheerfully.

"She could still be mad."

"'Sweetheart,'" David repeated in a breathy, high-pitched voice. "'Sweetheart, it's been—'"

"OK, she didn't sound mad." Katie grinned, despite herself. "I wonder what they're talking about in there," she added.

With that, the door opened. Two flushed and shining faces appeared behind it, beckoning Katie and David in. "Come on back," said their uncle happily. "The secretary wants to hear your story."

"Alicia," said the secretary, correcting him. Then she smiled joyfully at the children. "You must call me Alicia. And please, do come in."

They slid off their chairs and, clutching their drinks, Katie and David stepped between their beaming uncle and the equally beaming Alicia and back into her beautiful office. This room was so large that it had what appeared to be its own living room on one side of it, complete with sofas and overstuffed chairs and softly glowing lamps. Outside the secretary's enormous windows the night sky was black. Over on her desk half of a roast beef sandwich sat uneaten. They had interrupted her dinner.

"It's a good thing you work so hard," said Katie shyly.

They all turned to look at her. "I mean, it's so late. We were afraid you might have gone home."

"Oh, I never go home," said Alicia, laughing ruefully. "I just seem to live here. It's wonderful to meet both of you," she added warmly. "Katie, you're the image of your father. And David, I'm sure you've heard this before, but you look just like your mother. And your uncle, too," she said, and her voice deepened slightly as she gazed once again at Alex. She sighed. "I haven't seen either of them in years."

How strange it was to realize that the secretary—no, Alicia—knew their parents.

"Neither have we," David chimed in. "Well, not really years. It just feels like that."

The secretary's face grew grave. "Yes," she said. "Alex has just been telling me. Please sit." She ushered them over to the softest of the sofas. "And do begin at the beginning."

This time there were many interruptions as they told their story. The secretary had a number of questions about Trixie and her crew, and though she was polite, she did break in to ask. And when she heard about their race across Washington DC her face darkened.

"You won't be going back on the street until we have all three of them," she said in a voice that allowed for no argument.

In a kind way, Alicia asked Katie and David to set aside the story of their long journey to their uncle Alex's. She looked forward to hearing it, she explained, but their parents' situation was urgent and for now, they should tell her only about the Katkajanians. And they should say everything, holding nothing back.

"I think we have said everything," said Katie. "I think that's everything we know. But now"—she paused, surprised to feel the waters rush up behind her eyes—"now we're just afraid—we're worried that—"

"They said they'd kill our parents if we told," said David bluntly. "And we've just told you, and by now those guys on the street know it. So we're really glad you're going to help. But it would be great if—I mean, thanks, and everything—but it would be great if you could help *fast*."

Katie leaned forward. "What he means is—"

But Alicia covered Katie's hand with her own, stopping her. "I know exactly what he means," she said. "And he's exactly right."

Rising to her feet she walked briskly across her office to her desk. She stepped behind it and picked up a phone unlike any David or Katie had ever seen. She pushed a button on this strange phone and spoke into it.

"It's Alicia," she said. "I need Security in my office, now."

Almost instantly the gilded doors of the secretary's office swung open. In swept a grim-faced man carrying a hard plastic case, a frowning woman clutching a laptop, and a couple of boulderlike guards. The guards appeared to be wired for sound. Tiny microphones were mounted beside their unsmiling mouths and small, flat speakers were strapped over their ears.

In rapid, no-nonsense tones, Alicia told them about the three Katkajanians who were lurking outside the building. The grim-faced man turned immediately to the children and Alex. He seemed to be in charge.

"How many?" he ordered. "Height of the male? Approximate age of the first woman?"

The frowning woman dropped onto a chair, flipped open her laptop, and began furiously typing as David and Katie and their uncle tumbled over one another in their rush to describe Trixie, Hair, and Nose.

"They're occupying a house as well," added Alicia, breaking in. "You'll need to get a team out there ASAP. Kids, your address?"

The man tossed his plastic case onto a tabletop, snapped it open, and removed the largest cell phone the kids had ever seen. He repeated their address into the phone.

"It's a secure line," explained Alicia in a low voice.

The security team was in overdrive now, communicating the information they'd just received to squad cars outside. Down on the street seven stories below, a siren began to wail. Even from the secretary's office they could hear the car burn rubber as it peeled away from the State Department and out into the surrounding city streets. From a distance they heard other sirens answering the first one's call as the hunt for the three thugs began.

"Is that a good idea—the sirens and all?" asked David. "Don't you want to do this on foot? Because—"

Katie interrupted him. "But what about Mom and Dad?" she asked anxiously. "We don't just have to catch the guys outside. We also have to—"

Alicia silenced her with a quick sharp look and a finger across her lips. Her eyes gestured to the security team and she shook her head very slightly. Katie stopped in confusion. They weren't supposed to know?

"Mario, are you guys set?" asked Alicia, looking inquiringly at the grim-faced man.

"We'll bring 'em in for ID as soon as we catch 'em," said Mario and, rising, he beckoned to the frowning woman and the two guards to follow him out. The frowning woman balanced her laptop on her arm and kept on poking at her keyboard, even as she backed out through the mahogany doors.

No sooner had the doors shut than Alicia turned to David. "Don't you worry," she said proudly. "Our security is the best, and they will catch your Trixie and her friends." Then she turned to Katie with a reassuring smile.

"And as for you: Mom and Dad indeed," she said. Once again, she picked up her phone. This time she seemed to straighten her posture so that she stood tall and strong. She punched in a number she obviously knew by heart.

Alicia's enormous office seemed very still in the wake of the clattering security team. Her three visitors waited in this hush, wondering.

"Thank you," Alicia murmured after a moment, to someone who had apparently answered. "Yes. Yes, I'll hold."

Then she snapped to attention and stood, if anything, even taller.

"Mr. President," said the secretary of state in a strong, clear voice.

Katie gasped softly.

"I am sorry to disturb you after dinner. Thank you for taking my call."

She paused. Then she said, "It's about Katkajan. They have the Bowdens."

THE PREDATOR
BECOMES THE PREY

With the president himself involved in the search for their parents, Katie and David should have been relieved. But they were not. By the time they left the State Department that night, they knew their troubles were not over. Trixie, Nose, and Hair had not been found.

The government would keep on searching. The Katkajanians were now wanted criminals. But until they were arrested, Katie, David, and their uncle Alex would have to be protected.

The night before, they had slept in Alex's small house on the mountaintop. That night they were to sleep in a State Department safe house in Washington DC.

It was practically dawn by the time they finally went there. Alicia herself escorted them from her office, with

Mario the security chief, the laptop woman, and the two armed guards swarming after them. Squeezing themselves in, they all rode a special elevator to an underground garage. Then Katie, David, and Alex were ushered into an unmarked, dark car.

"This is the way I travel," said Alicia, hugging them. "I and my most important foreign visitors. I don't want you to worry, kids. You're completely safe."

"I know. Thanks," said Katie, hugging her back. But she climbed into the backseat and slid across the slick upholstery with a heavy heart.

The kids and Alex slammed the doors and waved. The two security men with the earpieces and microphones climbed into the front seats. There was a thick, plastic privacy wall between the backseat and the front seat, so they could not talk to their drivers. But as the car rolled up the ramp of the garage toward the exit, they could see the men muttering into their microphones, issuing instructions to security personnel who were waiting in their vehicles above them on the street. As soon as they were out, these cars were supposed to follow them inconspicuously to their destination.

"I knew that was a bad idea," said David as their car emerged into the night. "Sending out all those sirens and everything!"

"It's too late now," said Katie wearily.

"Trixie and the other two—they had a head start of,

like, an hour! By the time the security guys got on it, they were probably sitting in some restaurant eating dinner somewhere! What you have to do is walk around on foot and just—"

"Uncle Alex!" said Katie.

David ignored her interruption. "Of course, security's probably checking out the restaurants now," he continued bitterly. "And Trixie and those guys are probably done with dinner and back in the bushes, watching our car."

"David, quiet," said Katie. "I mean, you're right, but we know. Uncle Alex? Why did Alicia tell me to shush when I asked about Mom and Dad?"

"Because that information is need-to-know, Katie," said her uncle. "And those people in her office—the security team—they work *here*. They can't help us find your parents in Katkajan. So they had no need."

"Right, 'need-to-know,'" said David. "I remember about that. It's why we never get to hear about Rover." He was still fuming about the way the search had been bungled, so he spoke more angrily than usual.

Alex's face closed up, the way it always did when Rover was mentioned. "That is correct, David," he began. "There is no need to—"

David cut him off. "I want a gun," he said.

Alex was stunned. After a moment he responded. "No," he said.

"Trixie and those guys are out there," said David.

"You will be perfectly safe," said his uncle. "Sometimes—very regrettably—it is necessary for adults to have guns. But children with guns? That is an abomination."

"I want one too," said Katie.

At this Alex gave a strangled sort of yelp. For a minute or two they rolled toward the safe house in silence.

"Mace," said Alex, recovering at last. "It's like a pepper spray. If someone tries to attack you, you squirt it in their eyes and it buys you some time. It's illegal, but with a permit—"

"We know what it is," said David. "We want real weapons."

"I'll get you some mace," said Alex angrily.

"Thank you," said Katie. "Thank you for the mace." And she crossed her arms and looked out the window.

"Me—no thanks," said David hotly. "A spray, when my enemies are armed. Why don't I just trip 'em instead?"

Luckily for all of them, they had arrived. And at this point in their wanderings—exhausted as they were—just to arrive at a place like the safe house was enough to distract them. Nobody who wandered past this house would know there was anything unusual about it. It looked like an ordinary family home and it was located in an ordinary Washington neighborhood. But it was secretly protected by armed guards day and night.

And almost more important to Katie, David, and Alex, despite being owned by the government, it was a *house,* with private rooms and showers, toilets and television.

The next day, a woman from the State Department was even going to bring them clothes.

To Alex's disgust, the house was also kept supplied with fantastic foods: frozen pizzas and marshmallow fluff; garlic 'n onion chips and double-stuffed cream-filled cookies. Late though it was, and tired though they were, the kids broke open this stash as soon as they arrived. They were famished. Taquito Frito had been their last meal, and that had been practically yesterday. It was only a moment's work to turn a bag of corn chips and a jar of microwaveable cheese sauce into a platter of nachos.

There were no two ways about it: It was a huge relief to be sitting at their new kitchen table and demolishing the nachos without looking over their shoulders and wondering who might be creeping up to snatch them. But it was a short-term relief: a here-and-now relief. Out there—beyond the guards who protected this house— Trixie and the others still lurked. And out there, their mom and dad and Theo were still captive.

For the first day or two David and Katie were tired and they did very little. People from the government were looking for Trixie and her gang in the streets of Washington, and for their parents and Theo in Katkajan. Katie and David slept, wandered listlessly on the Internet, and watched TV. Alex—who despite their troubles found time to disapprove of the computer and the TV—brought them some books.

They were comfortable and that part was good. But they were no better than prisoners, and they had no idea how long it would last.

Even worse, they had no idea how the search for their parents was going. This was especially hard for Katie. She always felt better when she knew what was happening, and just when things were getting very, very important, it seemed she was to know very little. A few days turned into a week, and one week turned into two. Yet she found that no matter what she asked or how badly she needed to know it, her questions were turned aside with soothing words that said nothing and reassurances that did not help.

And that was when they saw their uncle. Most of the time they did not see him. Technically the house was for him, too, but he was working closely with the government to solve the Katkajanian problem, or "manage the crisis" as he put it. That kept him busy night and day. The government had set up what it called a War Room in a top-secret location, and Alex had a desk there.

"With Alicia, I guess," said David, grinning. He shared Katie's concerns, but the steady supply of snack foods and cable TV had improved his mood.

Katie, though, was not amused. "It's a war?" she asked

Alex when he told them how things would be. "There's a war in Katkajan?"

"Not really," said Alex cautiously. "Not yet, anyway, and we hope not ever. But there's a plot, as you know—a very fast-moving plot. Your parents are caught up in this. And that's all I can say."

This irked Katie. They had wanted him to help. That's why they had gone to find him! But they had not wanted him to take over and to shut them out. "So where is this War Room?" she asked. "I mean, is it in the city or what?"

"I can't discuss that, Katie. The location of the War Room is top-secret."

"Like I'm going to tell!"

"How'd the president meet Mom and Dad?" asked David. He continued to think this part was very cool.

"Rover was kind of a big deal," said Alex modestly.

"Obviously," replied Katie, rising to her feet in anger. "Not, of course, that we know what it *is*."

Her uncle looked at her reproachfully.

"They treat kids like hamsters around here," she said, and she stomped off to her room and shut the door hard.

But as the days passed, the strain of waiting began to wear even on David. Two weeks became three. They could go nowhere. School had begun, and for the first time ever they wanted to go, but they were not allowed to. Tutors were sent to them at the safe house instead.

■ ■ ■

Katie usually liked math, but she stared listlessly at the problem before her. It was a pretty hard one, and there were seven to go.

Since they weren't going to school in the usual way, and their uncle was gone all day long, it was up to them to decide when to do their work. David had already taken to doing his in the last few minutes before their tutors showed up. Katie, though, wanted to make this life she was living feel a little less weird, so she clung to a semi-normal schedule. This meant that now, at ten in the morning, she sat in her safe-house bedroom at the small desk they had provided, fighting with homework.

And it was completely impossible to concentrate and completely, *completely* impossible to feel even halfway normal.

She dropped her pencil in disgust and tossed herself backward onto her bed. For a moment she lay staring morosely at the ceiling. Then she rose and crossed the room to the window. Katie's window faced the street, and the security team had ordered her to keep her blinds closed. She never did, though. Her life was bad enough without sitting in the dark.

It was nice out: blue sky, puffy white clouds, and the trees autumn red. Of course it was nice! Why wouldn't it be, with her trapped inside?

She looked down the street. There was the mailman. Soon he would be at their house—not that they ever got mail here. And across the street and one house down, a cute dog was out in his yard. Despite their recent experiences with Chester and that dog in Melville, Katie actually liked dogs and wouldn't mind meeting this one. That would never happen either.

The dog had started barking, though. A woman was walking up the sidewalk, approaching the house across the street from Katie's window. Katie was pretty sure those people weren't home, but the woman was fishing in her enormous bag for a key. Probably she worked there, as a cleaner or something.

Katie could not see this woman's face, but she was short and squat with a heavy, thudding footfall. It was not Trixie. This woman's hair was brown with blond streaks, and very curly. Nonetheless, she looked enough like Trixie that Katie felt slightly sick, even just seeing her walk.

Would she be like this for the rest of her life? Was she doomed to get a stomachache every time she saw a short, squat woman? Well, she would overcome it. She would make herself watch.

The stranger's bag was deep and wide, but she had found her key. She opened the gate and stomped—*thud, thud*—up the front walk. As she turned to fit the key into the lock, something glittery on the back of her hand flashed in a shaft of the bright morning sunshine.

Whoa. That was a heck of a flash. Katie had caught the gleam even from the second story of the house across the street. She wondered why this woman was wearing that kind of ring to clean the house.

The woman dropped the key back in her bag and put her hand on the doorknob. *Flash*—there it was again. But as her hand turned, the ring stopped reflecting and for a split second Katie saw the color beneath the sparkle. It was a brilliant purple.

With a gasp that seemed to tear itself from her chest, Katie threw herself onto the floor. Was she too late? Had she been seen through the window?

For a second or two she lay there with her heart pounding. Then a terrible thought occurred to her. David. Where was he? Was he sitting in a window somewhere?

She had to find him. She rose to a crouch and—staying low—crawled to her door. The moment she reached the hallway she leaped to her feet and broke into a run.

The daytime security guard was a youngish, round-faced guy named Curtis. Curtis was in the kitchen, sipping a cup of coffee, munching on a doughnut, and tapping at his laptop, and he did not so much as look up as Katie sprinted through. Not the sharpest tool in the box, she thought, passing him by.

David was sprawled on the sofa in the basement, watching extreme skateboarding on TV. Katie burst in. He only had to see her face to know that whatever it was, it was bad. He, too, leaped to his feet.

"Mom and Dad—are they—"

She cut him off. "No, it's Trixie! David . . ." Katie was panting so hard that she could scarcely speak. "David," she repeated, clutching at her chest. "She's *across the street.*"

He went pale. "How do you know?"

This was too infuriating in her current state of mind. "I saw her, stupid!" The skateboarding program switched to an ad for some kind of power drink and the sound of it blared over their voices. "Would you turn that thing off?" she cried.

David fumbled for the remote and pushed the button as Katie struggled to catch her breath.

Gripping the back of the sofa for support, she continued. "Trixie," she said. "She walked right into that house—that yellow one there. Right in through the front door—she let herself in with a key! She must be pretending to be a cleaning lady or something. At first I didn't recognize her. I mean, I *did* recognize her, right away, but she's wearing a wig so I thought it wasn't her. I was so *dumb*! But then I saw that ring!"

"What ring?"

"That big purple one—the one she stole from Mom. She's wearing it, David! It's her!"

At the mention of the ring, David sank back onto the sofa. "Oh," he breathed. "Oh, man." He thumped the sofa with his fist. "What an *incredible* coincidence."

"David, get *real*! It's not a coincidence! She's there on

purpose! She knows we're here. She must have gotten some kind of job there, as a cleaning lady or something. She's pretending to work there so she can watch us."

"Oh. Right," he said, recovering quickly. "You're probably right!"

"Of course I'm right!" Katie dropped into an overstuffed chair but instantly realized that she was too agitated to sit. She rose and began to pace.

For a moment her footsteps were the only sound as both of them pondered this development. Then a smile crept across David's face.

"It's fantastic," he said.

Katie stopped her restless pacing and stared at him, stupefied. "You're kidding. What on earth is so fantastic, David? This safe house is terrible! We've been stuck here for weeks, just so we could have this protection that's supposed to be so great, and Trixie found us anyway! It's a good thing we didn't get kidnapped. Or shot! We know she has a gun!"

"Katie," David said patiently, "you're missing the point. She didn't find us. I mean, she did, of course; that's true. But we also found her, *and she doesn't know*! We know where she is, but *she doesn't know that we do*. She's a sitting duck! All we have to do is tell Curtis, he'll get some reinforcements, and they'll pop across the street and grab her."

"*Them*, David. We need to grab *them*."

David was silent. She continued. "Nose and Hair? If our guys surround that house, the first thing she does is pick up her cell and tell them to run."

"Oh." This problem took David only a moment. "That's not a problem, Kat," he said decisively. "That's just a matter of following her. It means instead of grabbing her right here, our guys just have to follow her when she leaves."

Katie thought intently about this. "You figure they're all living together somewhere," she said. "So when Trixie goes home—wherever home is right now—Nose and Hair will be there."

"Right."

"Well, that makes sense."

"Sometimes I do," he retorted sarcastically. But David wasn't really mad. He was too excited. It was so incredibly beautiful that Trixie was right across the street. "Which house?" he said. "Is it the one with the dog?"

"No, the one next door. The yellow one."

David looked blank.

"You can see from my window," Katie said. "David, let's go call Alicia and Alex."

"I want to see the house first," he said. "After we tell, they're going to lock us in a closet or something, and I won't get to see anything."

Katie sighed. "C'mon," she said. "But you have to stay low." And leading the way, she headed for the basement stairs.

Curtis did not even seem to notice their stooped posture as they shot past him toward the foyer and the stairs that led to the second story.

"Observant guy," muttered David, crouching as he took the stairs two at a time.

Katie was already in her room, skittering across the floor toward the window. She collapsed on the rug beneath it, with her back to the wall.

"There," she said, panting as David shot to a stop beside her. "It's that one right there, straight across."

He turned and rose on his knees to peer over the windowsill.

"Stay *low!*" she barked, seizing the back of his shirt and pulling hard.

"Katie," he said patiently. "Relax."

"There's a wide-open line of sight between the front of that house and this window," she retorted. "Just take my word for it, OK? Trixie's in there."

"I'm looking. She's not going to notice the top of my head!" And gripping the edge of the windowsill, he rose until he could just see the house.

"Oh, that one!"

"Like I said. You don't have to see this, David."

"Which direction did she come from?" he asked. "I mean, where exactly was she when you first noticed her?"

Katie sighed. She guessed it was OK. Only a tiny bit of David's head was showing, and Trixie would not notice that from inside the other house. Still crouching, she joined him at the windowsill.

A quick glance across the street revealed that the coast was clear. Good. "She was coming right there, see?" said Katie, pointing up the street. "And the dog was out and it started to bark, so I looked that way." She hitched her body a little higher so she could point.

"Is that her car?" asked David, also rising a bit so he could point too.

"No, she was walking. She must have come by bus."

"I don't see a bus stop."

"So maybe it's on that big street. Down that way, see?" But to see where the big street was they had to crane their necks.

They both hitched just a tiny bit higher to do so.

Both of them saw the quick whoosh of the shade at exactly the same instant. Both of their heads whipped around when someone in the second-story window of the yellow house suddenly snapped the shade open. Only then did they realize that they were no longer crouching but were fully visible in Katie's window.

She still had that freaky wig, but it didn't matter. At that moment, they felt that they would have known her with a mask on. The street was very narrow, so the two houses were actually quite close, and they were staring straight into Trixie's eyes.

■ ■ ■

They threw themselves onto the floor, but it was too late. Katie turned on David in a fury.

"You had to see!" cried Katie. "You had to—" Unable to express her rage in words, she shoved him.

"Hey!" For once he was just as upset as she was, so he shoved her back. "We both got seen! You were standing there too."

"Oh, it doesn't matter," Katie wailed. "We've ruined everything. We had this fantastic advantage and we've trashed it!"

"No, we haven't," David said, scrambling to recover. "We haven't trashed it. We just have to hurry—that's all."

"She's going to run, David! She's going to leave in, like, a *second*."

"So why are we sitting here? And why"—he suddenly realized—"why are we hiding?" He leaped to his feet.

"So we don't get shot?" she said, lunging for his knees.

"In broad daylight? With a guard right here, who'd hear it happen?" And he kicked himself clear of her and sprinted for the door.

"Watch the house," he barked. "I'll get Curtis. Make sure she doesn't go anywhere!"

His last words flew back to her from the stairs. He was already gone.

For a moment Katie remained in her crouch, still

thinking about Trixie's gun. But David was right and she knew it. Now that Trixie knew she'd been found, she was sure to flee. They must monitor the yellow house. Mastering her fear, Katie turned and raised her head once again over the windowsill. The second-story shade was still up, but the window was empty.

Had she already left? Katie scanned the street, but it was empty. Good. Maybe they were not too late.

In the meantime, David had reached the kitchen. Curtis looked up, blinking, as he burst in.

"Trixie," said David. "The lady who's been after us. She's across the street."

Curtis put down his coffee cup. "What?" he said. "Who?"

David did not have time for this. He took a deep breath and spoke as patiently as he could. "Trixie," he repeated. "This is an emergency, so we're going to have to move fast, OK? You are guarding us from a woman named Trixie, and two other people who help her. My sister and I have just seen Trixie across the street. And Trixie knows we've seen her, so she's going to run, any second. You need to catch her before she does."

That was pretty clear, he thought.

At this Curtis rose and looked around. Then he sat back down. "OK," he said, as if he were thinking. "OK. I'd better take a report on this." He gave David a nervous look. "Now, don't you panic," he said. "Everything's under control."

"I'm not panicking!" David said, though at Curtis's

useless words panic did, in fact, start to bubble up within him. "And we don't have time for a report!"

"I'm going to take a report," repeated Curtis firmly. "Gonna have to call Manny, too."

Manny was the guard who patrolled the outside of the house. Curtis pushed a button on the two-way radio that hung from his belt, and the familiar staticky sound came out.

"Officer two-six-one; this is officer two-six-nine," Curtis said into the static. "Would you step into the kitchen please, two-six-one?"

"Roger, two-six-nine," said a crackly voice.

Curtis shut down the radio and drew his laptop toward him. "OK," he said, tapping a few keys and frowning. "You hold on just one second while I get to the right page, here."

"Never mind," said David abruptly.

The guard looked up, confused.

"Never mind," he repeated. This was not going to work. He would call Uncle Alex and Alicia instead. But first he had to get rid of Curtis. "Maybe it's not an emergency," he said hastily. "We'll wait and see. Thanks anyway!" And he fled.

Phone, thought David. Private phone. There was one in Alex's room, where he could speak without Curtis overhearing. But on the stairs going up he met Katie coming down. One look at her face told him everything he needed to know. She said it anyway.

"She's leaving!" cried Katie. "Go get Curtis—she's leaving right now!"

"Forget Curtis," said David tightly. And grabbing Katie's arm, he pulled her off the bottom step and yanked her across the foyer toward the front door.

They were under strict orders not to leave the house. Were they actually locked in? Slowly—Curtis must not hear—David tried the knob that opened the deadbolt. It turned. Their captors had obviously assumed they would not *want* to leave.

Because we're so safe here, David thought sarcastically.

While he was trying the door, Katie was peeking from behind the edge of a curtained window. "I see her," she hissed. "She's headed down the street. She's moving *fast*."

"Is she looking?"

"No. You're clear—go *now*."

David slipped out. Behind her Katie heard the back door opening and Manny's footsteps heading to the kitchen. There was no time to lose. Without further delay, she followed David and gently closed the door behind her.

Once outside both of them hesitated. They had emerged onto the top of a flight of stairs that led to the ground. Trixie might look over her shoulder at any moment, and these stairs were highly visible from anywhere on the street. Turning to the side, David swung under the railing and dropped down to the dirt below. Katie followed.

They scooted across the lawn toward a hedge that

ran the length of the front yard along the sidewalk. In the shelter of this shrubbery they began pursuing Trixie down the block.

Back in the safe-house kitchen, Curtis told Manny it was a false alarm.

Manny rolled his eyes. Kids. It was good to be in the kitchen, though. Curtis had the easy job, indoors and all. "Mind?" he asked, gesturing toward the coffee pot. "Since I'm here?"

"Mugs are by the sink," said Curtis. "Get a load of this." And he twisted his screen around so Manny could see. It was open to YouTube, where there was this dog who knew how to ride a surfboard.

David crept behind their front hedge, peering down the street and swiftly assessing the situation. How could they manage to follow Trixie without being seen?

The street was lined with sleepy houses and neat front yards. Some of these yards were bordered with bushes or fences—good—but others were not. To add to their difficulties, it was fall. Many of the neighborhood shrubs had lost their leaves and now offered no cover at all.

David slipped across to the neighbors' yard, where a stone wall along the bottom of the lawn offered useful protection. Fortunately, he thought, it was windy. All these dead leaves blowing around might—might—mask their noise. But the wind would not mask the sight of them as they passed houses like the next one, where the grass ran straight down to the sidewalk and there was nothing to hide behind at all.

For one brief moment he and Katie hovered, thinking. What they were doing wasn't going to work. Their only hope of successfully shadowing Trixie was to creep behind the parked cars that lined the road. This wasn't a perfect solution. It meant dashing across open space to get to the curb, and there were spaces between the cars as well. But they had no choice and no time.

While these thoughts raced through David's mind, Katie slipped under his arm, glided across the sidewalk, and landed in a crouch behind a battered station wagon. So he guessed she'd figured out the same thing. He followed.

They had only hesitated for a moment before leaving the yards for the cars, but even that brief delay had cost them. When they looked up, Trixie was farther ahead.

"Hurry!" whispered Katie, still crouching. Staying low, she checked to see that the coast was clear and then scooted along the sidewalk side of the parked car. When she reached the end of it, she darted to the next one.

And so they slipped into a rhythm: darting from car to car; checking that they had not been seen; and darting again. Dart. Check. Dart.

The wind whooshed and in the swirl and noise of

blowing leaves, Katie whispered to David. "Trixie—look at her hair!"

Her hair? David was too busy making sure Trixie wasn't looking backward. "What about it?"

"She took off the wig," hissed Katie.

He glanced up quickly. So she had. And . . . ?

"She's afraid," said Katie.

"Huh? Why do you—" But David did not finish his question. Suddenly he got it.

That wig had been Trixie's disguise. They blew her disguise when they caught her wearing it. Now she was hiding in her own hair, hoping her pursuers would look for brown and blond curls.

What this meant was huge, and David had almost missed it. He'd almost missed it because he was scared. It had been very scary when they met Trixie's eyes in the window. They were scared now, just thinking that she might turn around and see them. By now, David was so used to being scared that he had almost overlooked what had just happened.

David glanced again at the woman they were following. She was calm—chillingly calm. She was not rushing or calling attention to herself in any way. But she was *moving*. She was trying to get away. And every so often—just casually, as if she were looking around—she seemed to be scanning the street for someone who might be after her.

Someone like them.

They were still in danger, and David knew it. Trixie had a gun. She would probably prefer not to use it in such a public place, but she had it. And she had friends— Nose and Hair and the others. She had probably told her friends that she'd been seen. They might be coming to her rescue right now.

But it did not matter. David's heart still soared. Katie was right. Trixie was afraid, and with good reason. For the first time, she was not chasing them. They were chasing her.

The tables had been turned. The game had been flipped. The predator had become the prey.

"SOON"

Trixie stopped. She stopped at a corner where their street crossed a busy boulevard. There was a traffic light beside her. Was she waiting for the light to change? Was she uncertain where to go?

Katie and David stopped too, taking shelter behind a red minivan and fearing to move until they knew what Trixie would do next.

Yet they needed to move. Though they had managed to shadow Trixie from their house to the traffic light without losing sight of her or being seen themselves, they had fallen very far behind. That was because their progress had been stop-and-start, while Trixie had walked at a brisk pace with no pauses. Now that she had paused, they needed to gain some ground.

David assessed the situation. Trixie had looked from side to side as she walked, but she had not once turned around. Probably it was safe. Slowly, tentatively, he eased his head out from behind the minivan.

The instant he did so, she pivoted.

He would never have believed that such a lead-footed person could spin so fast, especially with her hand in her pocket. That would be her right hand in her right pocket—the pocket where she probably kept her gun.

David yanked his head back, his heart drumming in his chest. He closed his eyes tight. She hadn't seen him, but man, that had been close. Venturing out, gaining ground—this was a bad idea: bad, bad, bad.

He opened his eyes. To his horror, Katie was slowly inching forward. He pulled her back. "She's looking!" he cried in a hoarse whisper. Thank goodness for the wind that would carry away his voice. "*She has a gun.*"

Katie turned on him in a fury. "She'll get away! Did you see that corner, David—where she is? It's totally blind! If she turns it, she's gone!"

He had seen it, and what Katie said was true. The people who lived there had planted a thick wall of tall bushes around the edge of their front yard. This enormous bank of shrubbery made it completely impossible to see what might be happening on the other side of the corner. If Trixie headed to her right, they would not be able to watch where she went.

But at just this moment, David could not have cared less. "First priority?" he said. "Don't get shot."

Katie did not listen. She jerked her arm free of his grip, half rose, and peered out. When she looked back at David there was panic on her face. "She *is* turning—she's turning the corner now! Go!" And she took off.

David followed. He had no choice. And instantly, he saw what Katie had meant. Trixie had slipped completely out of sight.

There was no darting and checking now. Forgetting all danger they ran, desperate to reach the corner.

But they were too late. On the other side of it they found nothing. Katie peered down the boulevard, searching desperately for the short, aggressive stance and the glossy black hair.

"She's probably there," Katie said tensely, pointing toward a shopping center that lay ahead on the left. "At that little mall. Let's go." And she started.

"Katie, *wait*." Again David jerked at her arm, stopping her.

"We have to *hurry*." Again she tried to free her arm, but this time her brother held tight. He dragged her under the bank of shrubbery that hung over the corner.

"Katie, get real! She can't be all the way over there. She didn't have time to get that far! She'd still be walking, and we'd see her. We don't."

"She didn't just vanish!"

"No, she got picked up. She probably called 'em as soon as she saw us in the window—that nose guy, and the weird-hair lady," said David. "They met her right here— I'm sure they did. That's why she waited when she got to the light. Then she got in the car and now they're gone."

The truth of this was instantly obvious. Their prey had slipped through their hands. They'd had Trixie, and they had lost her.

It was very hard to bear. Katie seldom cried, but now David saw with surprise that her eyes were filling.

"We tried," he said. "Stuff happens."

"But why does it happen to *us*?" Katie asked in a thick voice as the tears began to roll down. "It's *always* us—and why? First our parents—What are you looking at?"

The light beside them had turned red. Everybody had braked and a line of idling cars was stacking up, waiting for the green.

David's eyes were fixed on these cars. Katie's gaze followed his. The second car in line was a black SUV. Its front fender was missing. Where the fender ought to be was a deep dent.

Both of them lifted their eyes to the windshield. Hair was behind the wheel. Nose was in the passenger seat. The back of the car was shrouded in tinted privacy glass, but that did not matter. They did not need to see to know who was inside.

"They must have gotten turned around and circled the block," said David in a low voice. "But it's OK—just walk. Walk back toward the house. They won't notice we're here."

But Katie did not walk toward the house. Instead she lifted her chin and straightened her shoulders so that she stood very tall.

"I want them to notice," she said with composure. The tears had not yet dried on her face, but her voice was strong and clear. She marched across the sidewalk to the SUV, peered into the rear passenger window, and rapped smartly on the glass. Then she stepped back and waited.

There was a brief pause. Then the door opened. Inside was Trixie. The familiar oily smile slid around on her face on its slick coat of syrup.

To their astonishment, Trixie opened her arms toward Katie, as if to fold her into a great big hug. "Honey?" she said. "So good to see you? We were so, so worried!" She turned to loop David into the same slippery smile. "You too!"

Katie and David let Trixie's open arms hang empty as they stared. They'd had weeks to consider what it might be like to come face-to-face with her again. They had imagined this moment many times and many ways. They had imagined Trixie shouting, Trixie snarling, Trixie shooting.

But this?

Trixie dropped her arms. Then she seemed to notice the traces of tears on Katie's face. "Oooh, you're sad," she said with a little pout of sympathy. She gave the seat beside her a comfortable pat. "Come. You kids just get in the car, and we'll drive you home."

Uh-oh.

Katie took a big step backward. "No thanks," she said, shaking her head.

The light was still red. Nose rolled down his window, stuck his head out, and glanced nervously up and down the street.

Trixie ignored him. She continued her talk with Katie.

It was all back: the black brows that arched coaxingly up her forehead; the wheedling question marks where they did not belong; the laugh like splintering glass.

"That little house?" Trixie said. "Where we put you, to keep you safe?"

David needed a moment to figure this one out. When he did, he was appalled. The house with the rats, that was *to keep them safe*? But Trixie was still talking.

"We went back there to help you?" she said. "And you were gone. Gone! We were so scared! We thought someone would get you and hurt you. And I felt worst of all, because your mom and dad? They told me to take care of you! So!" Trixie laughed her brittle laugh. "Now we'll take you home."

"That's funny," said Katie. "My mom and dad told *me* not to get in cars with child abusers."

"Get in now!" Nose said menacingly.

Trixie turned her head briefly in Nose's direction. Her broad smile did not falter. "Shut up," she said through her gleaming teeth.

The traffic light ahead of them turned green, but Trixie, unhurried, turned back to Katie. "Honey," she repeated, ignoring the light. "Nobody here is mad at you? We're just glad we found you!"

The cars in front of the black SUV rolled forward. The cars behind it began to honk. Katie took another step backward.

"Trixie." Hair spoke up in her nasal voice. "Da light. Id's 271 chadgig."

Trixie continued to speak to Katie, and she continued to smile. Now, though, her voice was growing just a tiny bit tight. "We're running out of time, sweetie," she said very softly. "Don't make me come out and get you."

"Suit yourself," said Katie, and she stepped back again.

Trixie's smile vanished. "You little—" And with a grunt, she swung her short, heavy body out of the car, planted her feet on the pavement, and rose to her full, if brief, height.

As she did so, Katie gave a strange snap to her wrist. A small silvery capsule slid out from her sleeve. As Trixie lunged, Katie raised her arm and released a blast of noxious mace straight into Trixie's eyes.

Trixie gave a hoarse shout and clutched at her face. She dropped to her knees and collapsed on the ground, rolling in agony.

"That does it!" cried Nose, and he flung open his door and strode out of the car. But he did not make it to the sidewalk. Instead, he tripped headlong and landed nose-first on the pavement. There was a sickening crunch and a blood-curdling cry as this already-broken part of his body shattered yet again.

David withdrew the ankle that he had deftly slipped under Nose's feet and shook his head, disgusted with himself. He hated to resort to such primitive tactics, but when you aren't armed . . .

Now shouts of alarm rose from the honking cars behind them and doors began to slam. Adults ran to the children's aid. In the hubbub, Katie and David almost forgot about Hair. Fortunately, she reminded them.

"Dode shoot!" she called, putting up her hands in surrender. "Please dode shoot."

"Oh," said Katie happily. "I almost didn't remember!" And reaching down to Trixie's writhing body, she patted her pockets and extracted the gun. As she did so, a purple flash caught her eye. She tucked the gun under her arm, grasped Trixie's wrist, and tugged the ring off her finger.

But by that time she and David were surrounded. A pantsuited woman who had leaped from a beige sedan folded Katie into a tight embrace. A young man with tattooed arms raced to the driver's-side door and pulled Hair from her seat. A man clutching a cell phone yanked David away from Nose's prone body. Planting his foot on Nose's back, the man barked, "Don't get any ideas, buddy!"

All three of their pursuers now lay facedown on the pavement. Katie wriggled out of her rescuer's grasp and made her way to David's side. "Nice footwork," she said.

"Don't start," he retorted testily. "I totally could have used a gun." Then he sighed. Just thinking about that gun made him remember Alex. Despite their success, David had a feeling that his uncle would not be happy.

He turned to the man with the cell. The guy was still hovering over Nose on a personal mission to prevent him from getting up, ever in this lifetime.

"Um, borrow your phone?" said David wearily. "I think I'd better make a call."

David was more right than he knew. It turned out that no one was happy. Katie and David thought this was more than a little unfair, seeing as how they had caught three dangerous armed fugitives. Thanks to them, Trixie, Nose, and Hair were all under arrest.

But back at the safe house, no one seemed particularly interested in this good news. All they wanted to talk about was how Trixie had found them and how Katie and David had gotten out.

"Um, by opening the door?" said David.

All that afternoon the police and the State Department people investigated. Everybody was questioned. The Katkajanians were interrogated down at the station. Apparently—or so Katie and David were later told—Trixie and Nose wouldn't talk, but the clueless Hair did. From her they learned that David had been right about what happened the night the kids and Uncle Alex met Alicia at the State Department. When the cops went out to search for the three thugs, the thugs themselves were dining peaceably at an Italian restaurant. After their dinner they had retrieved the black SUV, slipped back to the State Department, and followed the Bowdens to the safe house.

The police also questioned the owners of the yellow house across the street. They turned out to be a harmless older couple. This couple was horrified to learn that the new cleaning lady who had knocked on their door—telling a hard-luck story and begging for a job—was actually a wanted international criminal.

While all this was being discovered, Mario and his team were busy at the safe house. There they had a long, private meeting with Alex, who was furious to learn that there was no other residence to which he and Katie and David could be moved, now that this one had been compromised. Even through the closed door Katie and David could hear their uncle's uncharacteristically raised voice.

When that meeting ended, Mario, the laptop woman,

and the guards with the tiny microphones swarmed over the place, replacing locks, tightening procedures and, of course, phoning and typing furiously. Before they left, they sent Curtis and Manny packing. A new pair, who looked much more dangerous, took their places.

But it wasn't just the Katkajanians and the neighbors and the safe house that got worked over. Katie and David did too. Late that night, when everyone had gone home and the house was quiet again, they were called to the living room for a long lecture from their uncle Alex. Alicia sat beside him, backing him up as he alternately ranted and wrung his hands.

The point of Alex's lecture was that the kids should never do anything like what they'd done that day—never, ever again.

"I know you got them," said Alex, who could tell that Katie and David were not happy. "That's not the point."

"Funny, we thought it was," said David.

"I'm glad about that part," said Alex, correcting himself. "Don't get me wrong."

"We're both glad," Alicia chimed in. "It's just that you took a terrible risk. When we think what might have happened to you, leaving the house like that . . ."

"What if Trixie hadn't gotten out of the car?" demanded Alex. "What if she'd pulled you in, instead?"

"Look, we've been all over this," said Katie. "We won't do it again, OK?"

"We can't do it again," said David angrily. "We're locked in now."

This was perfectly true. The State Department's new locks could be opened only with codes, even from the inside of the house, and these codes had not been shared with David and Katie.

"We're locked in," he repeated. "And why? I mean, we're not in danger anymore! Nobody's after us now. We got 'em! In fact," he added, warming to his topic, "why do we have to stay here at all? Why can't we just go home, at this point?"

Katie and David actually knew the answer to this. The idea had already been discussed, and Alex was firmly opposed to it. Bad things had happened in their house, he said—things it would scare them to remember. And the Katkajanians had trashed the place. Alex was sure the children would find it upsetting to see what had become of their home.

"Not now," Alex said after a pause.

"We can clean it up!" argued David.

"Eventually," said Uncle Alex. "But for now we want you to stay here. Just until this is all over."

"You mean, just till you find our mom and dad," said Katie.

"Right," said Alex.

Ah, thought David. This got them to the main point— the big, ugly problem that lay behind this whole business.

He and Katie had no parents, and nobody seemed to know what to do about that. David had been perched on the edge of the sofa, but now he threw himself back into it and fixed his gaze stonily at the ceiling.

"Uncle Alex?" Katie's voice was polite, but there was pleading in it too. "And Alicia? I'm not mad about the locks—really, I'm not. And it's OK with me to live here for now. I mean, it's OK with *me*," she repeated, glancing at David. "But about Mom and Dad. When do you think you'll find them?"

Alex and Alicia exchanged anxious looks.

"Soon," said her uncle painfully. "We know you're waiting and—and I'm sorry."

There was nothing that either Katie or David could say to that. So moments later, Alicia said good night, and the three residents of the safe house headed off to bed.

"I should be happy," said Katie gloomily as she and David climbed the stairs. "I mean, we did this huge thing today."

"What?" said David sarcastically. "You're not happy?"

She ignored the sarcasm. "I know he said 'soon,' David, but did you see their faces? What was that about?"

"I don't know."

"Does 'soon' mean tomorrow, or the day after that? Does it mean, 'Soon we'll tell you they're dead?'"

"Look, I don't know," her brother repeated. "But I do know this: This can't go on forever."

277

"Which means . . . ?"

David sighed. "Which means I don't know if it'll be tomorrow, or the next day, or next month, for that matter. But eventually, we're going to find out. Eventually, they have to tell us *something*."

ROVER

But they did not find out the next day, or the day after that, or the day after that. Instead, the most frustrating part of living in the safe house—the information blackout— continued.

If anything, in fact, it was worse. Before the capture of the Katkajanians it had been aggravating not to know what was happening. Now it was scary, too. David and Katie had seen too much. They could no longer assume that the adults who were managing this crisis knew what they were doing. They could no longer simply trust.

What they saw in their uncle did not reassure them. Alex looked weary and tense. He tried to come home for dinner, and most nights he did. But he was never there on time, and he never seemed to finish his meal before rising from the table with a distracted face and returning to the War Room to resume the search.

Then came a night when Alex did not go back to the War Room.

For the first time since they had been at the safe house, he joined Katie and David for dinner on time. He sat down to eat with them, and tried to ask them questions about their schoolwork. But his conversation and his smile were strained. Though they tried to answer what he asked, they sensed his mood and soon a gloomy silence fell over the table. At last Alex put down his fork, pushed back his chair, and sat staring at the floor.

Katie and David exchanged a look. "It's not going well, is it, Uncle Alex?" asked David bluntly.

"No," said Alex after a moment. "No, David, it's not."

Katie flushed with fear. "Are they—are they—"

"They're not dead," said her uncle woodenly.

"Then there's still a chance!" said David.

"They're not dead," Alex repeated, and his voice was terrible. "But Katie, David: I'm afraid we're running out of time."

"Uncle Alex," said David fiercely, "what is it? What is—"

"They're our parents!" cried Katie. "We need to know—"

"You're right," said Alex, interrupting her. "You're both right. You do need to know. Kids, it's time we talked about Rover."

■ ■ ■

None of them could eat, so they retreated to the living room for this all-important and long-delayed conversation. Outside the window the autumn sky was just beginning to darken. Alex sat tensely on the edge of the sofa, and Katie and David pulled their chairs up close, trembling with anticipation.

Their uncle spread his fingers wide and ran both palms through his hair. Then he sighed, lowered his hands to his knees, and plunged in.

"I'd better start from the beginning—the beginning of this search," he said. "Which means the night you met Alicia."

"*Weeks* ago," Katie broke in.

"Correct," said Alex gloomily. "Kids," he continued, "when we first told our story to Alicia, you warned her that she had to hurry. You remembered what the kidnappers told you on the phone the day you discovered your parents were taken. You remembered that they threatened to kill their captives if you told anybody what they'd done."

"Right." We know this part, thought David.

"You said to Alicia, Find them fast, because now we've told."

"And Alicia said they would," said Katie. "She said they'd hurry."

Alex nodded slowly. "She did hurry," he said. "That very night, our government spoke to friends of the kidnappers in Katkajan."

"We know their friends?" Katie was aghast. "We know who they are?"

"It turns out we had a pretty good idea," said Alex grimly. "We knew there was political trouble in Katkajan, we knew who was behind it, and we'd been watching 'em for a while. So we asked some people on the fringes of that group to pass a message to the guys who have your parents. The message—well, it hinted that we'd negotiate. We sort of implied that we'd cut a deal. You know"—he searched for words—"we let them think America would do what they wanted, politically, if they'd give back your mom and your dad and your sister."

David was both relieved and confused. He wanted his parents and Theo back, of course. But could this be right? "Great," he said uncertainly.

282

"We won't really do what they want," added his uncle hastily, seeing David's confusion. "We never do, with kidnappings. You can't. You encourage these people, and then there's no end to it. They kidnap again and again and again—"

"We get it," said Katie miserably.

"But if they *think* you might negotiate, then you've bought some time. That's the idea, anyway. You *pretend* to negotiate. You do it slowly. And while you're going back and forth, you're quietly searching for them. You figure out where they are, and then you pounce."

"How do you search?" said Katie, beginning to see.

"Rover," said David eagerly. "Uncle Alex, I bet you use Rover."

"You're right," said Alex. "You're absolutely right. David, Katie, Rover is in the War Room, and we've been working with it to find your parents."

"Working how?"

"I'm getting to that. Kids, do you know how they used to find missing people in the old days? How they still do, in some places?"

David and Katie were silent.

"They used dogs," their uncle said. "They used a special kind of hound that was trained to sniff people out. The reason hounds can do this is that no two people are alike. Each of us has our own unique smell, and the dogs perceive that. So you give the hound something that belonged to the missing person—a shirt, for instance, or a jacket. The dog sniffs the thing, registers the smell, and follows the scent to wherever the person—"

"Rover!" cried Katie. "That's why it's called Rover!"

"Exactly," said her uncle. "Our invention is called Rover because it's like a hound dog—a very high-tech one."

"It smells?" Despite himself, David was impressed.

"Yes, actually," said Alex with modest pride. "As far as we know, it's the only thing like it that does smell. But it's better than that. A dog can only smell what's in front of its nose. Our Rover, though, can smell what's miles and miles away. You just have to load in the scent you want it to find—from an old sock or whatever you have—and then it sends out its sensors and matches that smell to the real person, wherever that person may be."

"That's very cool," said David, impressed despite the circumstances: His mom and dad had made that.

"And that's not all," said Alex. "You know, a person's scent isn't the only unique thing about them. It's not the only thing you can use to search them out."

"Fingerprints," said Katie.

"Yes. But those are pretty hard to detect from a distance. Not that we didn't try."

"So what are we talking about?" said David.

"Well, each face is different," said Alex. "That's easier, because while fingers point down, faces point up and out. So Rover can see them better. And not just faces, either. Each eye is different. And each gait."

"Gait?"

"Yes—meaning the way you walk. If you give Rover a video of someone walking, it can pick that person out on a city street, miles away, by their gait."

"OK, I'm impressed," admitted David.

Katie was not surprised. After all, she had recognized Trixie's distinctive heavy footfall from across the street. But she didn't pause to consider this. She did not want to be distracted with their parents not yet found. "Is that all?" she asked.

"Not quite," said Alex. "Voices work too. They're just as

unique as smells and faces and gaits. And they're unique from the first day of life, by the way. Each and every baby, even, has his or her own special cry. If you feed that cry into our Rover, Rover can find that baby."

"Theo!" said Katie. "What about her cry?"

Uncle Alex's face had begun to brighten as he pursued the distracting subject of Rover. Now it collapsed again into gloom.

"Well, that's just it," he said. "We don't know Theo's cry. There's no recording for Rover to work with. It can't find what it's never heard. It has to have something to recognize."

"Mom and Dad have socks and shirts," said David. "Lots and lots of socks and shirts. And most of them are still at home."

Uncle Alex nodded. "We've been trying that," he said. "We've been back to the house—we've been all over it. But everything we've found has been corrupted."

"What does that mean?"

"Corrupted . . ." Alex searched for words. "Messed with; touched. It's got other people's smells on it now. Rover can't get a clean read of your parents' scents. Those animals," he added angrily. "They're thieves; they're snoops; they're rummagers. They handled every single object in your house."

"Keep looking," said David fiercely. "Don't give up."

Alex shifted unhappily in his seat. "Well, that gets me

to the problem," he said in a miserable voice. "I'm sorry to say that it's getting rather late. The kidnappers won't negotiate forever." From the struggle on his face, Katie and David could see that he had reached a part of his story that was very hard to tell. "They've given us a deadline, kids. They've named a date and a time, and they've said if we don't meet their demands by then, well—"

Katie screamed, and buried her face on her knees.

"When?" demanded David. "When is this deadline?"

"The deadline is tomorrow," said Alex bluntly. "Tomorrow morning at six."

Now Katie lifted her head and rose to her feet. Her hands were balled tightly into fists and her face was a mask of fury.

"And you're telling us *now*?" she demanded. "Our parents and our baby sister are supposed to die tomorrow—and you're telling us *now*?"

"If there was anything we could have used . . . ," said Alex.

"All this time we've been begging! Begging for news. And you said nothing?"

"A movie of them," continued Alex helplessly. "A recording on an answering machine. Or—"

"Or a song?"

Both of them turned at David's words. He, too, had risen and was frantically pacing the room. Now he wheeled around to face his uncle.

"Uncle Alex, we do have something. We have a song."

"Your parents recorded a song?"

"No, we did. Katie and me."

Alex was bewildered. "We're not trying to find you," he said.

"Uncle Alex," said David. "My mom and dad have our song with them. If we find it, we find them."

Katie leaped to her feet, elated. "Oh!" she cried. "Oh, David! That's brilliant!"

"Somebody's going to have to explain," said Alex.

"Our parents' cell phone plays a recording of Katie and me singing. It's their ringtone. We're playing the piano and singing this dumb song. The phone is in Katkajan, and the original recording is here, at home. So if we load that recording into Rover and then call the phone, then it'll ring and Rover can find it—"

"And wherever it is, our parents will be there. Oh, David!" said Katie excitedly.

"It'll be easy for Rover," continued David, "because it's a perfect match. It's the same recording! And it's—"

"And you could have had it *days* ago, Uncle Alex, but you didn't tell us! You didn't think we 'needed to know'! You didn't—"

"Katie, stop," said Alex. "Where is this recording? Where's the original?"

"It's on our mom's computer."

Alex collapsed backward onto the sofa. "Then kids,"

he said miserably. "I'm afraid it's gone. Your parents' computer—it was wiped out."

"I don't get it," said David.

"I mean they wiped out the hard drive," said Alex. "We looked there. We figured your parents would have stuff stored there—video, audio, something. So we looked. We found absolutely nothing. Trixie—she took what she wanted from that computer and she destroyed the rest."

David felt as if he had been slugged in the gut. The wild hope that had propelled him to his feet drained from his body and he collapsed back onto the sofa. But through his pain he heard his sister's steely voice.

"Did they take us?" she asked.

Both of them looked at her.

"Did they take our voices? Because we can sing it again. We did it once; we can do it again."

David came back to life at his sister's words. "Perfect!" he said. Rising, he rushed to Katie's side, seized her by the shoulders, and shook her from sheer joy.

But for some reason, Uncle Alex did not share in the children's excitement. He looked, if anything, more dismayed than before.

"Our voices haven't changed, Uncle Alex," said David. "The ringtone's only a couple months old!"

"And we've heard that recording a million times," added Katie. "We know it by heart—we can even make the same mistakes on all the same notes!"

"It's not that," said Alex slowly.

Katie felt her panic returning. Maybe their parents' phone was not in use. Maybe its battery had run down. Maybe the kidnappers hadn't even kept it. "Their phone," she asked. "Is it their phone? Is it still—?"

"Their phone is fine," said Alex. "We've used it—we still use it—to contact their kidnappers. It's just . . ."

"Then what?" demanded Katie. If the phone was good, there was no problem. "Uncle Alex, this will work!"

"It's not your idea, kids. The idea is good. I'm just worried that we don't have time."

"You said six o'clock tomorrow morning. It's only seven p.m. now!" she said.

"Six fifty-seven," David corrected his sister. "To be exact."

"Six fifty-seven! So we have eleven hours!"

"Katie, that's six o'clock Katkajanian time." Alex's anguished words stopped her in her tracks.

"*What?!*"

"They're nine hours ahead of us. We have two hours, not eleven."

At this David exploded. "Well, thanks for letting us know!" There were daggers in his voice. At this moment, he hated his uncle. "How long does it take?" he demanded. "To use Rover—how long? After we get the song, how long does it take to load it in? After we load it in, *how fast does that dog hunt?*"

"Depends," said Alex. "The closer the match, the faster the search."

"So we'll make it exactly the same," said Katie desperately. "We can sing it with the piano—we can go back to the house, even, and use the same piano. Are pianos like voices, Uncle Alex? Is each one different? Because we can use exactly the same one!"

David paced, ticking off the remaining time on his fingers. "We have two hours," he said. "We can be at the house by seven thirty, seven forty. Give us half an hour to record the song—but it won't even take that long. Fifteen minutes! Then we're back at the War Room by—"

"But kids," said Alex. "Once Rover finds your parents, it's still not over. Finding's only the first part. The other part is the rescue. Your mom and dad aren't saved until the Katkajanian police can get to wherever they are. That'll take time, too."

"How much time?"

"Again, it depends. For a while we thought the kidnappers were holding your parents in the mountains. If they're still there, then it's certainly too late. It's just so remote and there are no police—"

Alex broke off, seeing the anguish on the kids' faces. "But we think they aren't there anymore," he said hastily. "With the cooler weather coming, we think they've been moved back to Taq—to the capital. And if they're right there, well, it's not that big a place. But I figure you need thirty minutes at least. If we find them by"—he calculated quickly—"if we find them by eight thirty our time, we might have a chance. Any later than that and I'm afraid—"

"Stop talking!"

David and Alex both stared at Katie. "Uncle Alex, you can tell us in the car! Would you get your keys and drive? Would you *hurry*?!"

HURRY, HURRY

Yet in the maddening world of adults, some things, it seemed, could not be hurried. They could not be hurried even when lives were at stake. And it soon became clear, to their deep consternation, that the hardest thing to hurry was their uncle Alex himself.

He meant well; there was no question about that. And he certainly *could* move fast. They had not forgotten how quickly he had whipped out that pistol back on the mountain.

But now they began to see that the Uncle Alex they had met in Vermont was one man, and this Uncle Alex was another. They had already learned that here in the city Alex tended to worry. Now they saw that worry made him dangerously slow.

Katie had asked him to get his keys, but Alex felt that the safest way to travel would be under police escort. With cruisers in front of them and cruisers behind them—blue lights flashing—they could move at top speed and rip through intersections, disregarding red lights without risking an accident.

David and Katie reluctantly accepted. But that meant they had to wait for the police to get there. And then when they did, their uncle was on the phone with the War Room, arranging for a recording crew to meet them at the house.

So for four agonizing minutes after the police arrived, Katie and David sat while Alex talked. Unbelievably, he had placed his call from a landline.

Five police cars were idling outside the door, motors running. Almost fifteen minutes had passed since Alex had given Katie and David the dreadful news that they had just two hours to save their parents' lives. But they could not leave the safe house until Alex had finished his conversation.

"4556 Lilyview Lane," he was saying. Then he fell silent, listening. "No," he said, in response to an apparent question. "'L' as in Larry. L-I-L—"

Katie thought she would go mad. "Uncle Alex, have you heard of cell phones?!" she hissed.

"I'll call you from the car," he said abruptly, and hung up.

Katie and David were already there when Alex slid into

the cruiser beside them. The cop behind the wheel was a wiry guy with a deeply lined face, forearms like steel ropes, and a seen-it-all expression that gave David hope. While waiting for Alex, David had had a talk with this cop about the need for speed. They had understood each other perfectly. The man began pulling forward before Alex had even shut the door.

"Wait!" barked Alex. "Stop."

The cop stopped sharply, causing all three of his passengers to lurch forward.

"Katie, David, fasten your seat belts."

"You've got to be kidding," said David.

"Certainly not," said Alex. "We're going to be moving very fast."

"Uncle Alex," said David, his voice tight, "our driver— he used to race motorcycles. Professionally. We won't have an accident."

"David, just do it," begged Katie, fastening her own. She was almost in despair.

"I am still in charge here," said their uncle. "We aren't going anywhere without seat belts."

Katie reached over David's lap and snapped his belt for him. "I did it. Drive!" she ordered.

"He *jumped* motorcycles," David said, fuming as the cruiser peeled away from the curb. "Tell him," he begged the driver. "Would you please tell him, Tyrone?"

But Alex was not listening. He was back on the cell phone,

finishing his instructions about the recording equipment they would need at the house. And Tyrone, so talkative while the car had been idling, was now hunched over the wheel and silent, his eyes locked on the road ahead.

David looked at his watch when they finally peeled away from the curb—7:13. The movement of the clock was relentless and terrifying.

On the other hand, none of them had ever traveled the way they did then up the famed avenues of Washington DC.

The rush-hour traffic was still thick enough that in an ordinary car, they would be moving at stop-and-start speed. But not tonight. They were in a pack of five cars, and they were at its dead center. A cruiser rode on either side of them, a third cruiser rode behind and a fourth ran ahead of them. The lead car's job seemed to be to clear a path, like the tip of a wedge. Every car in their pack had its lights on and its siren wailing. Katie and David watched in awe as the thicket of traffic parted to make way for them, peeling to the sides of the road like a zipper opening up.

David's heart swelled with admiration. The government had messed up big. A few cracks were turning up in their uncle Alex. But the cops—the cops were *great*.

And then they hit trouble.

They had left downtown behind and were on their way to the suburbs. The office buildings and embassies that had lined the road had turned into houses and the road itself had slimmed. Now there were just two lanes: the left one where their convoy of five could travel single-file, and the right one, where all the other cars could go to get out of their way.

But up ahead, that right lane was blocked.

For someone on that all-important avenue, today was moving day. A gigantic van was stationed at the curb in front of a house. The van's back was open, its ramp was down and fastened onto the pavement, furniture was everywhere, and no one was behind the wheel.

The moving van took up half a city block. Cars scrambling to get out of the way of the oncoming police convoy had no place to go. They clogged the left lane where the convoy needed to travel, their horns blaring and their drivers looking frazzled.

The car bearing Katie, David, and Alex was second in the convoy line. The police car in front of them stopped short. The cop inside it must have flipped a switch, because his siren launched into a different and more threatening wail. The cars in their path shifted nervously under this pressure, but the logjam packed itself in even tighter.

"Tyrone!" cried Katie, dismayed. She seized David's wrist and looked at his watch—7:22.

But Tyrone did not break a sweat.

Wordlessly, he swung his wheel and pointed the cruiser down a side street to their right. The three police cruisers behind him followed his lead. A detour!

"Yes," said David softly.

But unfortunately, the sleepy residential street down which they were now racing had not been built for a high-speed car chase. And unfortunately, Tyrone's motorcycle-jumping right foot had the gas pedal on the floor.

Just a few hundred yards ahead was a corner where he would have to turn left. It was a tight corner, a narrow corner, a square corner. It was a corner that could not be taken at sixty miles per hour.

Tyrone did not take the corner. He took somebody's lawn. And jumper that he was, he took it in a flying leap.

Ugh! They all grunted and lurched as the cruiser hit the curb with a bump, bounced into the air, and flew across the front yard of the house on their left. *Crunch* went the front wheels of the cruiser as it returned to the ground, digging deep tracks in the grass.

Apparently tomorrow was trash day and the unlucky family who lived in this house had already put out its cans. *Smash* went the cruiser into the nearest one, sending it flying and releasing a rain of garbage bags in its wake.

"Hey!" cried the owner of the house, who was standing on his porch and saw the whole thing.

But Tyrone did not stop. He was headed for the lawn next door. That would be the lawn with the beautiful cherry tree planted firmly in its center. That would be the tree with the heavy, low-hanging branch, from which a child's empty red plastic swing dangled innocently in their path.

Alex, white as a sheet and speechless, flung out his arms over Katie's and David's bodies. Katie covered her face with her hands. But David watched in sheer glee as the cruiser slipped beneath the branch, just catching the swing on its windshield and sending it flying after the garbage cans.

"Sweet," David murmured happily as they zipped, swaying, down the road, with three cruisers close behind them.

The next left turn brought them onto a wider street, so this time Tyrone was able to keep all four wheels on the ground. A few screeching seconds later they had returned to the main road they had left just seconds before, where a right turn put them back on their path with the moving van safely behind them.

"That was—that was—" Alex could not speak.

But Tyrone could. He did not unlock his eyes from the road as his right hand scooped up his radio. "Ten-four," he said tonelessly as the thing crackled to life.

"'Sup," replied a staticky voice, following an unintelligible jumble of numbers and codes.

"2707 Wildermere Road," said Tyrone matter-of-factly. "Damaged a civilian lawn."

"You read the address?" asked Katie, incredulous. "From midair? How did you manage to—"

"We'll check it out," replied the staticky voice, and Tyrone hung up.

"How did he see the address?" Katie repeated. "We were—"

But no one was listening. They were moving, moving. They were farther from the city now. There was seldom much traffic here at the busiest of times, and now it had grown late and almost dark. There was no need for sirens, and Tyrone and the other drivers shut them down. They were whizzing silently at highway speeds through the nearly empty suburban streets, and they were almost home.

While jumping lawns and scattering trash cans, they had not had to do anything but hold on. They had not had to think about the reason for their wild ride. But now they had almost arrived, and David and Katie remembered, and steeled themselves for what they had to do.

"Don't forget to sing that note hard on the third line—at 'happy,'" said Katie tensely as they approached the house. Mrs. Ivanovna had always made them emphasize that word. "We have to sound just like Mom and Dad's phone, and you know how we—"

But David was focused on speed, not quality. "I figure in and out in fifteen minutes," he said, looking at his watch. "We just have to be quick, and it shouldn't take longer than that."

"Right, but Rover searches faster if it's got a close match. So if it doesn't—"

And then they were there.

Yellow police tape barricaded the once-welcoming driveway. Of course. The house was a crime scene now. Tyrone crashed straight through the tape and screeched to a halt by the front door. The three remaining cruisers slammed to a stop just behind them in a flurry of brakes and flying gravel. All four cars cut their motors but kept their light bars flashing. The sudden stillness was disconcerting.

Alex looked around. "We'll just wait right here," he said.

Openmouthed, Katie and David stared at him. *Wait?*

"I don't see the recording team," he said tensely. "I don't want you sitting around in that disaster of a house while we wait. Not for any longer than you have to."

"Uncle Alex, we have to practice!" said Katie. "We have to—"

David looked at his wrist. "You're both nuts," he said tightly. "It's seven thirty-three. Why am I the only one with a watch?" He punched the door open with his foot, slid from the car, and hit the ground running. Taking the front steps two at a time, he reached the front door, grasped the knob, and pulled.

It was locked.

David wheeled around. "The key!" he shouted. "Who has the key?"

Katie and Alex had just left the car and gazed up at him, dismayed.

"I don't know," said Alex, blinking. "I'll have to make another call. I'll have to think—"

"We don't have *time* for a call!" cried David, furious. "We don't—"

But Katie had dashed past the stairs and was rummaging in the flowerbeds by the side of the house. Now she rose with a grim face, a baseball-sized rock in her fist. She backed away from the house, eyeing the living-room window.

"Let me!" said David.

"I can do it," she retorted.

"I have better aim!"

"But I have the rock," said Katie, and with that, she sent it sailing. It flew like a precision missile and struck the window squarely in the center. Shattering glass fell like rain and the sound of it split the night.

Alex's face was frozen in consternation. But all four cops were standing beside their cars, watching with open mouths. "Ball one!" said one of them softly.

They all looked up at the window. It was broken—so far, so good. But the bottom ledge was at least ten feet off the ground, and three deep rows of azalea bushes were planted beneath it, blocking their way.

"Now what?" asked David sarcastically.

Even as he spoke, Tyrone was slipping back behind the wheel. To everyone's surprise, he started up the motor.

"Where are you—"

Tyrone did not listen. Instead, he executed a neat, three-point turn, backing the cruiser up, swinging it around, and then pointing its nose toward the house. Everyone heard him shift and then—as they all watched in awe—he rolled straight toward the azaleas.

Shrubbery bent and snapped beneath his wheels as Tyrone's front bumper smashed through the thick rows of bushes and stopped with a gentle bump at the wall of the house, right beneath the broken window.

The cops, thought David again. The cops are *great*.

Katie scrambled up onto the trunk of the car. Then she scooted across the roof and down the windshield to the hood. With a boost she would now be able to hoist herself in. She looked around for David.

"Stop! That window's not safe!" Once again, it was Katie's uncle Alex, and this time he had a point. The center of the pane had vanished in a rain of glass, but jagged, unbroken shards lined the edges of it like teeth.

For a moment they all stared up at it, trying to think.

"Tyrone," said David urgently. "Borrow your nightstick?"

Tyrone's car had rolled to a stop in a sea of azaleas that crowded thickly around his doors and windows, blocking his exit. He was stuck like a nut in a bar of chocolate.

"I don't have mine, or I'd let you use it," said another cop, sounding worried.

With a mighty grunt, Tyrone shoved on his door. Yet more shrubbery snapped and branches scraped across paint with a noise that assaulted their ears. But the door cracked open and the cop twisted his body out and reached his nightstick over to David.

David climbed up beside Katie and, holding the sturdy club above his head in both fists, slammed it at the remaining shards of glass, clearing the window for entry.

"Still gonna need a tarp, or something," murmured a third cop, who was looking on with folded arms. A fourth booted cop stamped across the rubble of bushes at the back of Tyrone's car, opened the trunk, and withdrew from it a heavy, folded woolen blanket. Hand over hand, the police passed this blanket to Katie, who threw it over the windowsill to cover any remaining glass.

"I'm lighter," she said, as David, tossing aside the nightstick, dropped to one knee and clasped his hands together into a step for her foot.

She did not hesitate. With a grunt he shoved her upward. With a bend and a wriggle, she slid onto the rough blanket. A twist put her feet inside, and for an instant she sat on the windowsill, facing the darkened interior of the house.

"Don't land on the glass!" warned Alex.

"I won't!" And with a great push she disappeared into the silent house. For a fraction of a second the rest of them waited tensely. Then the blackened windows sprang to life and golden light poured out onto the driveway and the lawn beyond.

Katie had turned on the lights. "Whooee!" cried the cop who'd gotten the tarp.

They heard her footsteps within the house, running toward the entrance. There was a clatter of sliding bolts and then the front door swung open. David jumped off the car and headed for the stairs. Before he had even reached them, Katie was back in the living room and an exploratory scale could be heard from the piano.

David looked at his watch as he slipped through the door. It was 7:39. They had arrived at the house at 7:33. It had been locked up tight, with no apparent way in. Yet now they were inside, and it had taken no more than six minutes.

He still thought Katie should have let him throw the rock. He felt sure that if he'd thrown it, there would have been no shards left behind. Still, he had to hand it to his sister. *She* knew how to hurry.

She also, it turned out, knew how to freeze. Katie could not remember a single note of "You Are My Sunshine."

She sat on the bench, poised to play. The recording team had arrived. A silent, ponytailed man was setting up mikes and blowing gently into them, testing levels. His partner hovered softly in the background, watching the screen of a laptop computer. Outside on the grass they could hear the footsteps of the cops, who paced protectively on the gravel driveway, still lit by the glow from the open windows.

It was all systems go and the clock was ticking, but Katie could not begin.

"Think!" ordered David unhelpfully.

"If I could only remember the opening, I'm sure the rest would just come," she said desperately. "I had it memorized!"

"Are you nervous?" asked Alex anxiously. "Is it the house?" It was perhaps the fifteenth time he had asked.

No, Uncle Alex, she thought. It isn't the house. It's you.

To be fair, she did know what he meant. The place lay in ruins. There by the window was the glass that she herself had broken. The rock she had thrown still sat in a puddle of shards.

But the damage they had done was not the worst part. Looking behind her into the darkened rooms beyond, Katie could see that every object that had once sat on a table or a shelf now lay on the floor, broken. The pictures on the walls gazed out from behind broken glass. Someone had taken a knife to the cushions of the sofas and chairs, and each and every one of them was sliced open.

So it was definitely bad. But it wouldn't be nearly *as* bad if Alex would just stop talking about it.

"It's OK," she said. "The house is fine." On the wall before her was a photo of her father. Someone had driven the point of a knife through his eye. What hatred that person must have felt. Katie shut her own eyes tightly, drew a deep breath, and drove the thought from her mind.

"Because it must be very distressing," continued her uncle, "for you to see the—the hatred expressed by these—"

Katie exhaled. Thank you, Uncle Alex.

David, who had been listening, tried to remind them of what they had to do. "What key was it in?" he demanded. "The song."

"Well, if I knew that!" But prompted by his question, Katie tried again to remember the music she had once memorized. "Maybe G," she said, reaching for the keyboard.

"Or is it Trixie?" Alex again broke in. "I'm sure it brings back awful memories, Katie, just to be here."

Memories, Uncle Alex? Not really, but now that you mention it . . . And Katie was flooded by the recollection of the last time either she or David had played this piano. That had been the occasion of their first real fight with Trixie. She had emerged from that office, right there, and told David to stop, and wagged her fat finger . . .

Katie shook her head, desperate to clear it. "What key did I just say—F?"

"G," said David.

"But I'm sure that's wrong." And she dropped her forehead onto the keyboard in despair.

"Let's step outside," said Alex in a voice full of compassion. "You need to rest. This is a terrible strain."

Now David actually moved his body between his sister and his uncle. If Alex said one more word, he thought, he might have to slug him.

"Katie," David urged, giving her shoulders a light shake. "Settle down. You're tough, you know? You escaped from a locked house full of rats. Right? You stowed away on two different trucks. You stared down a woman with a gun and shot mace in her face! You can handle this!"

"I can't believe this is happening!" Katie cried. "I remember the middle part perfectly. But the part I need—the beginning—is completely gone. I can't remember how it starts!"

"So just play the middle," said David. "It doesn't matter!"

"Yes, it does!"

David took a deep breath and began to sing. *"You. Are. My. Sunshine . . ."*

"Don't forget 'happy!'" And she leapt in and sang with him. *My only sunshine . . .*

On the second line Katie's fingers suddenly remembered the notes and she began to play. This was too much for Alex, who emitted a small, emotional yelp. Distracted, they rolled over "happy" without emphasis. But they finished the song.

"That's a wrap," said David into the silence that followed their final notes.

"Got it," confirmed the man with the laptop, looking up at Alex. "It's all here."

"Great," said David. "Let's—"

"One more time," said Katie.

"You're crazy!"

"David, we had no piano at the top—but I can do it now! I just remembered the beginning! And later—we didn't do it the same way at all. We didn't—"

David thrust his wrist before her eyes so that she could see the gleaming face of his watch.

It was 8:04. Uncle Alex had said they would need to find their mom and dad and Theo by eight thirty their time for the Katkajanian police to be able to rescue them. And at nine o'clock . . .

"See you in the car," said Katie without further ado. And she jumped from the piano bench as if it were on fire.

Alex had been huddled with the sound men, who were e-mailing the recording to Rover. But now he looked at his own watch and the significance of what he saw seemed to register with him, too. With uncharacteristic speed he hustled after David and Katie. All three of them streaked out of the house, down the front steps, and into the car. It was not the same car—that one was still stuck in the azaleas—but Tyrone was behind the wheel. He was poised for flight, light bar flashing and motor churning.

Tyrone flicked a switch on his dashboard and the siren sprang to life, wailing into the silent streets. He peeled out of the driveway, and this time there was no stopping for seat belts.

Less than an hour to go. Just the thought made Katie sick.

"Uncle Alex?" asked David.

Alex was staring at the speedometer, his face frozen in alarm. The needle was climbing toward sixty-five and they were still on narrow residential streets.

The siren was very loud. David tried again, this time raising his voice. "Uncle Alex, does it have to wait till we get there, or can it start now?"

Dragging his gaze from the dashboard, Alex looked puzzled.

"Rover," said David. "I mean Rover. It already has our song; you e-mailed it. So while we're driving, can it start—"

But at the mention of Rover, Alex's distraction cleared and his eyes went wide with alarm.

David broke off. "What?" he said, exasperated. "What now?"

With a tiny movement of his head, Alex gestured toward Tyrone.

Oh, yeah. David had forgotten. Rover was top-secret. So without conversation—and on two wheels—they turned out of the neighborhood and back onto the broad avenue that led to the city.

Tyrone stepped on the gas, and the streets and houses around them dissolved into a blur as the screaming police car pointed its nose south toward Washington DC. Katie and David watched in silence. How far would they go? And where exactly were they headed? Despite their fear, both children were intensely curious about the location of the mysterious War Room.

They were not far from the center of the city when suddenly Tyrone flipped a switch. The light bar went dark and the siren was cut off in mid-wail. At the same time he swung to the left and began a series of quick, sharp turns that took them deep into the residential neighborhoods north and east of downtown.

Within minutes David closed his eyes. There was no point in keeping them open. He was thoroughly lost.

Katie was close to lost too. But she struggled to keep track of the sequence of turns they were making. It had been a left by that hotel, then three blocks and another left, then right at that red building . . . She was weary, and even without this additional challenge, her nerves were stretched to the breaking point. But she had learned her lesson. Until her parents and her sister came home, she would know everything it was possible to know. These people would never keep secrets from her again.

Night had fallen and the city had emptied. There was little traffic downtown and almost nothing to slow their course. In no time Tyrone swung to the right, bumped up a driveway, and glided to a stop.

David opened his eyes. They had arrived at a modest

brick row house. It sat in the dead center of a block of identical houses. David knew that there were dozens of blocks that looked exactly like this one in this part of the city.

So that was how they hid the War Room, he thought. They hid it in plain sight.

"This way," said Alex. And he kicked the door open and headed for the house.

David and Katie followed him up a short stoop and through the front door. There a sharp military voice ordered them to stop. "We're cleared," said Alex brusquely, thrusting an ID card at the guard.

Wordlessly, the guard nodded toward a door that led to a narrow corridor. At the farthest end was a closed door. In front of that stood another guard, alert and unsmiling, with a weapon in his hands.

Was it smart to run at full tilt toward an armed guard? Too late if it wasn't.

Katie and David broke free of Uncle Alex. Their footsteps pounded as they pelted toward the door where the guard stood. Just before they reached it, the soldier bowed his head and, with one arm, pushed the door open.

It was the War Room, and they were in it.

HUNTING DOG

But what was wrong? Supposedly, this was the red-hot center of the hunt for the missing Bowdens. Supposedly, too, the hunt was down to the wire. It was less than half an hour until Katie and David's parents and sister would be killed, and eleven minutes past the time when Alex said they had to find them if they wanted the police to find them alive.

So common sense said the place should have been frantic with activity. But it wasn't.

It had been busy, from the look of things. A bank of computer screens against the far wall scrolled seemingly endless lines of complex text, and a wilderness of tiny lights flashed green and blue. The tables, desks, and chairs were all askew; the tiny, windowless space was strewn with crumpled paper cups, and a crushed pizza box had been jammed into an overflowing trash can.

But everyone just looked depressed. Six people were there—no, eight—and every one of them slumped over a computer as if defeated. Alicia leaned haggardly against the wall. The secretary, who had been so crisp and in control at her office in the State Department, was now limp and unkempt, with great dark circles beneath her eyes.

David bypassed every normal greeting. "It's eight forty-one!" he shouted. "Why isn't anybody hurrying?"

Alicia pushed herself away from the wall where she had propped her thin, exhausted frame and picked her way through the scattered furniture to meet them. "David, Katie," she said, robotic with weariness. "Alex." She nodded toward the door, where he was breathlessly entering. "I'm so glad you've come. I'm sure—"

"Where are they?" demanded David, frustrated to the point of rudeness by these time-wasting preliminaries.

"I understand," said Alicia, looking grave. "First things first," she said. "Your parents and sister are still living. Or at least, we have no reason to think they aren't. But kids . . ." She took a deep breath and continued. "Kids, the news isn't good. We just aren't finding them. I don't want to—I won't lie to you. We—we've reached the end." Her face was full of compassion and shame.

"The recording?" asked Alex anxiously. He was now by their sides.

Alicia shook her head. "It's just not working. It's—I'm sorry, Alex."

"So you're giving up?" asked Katie in disbelief.

"We've tried it three times," said Alicia, "and—"

"Try it again," demanded David. "Uncle Alex, you try it."

Alicia and Alex shared an agonized gaze and Alex slipped into an empty chair before a gigantic console. Frowning, he tapped a few obviously familiar keystrokes.

Hurry, thought David, watching his uncle's careful fingers. But Katie's eyes were elsewhere. She was looking toward the front of the room, where a single enormous screen hung high on the wall, facing every desk and dominating the tiny space. This screen alone, among all the others in the War Room, had until now been totally blank. With Alex's keystrokes, it had sprung to life.

"Katkajan," Katie whispered. And so it was. A satellite photo of that country had filled the gigantic screen.

Just to the right of David and Katie sat a technician with headphones over her ears. This woman now read out a string of letters and numbers. Hearing them, Alex pushed another button and a small, green dot appeared on the screen. The dot hovered somewhere over a range of mountains that cut across the center of Katkajan like a slash.

"They're huge," murmured Katie, looking with dismay

at those mountains. If their mom and dad and Theo were still there, then there really was no hope.

But by now David had also found this screen, and he had focused on a different part of it. David was watching the green dot. "That must be Rover," he said to Katie in a low voice. "That dot right there."

Alex, still frowning, was punching more instructions into his keyboard. And as he typed—and as they watched—the green dot started moving. It had been perfectly still, but now it began to vibrate and tremble.

Rover indeed: The dot on Alex's machine looked exactly like a panting dog, straining restlessly at the end of its leash. Katie found herself whispering to this doglike dot. "Go," she murmured. "Go, Rover. Go get 'em."

Then Alex threw the dog a bone. He tapped a final key, and the song that Katie and David had recorded just moments earlier filled the room. The instant it did, he leaned to his right and pushed a button on a nearby phone.

The button dialed a number. Somewhere in Katkajan, a phone began to ring, and it was playing the same song.

You are my sunshine . . .

"Fetch," muttered David tightly. "Rover, fetch. Go find that phone."

It was almost as if the dot had heard him. Instantly

its faint tremble switched to a steady pulse. Instead of vibrating in one place, it began making tentative darting motions this way and that. Then slowly, shakily, the dot began floating away from the mountains. It began to draw nearer and nearer to Taq, the Katkajanian capital.

"It's working!" said David.

"They're not in the mountains!" cried Katie. "David, this is good! If they're in Taq, we might still have time!"

But at this Alicia spoke. "I don't like to disappoint you, kids," she warned. "But you need to watch what happens next."

She was all too right.

No sooner had the words left Alicia's lips than Rover stopped. The dot paused briefly, somewhere over the eastern foothills of the Katkajanian mountains. Abruptly, it then headed northeast. They all held their breath as just as abruptly it dropped perhaps a hundred miles to the south, hovered briefly, and began floating west.

Rover had heard, but it could not make sense of what it heard. The dog was tracking, but it could not pick up the scent.

"It's just wandering!" cried Katie in despair. "It's all mixed up!"

While the dot was drifting, Alex was holding the phone to his ear. Now he hung it up. "Voice mail!" he said bitterly. And the final notes of David and Katie's brief recording faded from the air.

"That's what it's been doing, Alex," Alicia said apologetically, as if she were trying to let him down gently. "At first it seems to hear, and then it doesn't."

"Have you tried Level 3?" asked Alex desperately.

"I'm afraid we have, sir," responded the technician with the headphones.

"It's so close, Alex," said Alicia. "It's so close to working. But it's not—it's just not—"

"It's just not enough." Katie broke in and they all turned to stare, their eyes drawn by the decision in her voice. "It's not enough," she repeated, "so we have to give it more. David, let's sing it again. Let's try it live."

"But what about the piano?" asked David.

"Forget the piano. It can work with just our voices. That recording we just did—it's not good, David! It isn't right at all!"

Alex stopped her. "It won't make any difference, Katie," he said mournfully. "Rover isn't about details like that. It listens for tones, the unique vibrations—"

But Katie spoke only to David. "What do we have to lose?" she demanded. She seized his arm in her two fists and shook it. "David, what's going to happen if we *don't* try?"

David spun around to face his uncle. "Where's the microphone?" he barked.

"The mike?" asked Alex.

"We're doing this one more time," said David. "We're

going to sing it again, right here and right now." He gestured toward the big screen, where the green dot still wobbled forlornly. "That dog needs fresh food," he said, and for a moment—from the indignation in his voice—it was almost as if he were talking about a real dog.

"It's here!" said a voice near the front of the room, and a wireless mike was passed, hand over hand, to where Katie and David stood.

Katie snatched at it. "How do you turn it on?" she asked, even as she found the switch and flipped it.

"Wait!" said Alex. Seizing the phone, he held his finger over the button that dialed the number. He was ready to go.

Then Katie's and David's eyes met and the room went absolutely silent. They clutched the microphone between them, and Katie whispered. "One. Two. *Three.*" And Alex pushed the button, and strong and sure they began to sing:

> *You are my sunshine,*
> *My only sunshine . . .*

They reached the third line. Katie stomped hard on David's foot, reminding him of the word they had to hit with special force.

> *You make me* happy,
> *When skies are gray . . .*

That was it. That was exactly the way Mrs. Ivanovna had made them do it. Katie squeezed her eyes even more tightly shut. She was concentrating on the rest of the song, remembering. She was disappearing into her own world, throwing every ounce of herself into what she was singing.

You'll never know, dear . . .

So intently was Katie focused that she forgot to watch the dot. But David's eyes were open. David could see the dot, and the dot was changing. It had begun to vibrate.

How much I love you . . .

With that, the dot began to move. Jerkily at first, then more steadily. It was hiking itself to the right, to the east.

Please don't take my sunshine away.

Why wasn't Katie looking? David wondered. It was uncanny how much the dot resembled a dog jerking and pulling at a rope to which it was tethered. Now David stomped on his sister's foot, and her eyes flew open. He did not stop singing, but he gestured frantically toward the screen, where the green dot was now sailing with a steady, determined motion toward the east, where Taq lay nestled in the foothills.

The dog was on the scent. They could practically hear it baying. And then Alex hung up.

"Voice mail," he said again. But for the first time, there was excitement in his voice. His fingers visibly trembled as he began to punch in the number one more time.

The dot had stopped somewhere over the eastern slopes. David stared at it, willing it to hold on. Please don't quit, he thought. The music's coming back. Please don't give up. Please don't—

"Wrong number!" cried Uncle Alex, again hanging up the phone.

Wrong number? There was another phone in front of David and he scooped it up.

"I'll do it," he said crisply. And he began to punch his parents' familiar number into the phone.

Alex looked alarmed. "David!" he cried. "David, don't!"

"What?" said David, pausing. This was no time for one of his uncle's issues.

"I don't want you dialing, David."

"I know the number!"

"It's not that," said Alex urgently. "It's—there's always a chance they might pick up!"

Unexpectedly, Alicia spoke. "Alex is right!" she said. "Let *him* do it. We can't take a chance that you'll get a live answer!"

David did not hesitate. "Thanks," he said, "but no thanks." And he resumed dialing.

"This is important," said Alex. "Listen to Alicia!"

"We tried listening, Katie and me," said David. "For weeks we've been listening. Now I'm making a call."

Alicia sounded desperate. "These are kidnappers," she urged. "They're killers; they're dangerous. Dealing with people like this is a complex skill; it takes training."

But David punched in the last digit. His eyes focused on the map as he listened for the ring to begin. His mouth was set in a hard, determined line.

"If anybody answers," cried Alicia, "hang up! Promise you won't talk!"

"Say when," whispered Katie.

"Now," he said, and again they began to sing.

Somewhere in Taq, the Bowdens' phone was playing their song. This time the dot made a beeline for that phone.

The dot was racing toward the Katkajanian capital. Even as it did so, the satellite image behind it was morphing. The rest of the country began to disappear, sliding off the edges of the screen. The center of the screen, where the capital was, began to grow larger and larger. City streets and landmarks emerged. Rover was zooming in on its target.

You make me happy . . .

The dot picked up speed as it descended into Taq. It was sure of itself now; it knew where it was going.

When skies are gray . . .

Now the telescoping of the picture accelerated to a dizzying speed. Watching it was like being in an airplane that was coming in for a landing. Details loomed into view. They could see not only streets but tiny buildings as well. The dot hurtled downward like a missile that was about to strike.

You'll never know, dear . . .

The closer it came to its goal, the faster the dot seemed to go. Down it went, and down, down, down. They could see cars now, and bicycles, and people. Out of all that great country and that huge, teeming city, the dot was zooming in on a short, ordinary-looking street lined with small, ordinary houses.

Now they could see the tiles on the roofs of these houses. If the dot got any closer, it would crash.

And then it stopped. It stopped over the chimney of an inconspicuous gray house with shuttered windows and an abandoned appearance. And as it did so, the computer began to beep—an insistent, repeated beep.

"Found!" cried the technician with the headphones.

"Alert the Katkajanians," ordered Alicia, her voice shaking. "Get the address of that house. And get me the head of police in the—"

But Katie and David did not hear. They were intent on the phone, which David clutched tightly to his ear. It had stopped ringing.

"Hello?" said David. "Hello?"

"David, hang up!" yelled Alex. "Say nothing!"

He should have spoken to Katie, too. With a great wrench, she ripped the phone from her brother's hands and clutched it to her face. "Where are our parents?" she demanded with steel in her voice. "Where is our sister? What have you done with our family?"

Everyone fell absolutely silent. Behind them a technician flipped a switch and instantly the call was transferred to a loudspeaker, which broadcast both sides of the conversation at full volume into the War Room. Every man and woman there was eye-locked on Katie, and all were on the edges of their seats.

Aware that every sound they made could now be heard by the kidnappers in Katkajan, Alex put his finger to his lips and flailed his arms, gesturing wildly for silence. Whoever that was on the phone must not know where Katie was calling from.

Alicia, who had been finishing an urgent call to the head of the Katkajanian police, abruptly hung up. Then, except for the crackling static of the broadcast call and the sounds of their breathing, there was total silence in the War Room.

"Oh, so dis is de daughter?" The faraway Katkajanian voice sounded very near. "How sweet. How you find us, honey?" And he laughed.

"We haven't found you," Katie lied. A shrewd instinct told her to keep the kidnappers off their guard. "We've called you. It's different, unfortunately. I want to talk to my mother."

"Your mother, she beezy right now." And he laughed again. "She sayin' her prayers."

The small gray house in the satellite photo may have looked shuttered and abandoned, but clearly it was not empty. Behind the Katkajanian who held the phone, the voices of the other kidnappers could be heard. Now the man with the phone turned away from it and spoke to them in his own language. From the excited cries that greeted his remark, he must have told them who had called.

Katie strained to hear the voices of her parents, but she did not.

David, who had snatched a piece of paper and scribbled something across it, now shoved a note under her eyes. *Keep him talking*, said the note.

This advice was not necessary and Katie pushed it away.

"You're trying to upset me," she said to the Katkajanian, "and it won't work. Just give me my father instead."

"He a leetle tied up too." And the man laughed yet again. "Hey," he said abruptly. "Where you callin' from? How come you no call before dis?"

"I didn't want to talk to you, that's why," she retorted. "What's your name, anyway?"

The Katkajanian found this question hilarious. "Harry Potter!" he said happily when his mirth had died down. "My name Harry Potter! Nice try, honey. Oh—no, wait. Dat not really my name." He paused. "My name really Meeckey Mouse." And he laughed even louder than before. "My name—"

It was too much for David. The nerve of this guy, with his lame humor when their parents' lives were on the line. He snatched the phone from his sister's hand.

"Listen up, Mickey," he said.

"David," Katie hissed. "I was keeping him talking!"

"Listen up," David repeated. "And put your friends on. I have something you all need to hear."

Alex went pale. "David—no," he whispered.

"Whooee!" shouted the Katkajanian. "Now de son is talking!" And David, frowning, turned aside from his uncle's desperate face, while far away in Taq the kidnappers gathered around the phone.

"What you got for us, honey?" said the man a moment later with barely repressed glee.

"Advice," said David. "Just a little advice for all of you, about my mom and my dad and the baby, too." He took a deep breath, steadying himself, and when he spoke he was very calm. "If you harm so much as a hair on their heads," he said, "then you had all better watch your backs for the rest of your lives. Because one of these days, I am going to be behind you—I and my sister. If we have to wait till we're old—if we have to wait till we're *dead*—we will track you down."

At this the Katkajanian stopped laughing. Katie grabbed again for the phone but David would not let her have it.

"Got to go," snapped the Katkajanian. "Nice advice, but I got to go. We plannin' a little party in—oh, about one minute."

Katie looked at the clock. It was 8:59. She lunged and the phone was hers. "Hello?" she begged. "Hello?"

But then everything fell apart.

On the other end of the line there was a crash, as if a door had splintered open. Frantic shouting followed, and something somewhere fell heavily to the ground. A gunshot rang out, and then another and another.

Amid the chaos of yelling and struggle a woman screamed—a terrible, terrible scream. Then with a click the line went dead.

"What's happening?!" cried Katie. She wheeled around to look at the screen. Surely something would show. But the screen had gone black. "Who *was* that? David, who screamed?"

"The police! That must have been the police—they broke down the door! It wasn't Mom," he added, belatedly answering her question. "That scream—I know it wasn't Mom!" But there was fear in his voice.

"Alicia, call them!" Katie begged.

Alicia had already dialed, but in despair she held up the phone. They heard it ringing, and ringing, and ringing . . .

WHERE ARE THEY?

For once, they did not push their uncle Alex away. In the terrible aftermath of the phone call to Katkajan—in the anguish of not knowing what had happened to their parents and their sister—they yielded at last to his earnest and bumbling sympathy.

It was time for sympathy now. Now they needed it.

"Call them," Katie had pleaded. "Call the police again." And Alicia had, and she had called them again after that. But there had been no answer. Then she had called the ambassador to Katkajan, and had told him to call the Katkajanian president.

"But it might still be a while before we hear," she said gently.

"So?" implored David. "So what do we do?"

"We wait," said Alex. "We just wait." He stepped between Katie and David and put an arm around each of them. Overcome, they sank into his hug.

"Go back to the safe house," Alex continued. "You've done everything you could possibly do. We'll know when we know. And kids," he added. "You . . . you . . ." He stopped.

"What?" said David.

"Kids," Alex said, his voice breaking, "you were splendid."

"You, too, Uncle Alex," said Katie, her words muffled by her uncle's shirt.

"No, not like you," he said through tears. "I'm awed by you. I'm just in awe of my niece and my nephew: my two wonderful children."

And then, though they lingered for a little while, there was really nothing else to do or say. So at about ten o'clock, Alicia called Tyrone, and the car came for David and Katie and they returned to the safe house.

They left not knowing. They did not know what had happened when the police had broken down the door of the little gray house in Katkajan. They did not know whether their mom and dad and Theo were dead or alive. And perhaps worst of all, they did not know when they *would* know.

David and Katie had thought they would not sleep. They did not want to sleep. But the decision was entirely out of their hands. Despite their reluctance to close their eyes, sleep pulled them into a black, unconscious pit.

When David's eyes finally did open, it was broad daylight and the clock said ten. Seconds later he was downstairs and breathless for news. But Katie had beat him by twenty minutes, and she told him right away that there was none. Uncle Alex had promised to call as soon as he heard, but there had not been so much as a word.

"It's been more than twelve hours," Katie said. "That can't be good."

David made no reply. He could think of nothing to say.

Bright sunshine sparkled across the table. Katie had poured a bowl of cereal, but it looked like dust to her and she could not eat it. The newspaper was spread open and David was staring at the comics, but she knew he was not reading the words.

"David," said Katie, carefully crushing a sugary lump beneath the back of her spoon.

"Huh?"

"David, what are we going to do if they're dead?"

"Thanks," he said gloomily.

"I'm not being negative, David. I'm being a realist. We tried, but we might have failed. We need a Plan B. We need to know what we're going to do if our parents never come home."

"You and your plans."

"Right. Me and my plans."

David sighed, but his answer was quiet and calm. "We'll live with Uncle Alex, I guess," he said. "I figure he'll probably move here. To take care of us."

"Right," said Katie.

David continued. "He's not, you know, at his best in the city. But he'll learn."

"Good," said Katie. "That's what I was thinking too."

And at just that instant, the front door opened. A moment later, Alex walked into the kitchen. He was wearing the same clothes he'd had on the night before. He looked awful, and a musty odor hung about him. But there was a strange little smile on his face and his eyes shone with joy.

For an instant Katie stared, electrified. Then she leaped to her feet, throwing her arms wide, sending her bowl and its contents flying.

"THEY'RE ALIVE!"

Uncle Alex burst into happy laughter and David let loose with an earsplitting whoop that brought the security guard running.

"Where's the paper?" cried David. "Gimme that—" He thrust aside the comics and began hunting frantically for the front page.

"It's not in there," gasped Alex, who was still laughing

and, in fact, seemed unable to stop. Doubled over, he laid his hand on David's shoulder. "Slow down!" he said. "Slow down; you'll tear it. Just wait. I'll tell you everything!"

"David!" cried Katie, who was literally hopping up and down. "Sit or he won't tell us!" And with a final, irrelevant shriek she plopped into her seat.

"It's not in the paper, David," repeated Alex, finally recovering. "Though it will be. This is big news, kids—big, and not just because of your parents. Though, of course, that's the most important—"

"Where *are* they?" said Katie.

"What *happened*?" said David.

"Let me talk!" said their uncle.

With difficulty they silenced themselves, and Alex began.

"OK, this kidnapping," he said, apparently struggling for the right place to start. "Your parents' kidnapping was part of a plot: a big insurgency that tried to topple the government of Katkajan. See, your parents were supposed to be leverage. The kidnappers found out they wanted to adopt. So they knew the guys who invented Rover would be in Katkajan, and they figured if they grabbed them, then the United States would pressure the Katkajanian government to give up."

"And you couldn't have explained this, oh, a couple of weeks ago?" Katie hadn't meant to interrupt. But despite her joy over the rescue of her parents and her sister, her anger flared as she remembered how she and David had been pushed aside.

Alex ignored her. "But we caught the kidnappers!" he continued. "*You* caught the kidnappers. The police got there just in time! We were right: That crashing that we heard on the phone was them, breaking down the door. So they saved your parents and Theo, and they stopped the plot. It's over!" he concluded giddily.

"So where are they?" repeated Katie. "Mom and Dad and Theo?"

Now Alex's face fell. "I'd better not exaggerate," he said, apparently remembering something. "I'm getting careless. It isn't *quite* over."

This didn't sound good, and the children's smiles vanished. "Whatever it is," said David flatly, "I don't want to hear it."

"It's not about your parents or your sister," said Alex quickly. "It's about the Katkajanians. You know they're all in jail—all the guys who did this."

"Trixie and the rest. Right," said Katie.

"Well, they can't just stay there. They have to have trials. I wasn't going to mention this on such a happy day, but unfortunately, you'll be involved in that."

Oh. That was no problem. "Uncle Alex," repeated Katie, "where are Mom and Dad?"

But her uncle was still thinking about Trixie. "I've already had to go down to the police station," he continued, "to identify the ones I saw—you know, the ones who followed us that night. Well, you'll have to do that too, and I know it will be painful, after all you've been through." His brow furrowed. "You'll have to testify and answer a lot of—"

"Excellent," said David crisply. "And no problem about ruining the happy day and all that. It just makes it happier."

"It makes it perfect," agreed Katie, thinking about their house, and the photo of her father with the slash through his eye. "I *want* to see them again," she insisted with an urgency that surprised even her. "I want to see them, when they're locked up and we're not."

Alex looked surprised, but he looked impressed, too. "Well, you will," he said. "You'll see them in a court of law."

"But *where*," said Katie again, "are Mom and Dad and Theo? I'm asking and asking and asking," she added, starting to realize that she was. "Are they still in Katkajan?"

"No, they're not," said Alex, and as he turned to this question at last, a look of suppressed glee crept over his face.

He had another secret. Katie didn't think she could stand it. Once again she jumped to her feet and this time, she seized her uncle's arm and shook it.

"Don't even think about not telling!" she cried.

"They're right here in Washington."

Katie gasped and clapped her hand over her mouth.

"So we'd better get to see them," said David. "Like, yesterday."

"They've just landed. You'll see them in about one hour." But the smug look remained plastered across Alex's face. If anything, it was worse.

"*Tell us now!*"

Their uncle laughed again. He couldn't seem to stop laughing this morning.

"Guess *where* you'll be seeing them?" he asked. "At the White House!" he sang. "You're going to see your parents, and you're going to meet the president!"

"I don't get it," said David.

"I told you," said Alex. "A *big* plot was stopped. This Katkajanian story is huge! The president's holding a press conference later this morning so he can tell the public all about it. But before he talks to the country, he wants to meet you."

This time the children were simply too stunned to speak. There was a moment of total silence as they processed this amazing news.

"We'd better get dressed!" And Katie dashed from the room.

In a daze, David rose to follow her. As he did so, though, he remembered something. "Uncle Alex," he said.

Alex looked up expectantly. A crazy grin still played about the corners of his mouth.

"Uncle Alex, about Rover?"

The grin evaporated.

"I believe your questions have been answered, David," said his uncle severely. "As I've already said, anything else that you now want to ask about Rover will be subject to 'need-to-know—'"

But David cut him off. "About Rover," he repeated. "Pretty cool machine, Uncle Alex. Really, way cool."

And Alex looked rather pleased to hear it.

ALL AT ONCE

When the State Department provided them with clothes, it must have known that such a day would eventually come. Katie found a dress in her closet and David found a jacket and tie.

"Do I have to—" David began.

"Yes," Katie said firmly.

Hurry, hurry. As quickly as they could, they washed up and wriggled into their outfits. Then they were downstairs and outside. It was a glorious fall day. Uncle Alex, who had hastily showered and changed, paced in front of the door.

Someone else was there too, crouched in the driver's seat of a familiar-looking police car with badly scratched paint. It was Tyrone.

Katie and David were delighted to see him. Characteristically, though, he was all business. Tyrone received their excited greetings with a wordless nod and without relaxing his grip on the wheel.

It did not matter. For once even Alex was wearing his watch. There was not a moment to linger. They hustled straight into the car, Tyrone revved the motor, and they were whisked away through the morning streets.

This time they drove the speed limit—not that they noticed. Familiar and famous sights flashed by—river, monuments—but they seemed to see nothing. Their eyes strained ahead for the most famous building of them all: the White House.

At last it loomed before them. On day trips to the city they had often peered between those gates for a glimpse of the stately and gracious home of the president. It was thrilling now to see the gates part and to enter the green and well-tended grounds.

Then everything became a blur.

The car stopped on a circular driveway; gloved hands opened the door; they passed through an arched entryway. It was bright and cool. Katie noticed through a haze of excitement that the place seemed half office, half house; David noticed with disappointment how small it all was.

Where were their mom and dad?

Smiling men and women were offering them drinks.

Soldiers were everywhere, in splendid uniforms with polished rifles held stiffly at their sides.

Katie and David and their uncle were all asked to sit and wait, and they did. Phones rang. Yet more people came and went and smiled.

Where were their mom and dad?

Now they were asked to pass through carpeted, narrow corridors. In offices along the way people seemed to be working. A gloved soldier was ushering them into yet another room.

Mom and Dad? Their hearts lifted, but inside this new room there were yet more chairs and again they sat.

David, suddenly inspired, reached into Alex's pocket, removed a cell phone, and began dialing.

"Hey," said Alex, too distracted to protest for real.

"I'm calling Mom and Dad," said David.

"Calling them where?" demanded Katie.

"On their cell," replied David. "Maybe they got it back."

"Good luck," she said crossly, and she sat back in her chair.

David finished dialing and put the phone to his ear. And suddenly—very, very loud and very, very near—rang the notes of a now quite familiar song.

You are my sunshine . . .

But they did not hear it through David's phone. They heard it through the wall.

All three of them leaped up. The guard, startled, tightened his grip on his weapon.

"Where are they?" Katie's voice trembled. "They must be right here! Mom? Dad? *Mom and Dad!!!*"

And then they *were* there, hurrying in from the hall, wild-eyed and clutching their ringing phone. They were there in the living flesh, laughing and crying and hugging and kissing until all four of them nearly tumbled to the ground.

Four?

"Careful!" warned Mr. Bowden. "Careful! We'll crush her!"

David and Katie both gasped. For there in their

father's arms, barely visible within her many layers of soft wrappings, was a tiny fifth Bowden. Gently, their dad tilted the bundle and their mom lifted the blankets away from her face. Theo gazed at her brother and sister with bright and knowing black eyes, but they could barely see her for the tears that filled their own.

"She's a beauty," boomed a familiar voice. And when they looked up, right behind their parents, Katie and David saw the president: the president of the United States. Beside him was Alicia, and both of them were smiling from ear to ear.

The president wanted to meet Theo, too, but she cried when he tried to hold her, which made everyone laugh. Then Alicia tried to hold her and it worked, and everyone tried not to stare at Alex, who looked as if he might explode from pure pride.

But the president had words for Katie and David. "I've been wanting to meet the heroes who helped us defeat the Katkajanian insurgency," he said, shaking their hands. "Thank you for coming to see me today. This celebration wouldn't be complete without you."

"Happy to help, sir," said David, then he blushed to the roots of his hair. *Happy to help, sir. Yuck!*

But the president tactfully changed the subject. "I understand the two of you took quite a road trip," he said.

"We did," said Katie. "And oh, Mom and Dad, we did some bad stuff, too. We stole," she said.

"Flashlights and crackers," said David airily, his blush fading. "We needed 'em." His face clouded slightly. "And I guess some money, too, and some other stuff . . ."

"It's OK," said their mother. "We'll go over all of it later and we'll pay it back."

The president did not seem concerned. "What did you think of our War Room?" he asked. "That's quite an operation, isn't it? You know, you're pretty unusual kids, getting to see that. Most people don't even know it's there." He chuckled. "It's pretty well tucked away."

Katie coughed politely. "South on Sixteenth Street," she said. "Left by the brick hotel with the columns. Three blocks and then another left, then a quick right at the—"

But then she had to stop because Alex looked so

annoyed, the president looked so shocked, and everyone was laughing so hard.

"Gonna have to move it now," the president muttered. "Well." He coughed and moved on. "I know you had some help from some heroic police officers," he said. "I'd like both of you to know that a Mr. Tyrone Jackson will be receiving an award for special service."

That was excellent. Tyrone had been great. David wanted to tell how the cruiser had leaped over that front lawn. "Mr. President, he was fantastic. He—"

But David did not finish, because everyone's eyes had turned to the door, where an escort had just arrived with another couple: a nervous-looking woman whom they did not know and an enormous man who was bursting the buttons of a shiny blue suit.

"Mike!" Katie and David launched themselves at the taxi driver, who never even swayed when both of them landed on him at once. Then they had to meet the woman, whose name was Betty and who was Mike's wife, and they had to introduce Mike to their parents and their sister and Alicia, and everyone needed to shake hands all around.

"I know you all have a lot of stories to tell," said the president, "and I've got one to tell, too, to all those reporters who are waiting in our press room. So I won't keep you, though I do hope I get to hear the details someday. And you, sir," said the president, turning respectfully toward Alex. "Will you be heading back to the Green Mountain State?"

At this everyone looked at Alex. And when they did, they saw that somehow he had slipped over to Alicia's side and had taken her hand. What's more, he was blushing a deep, ruddy red and Alicia's face was shining.

"Not . . . not . . ." Alex was unable to speak. Then he lifted Alicia's hand and, grinning, held it out for all of them to see. Glittering on her finger was an enormous diamond engagement ring.

Mrs. Bowden yelped and the president clapped Alex on the back and kissed Alicia and there was another round of hugs and congratulations. They might never have stopped except that eventually Theo began to cry, which again made all of them laugh.

"That's a heck of a cry!" said the president. "Bet our Rover could find her with that!" Then he sighed. "Duty calls!" he said. And he straightened his tie, saluted, and headed off to the press room.

"I'm starving," said David, which made the rest of them realize that they had not eaten either. So they all headed out to breakfast together: Alex and Alicia, Mike and Betty, and all five of the Bowdens.

David got to carry his new sister, so he lagged behind. "What a lot of trouble you caused," he scolded gently, looking into her tiny face. But Theo simply yawned and went to sleep.

AUTHOR'S NOTE

The Secret of Rover is fiction. Many of the places in it are entirely imaginary. Other places in this story are real, but I've changed them for the benefit of my characters, Katie and David.

For instance, Katkajan is my own invention. Vermont is real, but the towns of Melville and Hawthorne are not. I made them up, and I chose to name them for two of my heroes: the great American authors Herman Melville and Nathaniel Hawthorne.

Yonkers is a real place, but the truck stop that I've put in it is, again, fictional. And as for Washington DC, I'm afraid I've invented a couple of places within it—such as the neighborhood of Katie and David's old house—and I've moved a few other places around.

Some of what I say about Washington is true, though. I have seen the office of the Secretary of State. Though the building that houses it is plain, not fancy, this office is indeed ornate and beautiful. I've also been privileged over the years to enter the White House many times, and I can report that the interior is very much as I've described it.

ACKNOWLEDGMENTS

"You've never heard of me, but I've written a novel." If you want to make publishers and agents disappear, those are your magic words. I'm particularly grateful, therefore, to three people who stuck around. They are Liza Voges of Eden Street, my kind and adroit agent; Howard Reeves, editor at large of Amulet Books, who took a chance on me; and Amulet's Vice President and Publisher, Susan Van Metre, who warmly embraced the project. The rest of the Amulet team confirmed my opinion that my book ended up in the best possible hands.

I'm grateful, too, to the many young readers who agreed to look at my book and tell me what they thought. In alphabetical order, these smart and insightful kids include Miriam Israel, Gabriel Javitt, Joseph Johnson, David Lane, Zachary Moser, Ezra Schwartz, Leah Schwartz, Nathaniel Schwartz, Jenny Shore, Aaron Troy, and Eli Weissler. Abigail Friedland and Francesca Furtchgott shared their thoughts and encouragement about an earlier effort. Publishing takes time, so many of these readers are in high school now, or even beyond.

Kelly Corrigan, who teaches the fifth grade at North Chevy Chase Elementary School in Chevy Chase,

Maryland, graciously read an early draft. Sarah Kass, who teaches seventh grade English at Westland Middle School in Bethesda, Maryland, welcomed me and Rover to her classroom. In the days before I found Liza, Jon and Aliza Lerner generously helped me circulate my manuscript, and Dan Troy patiently explained the meanings of various potential contracts.

My good friend Anne Himmelfarb has been an endlessly tolerant listener and an invaluable critic. I've lost count of the number of times Anne has taken home a manuscript of mine, and I can't quantify the benefit I've derived from her comments on what she has read.

My children, Eva, Aaron, and Saul Wildavsky, are my fiercest critics, but there is no one whose good opinion I value more. Their insistence on the highest possible standards has immeasurably improved this book, and their confidence that it would find its way into print has buoyed me up.

It takes time to write a book—time that must be pried away from other necessities. My husband, Ben, has watched me pry away a lot more of it than either of us expected when the book began, yet somehow he is cheering me on as we cross the finish line. I'm grateful for that and much more. The thought of trying to itemize it overwhelms me.

My debt to my parents, Arnold and Nancy Flick, can't be itemized either. In all my life, their love for me has never faltered. This book is dedicated to them.

ABOUT THE AUTHOR

RACHEL WILDAVSKY is a former journalist who has written for the *Washington Post* and the *Wall Street Journal*, among many other publications. She has also worked for the White House under two presidents. Today she works for a private educational philanthropy. She lives in a suburb of Washington DC, with her husband and their three children.

This book was designed by Maria T. Middleton and art directed by Chad W. Beckerman. The text is set in 10-point LinoLetter, a slab-serif typeface designed by Reinhard Haus and Andre Gürtler in cooperation with the Linotype Design Studio in the 1980s. Released by Linotype in 1992, LinoLetter is a highly legible typeface created specifically for mass-produced publications such as magazines and newspapers.

The display typefaces are Bullet Small Caps Alternate and Eurostile Extended 2.